Christmas with Elizabeth

A Pride and Prejudice Holiday Variation

Leah Page

Copyright © 2024 Leah Page

Copyright © 2024 Leah Page All rights reserved

The characters and events portrayed in this book are fictitious. Any similarity to real persons, living or dead, is coincidental and not intended by the author.

No part of this book may be reproduced, or stored in a retrieval system, or transmitted in any form or by any means, electronic, mechanical, photocopying, recording, or otherwise, without express written permission of the publisher.

ISBN-13: 9798343182316

Cover design by: Erica Weise

To Doug. You are my everything and I love you.

Christmas with Miss Gardiner

Contents

Prologue 4
Chapter 1 11
Chapter 2 18
Chapter 3 25
Chapter 4 33
Chapter 5 40
Chapter 6 47
Chapter 7 61
Chapter 8 69
Chapter 9 76
Chapter 10 85
Chapter 11 95
Chapter 12 104
Chapter 13 115
Chapter 14 125
Chapter 15 135
Chapter 16 145
Chapter 17 154
Chapter 18 161
Chapter 19 168
Chapter 20 176
Chapter 21 186
Chapter 22 194
Chapter 23 201

Chapter 24 210
Chapter 25 218
Epilogue 226

Prologue

1791

Edward Gardiner ran his fingers through his hair. "Harriet, you cannot be serious. She is your niece. I cannot countenance the idea of her being taken to an orphanage." He looked down at the dark haired, chubby child who sat near his feet happily playing with the toe of his boot.

Harriet Phillips, Edward's eldest sister, primly placed her teacup on its saucer before answering. "Do not be silly, Edward. Of course she must go. There is no room for her here. Jude's business has done well, but I cannot be expected to keep both of Fanny's girls. I will raise Jane as a remembrance to my sister, and Elizabeth must be taken away. It is a shame, of course, but it is the only solution."

Edward paced the length of his sister's parlor. "It is not the only solution. You have three empty bed chambers. Surely there is room for both Jane and Elizabeth."

Harriet shrugged. "Perhaps there is physical space, but it is very costly to raise a daughter. I admit I always wished for one, but dresses and dance masters do not come without a cost. No, my mind is made up. I will not keep the baby. She is young enough that some desiring couple will snatch her up right away. I do not worry that she will be made to live in the orphanage for long."

Edward came to an abrupt stop, his eyes locking onto his sister with a look that bordered on disbelief. "Think of our sister. She would not have wished her youngest to be put to a home. If Fanny had lived, she would have done everything in her power to protect these girls. *Both* of them. She would be very disappointed in you."

Harriet scoffed. "Hardly! She did not like Elizabeth at all. She was gravely disappointed when another daughter was born. They expected a son, you know. I believe Fanny would have given the girl away herself if it were not for Thomas. He insisted no child of his would be put from their home."

Edward did not doubt the veracity of his sister's claims. His youngest sister was as silly as his eldest and would have thought little of demeaning her second daughter, though he doubted she would have truly given her away, no matter what her claims may have been.

His feet took him back to the table where Harriet sat eating a small cake. Sitting in the chair nearest his sister, he leaned forward and took her hand in both of his. "Harriet, I beg you. I will assist with the cost for both girls, but I am not currently in a position to bring her into my home. My business is going well, but it is not yet in a situation where I can take on an infant and a nurse. I still live in the back rooms of my warehouse. That is no place for a child."

Harriet patted his hand with her free one. "Of course it is no place for a child. That is why I did not suggest you take her. But she cannot stay here."

Edward released a frustrated sigh. "If you can only raise one, then allow me to take Jane. She is older and will be easier for me to care for. Elizabeth cannot yet crawl."

His sister laughed at the proposal. "Do not think me stupid, brother. I know you only wish to take the pretty one. It will not work. Jane is the spitting image of her mother. I will not be stuck with the homely child."

Edward looked to where the girls sat. Jane, age three, quietly held a small teacup to her sister's lips and offered her a drink of imaginary tea. Elizabeth, surrounded by multiple pillows, gurgled and smiled and attempted to take the cup into her chubby hands. Harriet was correct, Jane was a replica of her mother, with blonde hair and bright blue eyes. But Elizabeth was nearly an exact copy of her elder sister, only dark where Jane was light. It rendered her no less lovely. And though she was only seven months old, the child gave every indication of growing up to be a beautiful young lady.

He looked back to his sister. "I am ashamed of you, Harriet. Our father and mother would be ashamed of you, too, if they were alive to witness your selfishness. Send the maid to gather the girl's things. I will take Elizabeth with me."

Harriet had the audacity to appear affronted by her brother's words, but she did as he commanded. "Mary," she called over her shoulder to the nurse who sat near the girls, "gather Elizabeth's things, she will be leaving with my brother." Then turning to face Edward once more, she added, "When you find it is too difficult to care for a baby, do not return her to me. I will have Jude send you the name and address of the facility. You can take her directly there. I will have him transfer half of her mother's dowry to you, as well."

Edward stood and walked to Elizabeth. She raised her arms to be lifted and offered him a gummy smile. He obliged her by picking her up and placing her on his hip. "Do not bother. Elizabeth has been my goddaughter since birth, and now she is my true daughter. I will see to her needs very well. Being raised by someone as crass as you, Jane will need all the dowry she can get if she ever wishes to find a husband."

Edward's anger did not lessen when he walked from the house, nor when he entered the carriage. His sister was as selfish a creature as he had ever met, even more so than Fanny had been, though it felt disrespectful to compare them since Fanny's life had ended three weeks ago in a carriage accident. She had died alongside her husband, leaving two young girls at home in the nursery.

Fanny may not have wished for Elizabeth, but Thomas Bennet had loved her from the moment he laid eyes on her. Edward sighed. Thomas had been his best friend since childhood. He had praised his youngest daughter who had all the good looks of her mother, but with his own beloved mother's coloring. *She will be a great reader,* Thomas had written in his last letter to Edward. *I can see the intelligence in her eyes. Do not laugh at me, friend, I know she is but a babe, but I have great hopes for this second daughter of mine.*

Elizabeth's fleshy fingers grabbed at his shirt and tugged, pulling him from his reverie. He offered his thumbs, which she clutched in her pudgy hands. With his help, she stood on his lap and bounced while singing a happy baby song that translated to no words but indicated her contentment. A bump in the road caused her to fall forward onto his chest where she rested her head. Her hands had come free of his thumbs, and she placed her plump arms around his neck. Edward placed his much larger arms around her small body and hugged her close. This tiny child had already wiggled her way into his heart.

"It will be difficult for us both, my dear, but I promise your life will not suffer. I will be as good a father to you as Thomas would have wished. And I will buy you every book in London. Together we will build a happy life together." Elizabeth snuggled her small head into his chest and soon fell asleep.

∞∞∞

1795

"Gardiner, after giving it much consideration, I have decided it is my best interest to invest further into your business."

Edward schooled his features. It would not do for the Earl of Effington to know how thrilled he was to receive the additional funds for his business. In the past four years, profits from Gardiner Imports had grown more than five hundred percent, but these additional funds would allow him to take on another ship. Within two years he predicted the profits would double from where they were today.

"I am pleased to hear it, my lord. These funds will allow the business to grow substantially. Both you and I will turn a very nice profit."

The earl smiled. "That is exactly what I anticipate. My man of business and I — " His words were cut off when a small child entered the room. "Who is this, Gardiner? I did not realize you had a child."

The girl stood next to her father's chair and looked at the earl with big, blue, unblinking eyes. "Is this your 'vestor, Papa?"

Edward lifted the child onto his lap. "This is Earl Effington, Lizzy. Where is your nurse?"

"Sleeping," she replied.

From his chair, the earl sniggered. "My daughter does the same. Lays down with the nurse in the afternoon, and as soon as the lady's eyes close, Susan sneaks away to find me or her brother. But tell me, I did not realize you were a married man."

Gardiner stiffened, understanding the implications of the man's words. No matter how many times he offered the truth, men and women alike often assumed Elizabeth was his by-blow. Would the earl choose to believe him?

"I am not married. My sister and her husband were taken in a tragic carriage accident when Elizabeth was but a babe. My remaining sister raised the oldest child, and I took Elizabeth. For the past four years she has been as good as a daughter to me."

The earl's eyes moved from Elizabeth to Gardiner and back again. The girl smiled prettily at him from her father's lap. There was a similarity in looks, but as the child's uncle, she could just as likely carry a resemblance as she would if he were her father. "I thought, perhaps, you were a widower, as I am. My Susan is of a similar age. Come to my house in two days to sign the paperwork. Bring your daughter. Susan would love a playmate. We might as well introduce them now. I expect we will be in company often."

And so they were. Edward Gardiner and Paul Corwell, the Earl of Effington, became great friends as well as business partners. When Elizabeth was six, the Earl, whom Elizabeth affectionately called "Uncle Paul" agreed to be godfather to the child.

Their daughters, taking their cues from the men, followed suit. Lizzy and Suzy, as the girls came to know one another, were together often. The servants at Effington House knew Elizabeth Gardiner nearly as well as they knew Lady Susan. The servants at the Gardiner's home on Gracechurch Street, and later at their mansion on Brook Street, were as likely to take biscuits to Lady Susan as they were the master's own child.

The duo both served as flower girls when Edward Gardiner married Madelyn Brown in 1797. The new Mrs. Gardiner served as mother to Elizabeth and surrogate mother to Lady Susan, who was as often at the Gardiner's home as she was at her own.

Lizzy and Suzy celebrated their tenth birthdays in Ramsgate in 1801. And they both made their come outs in 1811. Both had anticipated coming out the year before, but Elizabeth had been traveling home from India with her parents and did not return in time. Lady Susan refused to do anything without her dearest friend, and so, at the rather advanced age of nineteen, the girls entered the ballroom, each on the arm of her respective father, to much applause and many smiling faces.

Chapter 1

Sisterly Affections

"I do wish you would reconsider your decision to stay so long from home. Eight weeks is entirely too much. I daresay your sister will have little for you to do in Hertfordshire, anyway." With a huff to emphasize her annoyance with her friend's travel, Lady Susan Corwell, the sole daughter of the Earl of Effington, moved her bishop to capture Elizabeth Gardiner's pawn.

Elizabeth studied the board before replying. "I dare say the diversions in Meryton will not equal those in London, but I cannot deny my excitement for clean air and long walks in the sunshine. But most of all, I look forward to getting to know my sister better. We had so few opportunities when we were growing up. My aunt would not countenance Jane coming here for too long for fear that she would lose Mr. Collins' attention were she to stay out of his sight for more than a week. And, of course, I was not permitted to stay there given my father's continued anger with her." She picked up her knight and toppled Suzy's bishop.

"Drat. I had plans for that piece."

Elizabeth smirked. "I suspected you did."

Suzy studied the board before continuing the conversation. "I know you love your sister, but I do not trust that she will have your best interests at heart. Do you not remember how she acted when we visited Ramsgate for our birthdays?" She cautiously slid her rook over three spaces.

"Ramsgate! That was all of ten years ago. And you cannot blame Jane for her actions then. We were still young girls while she was blooming and moving into adolescence. Three years is not such an age gap now, but the difference between a girl of ten and another of thirteen is rather stark. It is no wonder she found our giggling and boisterousness displeasing."

"Then can you account for her actions last year when she came to purchase her trousseau? She was hardly the picture of sisterly affection."

Elizabeth sat back in her chair. "What do you mean? Jane was everything good and kind. There was nothing she did to warrant your scorn."

"Ha!" Suzy retorted. "I will admit she was polite on the surface, for she has a manner of speaking softly while wearing a smile that convinces one of her kindness. But I did not like how she spoke to you. *'You are so short, Elizabeth. You wear too many dark colors, Elizabeth. Having a tradesman father must materially lessen your chances for a good marriage.'* As if her own adopted father is not a tradesman, and not one half so well accomplished!" Suzy's ire had risen in earnest. "But that is not the worst of it."

Elizabeth giggled. "There is more? What else did she say that I failed to remember?"

"She implied that she is more beautiful than you. I nearly screamed when she said it. And you did hear it; you must not pretend otherwise. We both sat on the settee while she sat in the chair where your companion sits now. You had just served a lovely tea. That is when she mentioned that you were meant for the orphanage because you were too ugly to keep!"

Elizabeth sighed. "I cannot deny it. That was what prompted me to ask Papa about why he adopted me while Jane stayed with Aunt Phillips. But I do not blame Jane. She is a sweet and loving sister, and I hope to grow closer to her during our visit. She simply has not had the exposure that I have had to what is right and wrong. I have had all the luck to be raised by Papa and Mama, who are both intelligent and refined. Jane, unfortunately, has had little exposure to such polite society and had the distinct disadvantage of growing up in my aunt's home."

"That is hardly an excuse."

Elizabeth reached across the table and touched her friend's arm. "I am pleased to know that you are a staunch defender of my honor, but I must ask you to be kind to my sister. She has not had the advantages that we have had. She has been loved solely for her looks, whereas we have been loved for ourselves and valued for our wits and personalities."

Suzy's face softened. "I suppose her upbringing has been far different. It would be a terrible burden to be valued only for what people see on the outside."

Elizabeth smiled. "Exactly, though I cannot deny she is a beautiful woman. I do not pretend to be unaware of my own appeal, but I cannot compare to Jane."

Throwing up her arms in frustration, Suzy exclaimed, "Cannot compare! I declare you are practically identical except for your hair. You are dark and she is light, but aside from that you are nearly impossible to keep straight."

Elizabeth giggled. "So you think I am pretty, then?"

Suzy rolled her eyes. "You are certainly pretty enough for the gentlemen around Meryton." Abandoning the chess board, Suzy turned in her seat and called out to Mrs. Gardiner who sat at a far table reviewing the account books. "Mrs. Gardiner, you must promise me that Lizzy will take as burly a footman as you can spare with her to Hertfordshire. I do not wish to see her compromised by one of the ill-bred gentlemen of that county."

Mrs. Gardiner smiled at her daughter's lively friend. "Do

not fear, Suzy. My husband has assigned Howes to attend with Lizzy. And of course, she will take her companion, Mrs. Annesley."

∞∞∞

"Promise you will write me daily."

Elizabeth hugged her dearest friend close. "I cannot promise to write you daily, but I will write you often. Twice a week, at least."

Suzy frowned. "I cannot like it, but I must allow you to have your diversions."

"Very magnanimous of you." Elizabeth pretended to be serious, causing her friend to deliver a friendly swat to her arm. "I will miss you," she said before hugging her friend one last time. "I will return in time for our annual Christmas celebrations."

"Oh yes, I have already planned many diversions for us. And then after, we must visit Madame Etienne's for new dresses. Nicholas has already accused me of being an old maid. I must find a husband this season."

"We have only just turned twenty! Your brother was teasing you. And I believe Uncle Paul will wish to keep you in his home for at least one more year."

"Father would keep me in his home forever, if he could. Nevertheless, I do not wish to be an old bride, and I do not wish it for you either. This spring we will find our husbands."

"I will help you find a husband. I do not wish to marry for anything less than the greatest of loves. If I must wait until I am an old maid before I find him, then so be it."

"Oh, I shall also only marry for the greatest love. But I shall do it this year." Suzy's smile widened as she waited for her friend's resulting laugh.

The friends hugged one last time before Suzy stepped out to her waiting carriage. Since the Gardiners moved to Brook Street, Suzy and Elizabeth often walked to each other's homes, but the day was cold and rainy. Shutting the door against a gust of wind, Elizabeth turned to find her mother waiting for her.

"Darling, I would like to speak with you for a moment."

Elizabeth quickly acquiesced and followed her mother into the parlor. "What is it, Mama?" Her mother indicated she should sit next to her on the settee.

Taking her daughter's hands in her own, she began. "Elizabeth, I do not wish to alarm you, but I must admit I share some of your friend's reservations for your trip to Meryton."

Elizabeth scrunched her nose in confusion. "Why? Surely you do not fear that Jane will harm me in some way."

Mrs. Gardiner patted her daughter's hand. "Not intentionally. Jane is, as you said, a sweet lady, at least on the surface. But she has been too spoilt by your aunt and made to think too little of others and too much of herself." Elizabeth nodded, though she did not fully understand what her mother was trying to say.

"You worry she will do something to harm me, Mama?"

Her mother shook her head. "I worry that she will unintentionally hurt you. You love her unconditionally, simply because she is your sister by birth. When you love, Elizabeth, you love with all your heart. You are fiercely loyal. I think Jane loves you, in her own way, but she loves her comfort more. It is why she married that imbecilic husband."

Elizabeth laughed. "Mama, that is hardly a nice sentiment, but I must agree. Mr. Collins did not impress me as having a superior wit when we met at their wedding."

Her mother attempted to hide her own smile. "He most

certainly did not. But with Jane's paltry portion, he may have seemed the best option she had. Especially since your aunt was loathe to let her out of her sight."

"Her portion was five thousand. That is not so small a dowry, though I do wish my aunt and uncle had allowed her to keep the interest the money earned over the last twenty years."

Her mother scowled. "As I said, they are selfish, and they have raised a selfish daughter. It is only her nature that has saved her from being impossible to tolerate. But you are correct, that is not so small an amount. Given her birth as a gentlewoman and her good looks, your father could have easily found her a wealthy tradesman to marry. But she wished to be a gentleman's wife, and so she settled for the only one she knew."

"Do not fear for me on that front. As I told Suzy, I will only marry for the deepest of love and affection."

As her friend had done only minutes ago, her mother pulled her in for a tight hug. "You must promise that you will not wander off without Howes or Mrs. Annesley to protect you. Your dowry of fifty-thousand pounds is a mighty incentive for a gentleman, both in London and in the country."

"I promise, Mama."

Mrs. Gardiner released her daughter and reclaimed her hands. "You are not the daughter of my body, Elizabeth, but you are the daughter of my heart. I dare say I loved you even before I loved your father."

Elizabeth blinked away the tears that rapidly formed in her eyes. "I love you, too, Mama."

"Then you must promise to write me twice as much as you write Suzy. If she is to receive two letters each week, then I must receive four. It is only fair, after all."

Elizabeth agreed with a laugh. "Of course. I shall carry a pad of paper with me so that I can write down my every thought and experience as they happen. You will open my letters to find a flutter of unconnected comments and events on small pieces of paper that you must piece together to understand."

Chapter 2

The Assembly

"You are here!" Jane Collins hurried down the stairs to greet her sister before Elizabeth even had a chance to step from the carriage.

"Madam, if you will excuse me."

"Oh, yes." Jane stepped back, a tinge of embarrassment on her cheeks. "Forgive me." The hulking footman Mr. Gardiner had assigned to his daughter assisted his mistress from the vehicle, followed soon after by Mrs. Annesley, and finally by Milly, Elizabeth's maid.

When Elizabeth was finally on the ground, Jane closed in and clasped her sister in a tight hug. "My dear, dear sister. You can have no idea how much I have anticipated your visit. I have wished all my life for you to come and stay months with me so that we can be true sisters. But it was not to be. Mother insisted she did not have the time or money to house you, nor would she spare me for more than a few days to visit in London."

Elizabeth willed herself not to cry. This was exactly the type of welcome she had most hoped for in her heart. "I am so thrilled to be here. I wish we had arrived earlier, but there was a carriage with a broken wheel ahead of us. It took up much of the road and we were unable to get around it for the longest time."

Jane pulled her sister into the house. "That is no matter at all. I am only glad you made it in time, else you may have missed tonight's assembly."

"Assembly?" Elizabeth eyes widened. "You did not mention it in your letters. I dare say neither Mrs. Annesley nor I are prepared for a ball after hours of travel."

Mr. Collins, her sister's husband and, though she loathed to admit it, her brother-in-law, joined the ladies in the entryway. "Welcome, sister. It is good to have you here at last." He pulled his wife to him and gave her a wet kiss on the side of her cheek causing both Jane and Elizabeth to wince.

"I was just telling Lizzy about the assembly. She has indicated she is tired after so many hours of travel, but you must help me convince her to attend, husband."

Mr. Collins clapped his hands together, so delighted was he to practice the art of persuasion. "Oh yes, sister. Tonight will be a grand event. It may not be hosted in a private ballroom like those you attend in London, but I daresay there will be more gentlefolk than tradesmen in attendance, which must surely be a relief since you are so often attending parties with the opposite attendance rations."

"I believe you mean 'ratios'," Elizabeth suggested.

"No, no. Rations. I am certain that is correct." Mr. Collins jowls jiggled for a full two seconds after he shook his head to indicate his sister-in-law's mistake. Though he was not a heavy man, he did have an abundance of excessive skin. His face crept directly into his neck with no evidence of a jaw or chin. Elizabeth was shocked when she viewed him for the first time at the wedding. She had not anticipated that her beautiful sister would marry such an unattractive man, but she consoled herself that he was likely an intelligent and kind gentleman. Unfortunately, soon after the vows were said, Mr. Collins opened his mouth to speak, and all hope of his intelligence fled. That he showed every indication of being kind, however, must count for something, Elizabeth silently reassured herself.

Mr. Collins cleared his throat. "As I was saying, the assembly will offer you a chance to meet the people of the neighborhood and to dance, though I dare say you will not be as popular as my Jane. She always dances every set." Elizabeth was shocked. A matron dancing every set when surely men will be scarce due to the war — it was not what she would have imagined from her sister.

Jane smiled obligingly at her husband. "We purchased our tickets, but we did not obtain one for you or for your companion. I hope you do not mind. I am sure my uncle has sent you with ample funds. Mr. Collins asked Sir William Lucas to save you a ticket. I hope he does not forget, else you will not have a way in and will be forced to come back to the house." Elizabeth ignored the slight, for surely it was unintended. She could not, however, prevent herself from noticing the vexed look on her companion's face. She contented herself that Mrs. Annesley simply did not wish to attend an assembly. Certainly, the lady knew that Jane spoke without thought and no ill intent was intended.

∞∞∞

"Milly, I apologize for the rush, but it seems I am to attend a public ball tonight. I have asked Mrs. Annesley to assist with my hair. You must hurry and steam my gown."

"Aye, miss. I can have the violet gown ready in a trice. Mrs. Annesley already warned me that we would need to rush this evening. I asked the housekeeper to send up warm water. It will not be enough for a bath, but it should allow you wash away the travel grime and freshen yourself as best you can." So saying, Milly pulled the silk gown from the as-yet unpacked trunk and swept out of the room to find the laundry.

Elizabeth busied herself with unpacking the trunk until a knock at the door indicated the water had arrived. After emptying half the water into the basin, the young girl hurried to help Elizabeth from her dress so that she could cleanse herself.

Elizabeth thanked the maid and then set about washing her body as best she could. Though she would have wished for time enough for a proper bath, she could not blame the absence of a soak for the source of her discontent. No, that fault could be aptly assigned to her sister and Mr. Collins. Though she was certain her sister had meant no ill with her comments, it was still astonishing that she expected her guests to attend a ball on the first night of her visit! And to have failed to secure tickets for Mrs. Annesley and herself? Unfathomable! She could not bring herself to be angry with her sister, but her Aunt Phillips did not warrant the same generosity. *This is what would have befallen you, Lizzy, had you been raised by your aunt. Lucky for you, your mama and papa taught you to behave with impeccable manners.*

But soon, Elizabeth had coaxed herself from her ill temper. As the cloth in her hand served to remove the dust from her face and body, time did the same with her uncharitable thoughts.

After a brief knock at the door, Mrs. Annesley entered. "Miss Gardiner, I am hardly as adept as Milly, but allow me to fix your hair." Elizabeth smiled at her dear companion. The lady had long served as her governess. When Elizabeth turned seventeen it was decided she no longer needed lessons, but as a valuable member of the Gardiner family, she was loath to let Mrs. Annesley go. She convinced her papa she required a companion, and he, unable to deny his daughter anything, relented.

Elizabeth took the brush from the elder lady's hands. "Allow me to brush it out. I am certain it has become quite knotted today. It will be faster if I do this first part."

Soon, Elizabeth's hair was brushed and shining. Mrs. Annesley placed a few drops of lavender oil in her palms and then ran her fingers through her charge's dark mane. "There, you will smell as sweet as you are."

Elizabeth laughed. "Hardly. I would have wished for a full bath. If I had known there was to be an assembly tonight, I would have waited until tomorrow to arrive."

Mrs. Annesley deftly twisted and pinned Elizabeth's curls on top of her head. "Yes, I would have preferred to skip tonight's festivities, as well, but it is not to be. We are here and we must do as our hosts wish for us." She patted Elizabeth's shoulder. "It is only one night, dear. You will have many other opportunities to get to know your sister."

∞∞∞

"See here, sister, I will introduce you to all the best people." Mr. Collins pushed through the crowd before turning to give Elizabeth an imperious look, prompting her to follow.

"Sir William Lucas, may I introduce my sister, Miss Elizabeth Gardiner?"

Sir William had long been acquainted with Elizabeth. He had invested in her papa's businesses and had taken supper with them many times over the years. "Miss Gardiner, it is a pleasure to see you again." With a bit of nostalgia, he added, "I held you when you were just a babe. I have never seen a happier father than Mr. Bennet. He surely would have been proud to see what a fine jewel you have grown to be." Elizabeth smiled at the jolly man before her.

"Sir, I believe I need to purchase a ticket for myself and my companion."

Sir William looked affronted. "You did not obtain your sister's passage to tonight's event?"

Mr. Collins jowls shook with nervous energy. "I… I believe I asked you to save her a ticket."

Sir William scowled. "I do not believe you did. In any case, it is my pleasure to say that tickets are sold out, Miss Gardiner, so you and your companion must attend as my guests of honor."

Elizabeth's smile widened. "Thank you, sir, though I do have funds to pay."

He patted her hand. "No doubt you do. May I reintroduce you to my daughter?"

Elizabeth allowed Sir William to escort her to greet Miss Charlotte Lucas. They had been introduced at Jane's wedding the previous spring and had enjoyed one another's company very well. They had exchanged regular letters since then, but Elizabeth was happy to spend more time in her company. Mrs. Annesley indicated she would sit in the corner before bidding the party adieu.

"Miss Lucas, it is good to see you again."

Charlotte greeted Elizabeth as though they were old friends. "I believe you agreed to call me Charlotte."

Elizabeth smiled. "And so I did. And you are to call me Elizabeth."

"I have been so looking forward to your visit. When Jane mentioned that you were to stay with her for a full two months, I was beside myself with glee. I hope you do not mind my impertinence, but I anticipate we will become the best of friends."

"Since I am known for my own impertinence, I do not believe it would be wise for me to snub yours."

Charlotte called over two more ladies Elizabeth remembered from the wedding, Miss King, a shy young lady with bright red hair, recently moved to Meryton to live with her aunt, and Miss Goulding, a plump, pretty blonde of about Elizabeth's age.

"Is it true you only arrived to Longbourn this afternoon?" Miss King said the words in a breathy whisper.

"Yes, our carriage was delayed, so it was closer to supper hour when we arrived. I had less than an hour to unpack and prepare myself for the dance."

"My mother says that Jane and Mr. Collins together have less sense than a chicken in a pigsty." Miss Goulding laughed in a pleasing way, which made it difficult for Elizabeth to take offense. It did not matter, since Charlotte was quick to jump to Jane's defense.

"That is not fair, Constance. Jane is not senseless, she simply does not have the ability to say no. Because she is so easily pleased by circumstances, she believes others will be as well."

Miss Goulding only laughed more. "You say that for Miss Gardiner's benefit and not my own."

"It is quite shocking, though," Miss King softly added. "To require a guest to attend an assembly on their first night at one's home and then to leave them no sooner than they enter the room." All four ladies turned to look at Jane who stood next to her mother, Mrs. Phillips, and a group of other matrons.

A sensation of disappointment washed over Elizabeth, but she mentally shook it away. She planned to stay a full eight weeks in Hertfordshire. There was plenty of time to get to know Jane. Tonight she would dance and laugh and make new friends.

Chapter 3

New Friends

The ladies of Meryton were aflutter due to the imminent arrival of a party of affluent gentlemen from London. "My mother said there were to be four gentlemen and three ladies," Miss Goulding claimed.

Miss King, feeling more confident, raised her voice just louder than a whisper to refute her friend. "No, no. It is to be six ladies and five gentlemen."

Charlotte laughed. "I have it on good authority that you are both wrong. My father visited Netherfield today and there are to be three gentlemen, and two ladies. The man who leased the estate is a Mr. Bingley, and he is joined by his two sisters, his eldest sister's husband, and a good friend."

"Mr. Charles Bingley?" Elizabeth asked.

Charlotte nodded. "Yes, do you know him?"

Elizabeth indicated that she did. She told them that his father had been good friends with her own papa until his untimely death two years ago. "Since then, Mr. Bingley has often been at our home to discuss business matters with Papa. Mama has sometimes invited him to stay for supper. I am certain you will all like him. He is very amiable." This information was happily accepted by all three of her companions.

"Is he handsome?" Miss Goulding asked, causing Miss

King to blush a fiery shade of pink.

Elizabeth smiled at her new, bold friend. "I think most ladies will find him to be handsome. He is not so tall, but I cannot call him short. His figure is pleasing, his eyes are brown, and his hair is the lightest of red, one might mistake it for blond. I think you will be pleased with his looks."

"What about his friend, a Mr. Darcy? Are you familiar with him, as well? Father said he was not to arrive until today, so I have no information on him."

Elizabeth shook her head. "I am sorry, Charlotte, that is not a gentleman I know." The ladies were briefly disappointed, but their emotions rallied when the doors opened and in walked five new persons.

"They are here!" Miss King squeaked. "And he is handsome, just as you said, Miss Gardiner."

"Not as handsome as his friend. That is a gentleman I would like to get to know." Miss Goulding then laughed heartily at her own comment. Elizabeth's eyes traveled from the well-known face of Mr. Bingley to the tall gentleman who trailed behind. Her heart sped. Miss Goulding had not exaggerated. He was possibly the most handsome gentleman she had ever seen. His dark, curly hair, sculpted jaw, and broad shoulders greatly appealed to her.

Charlotte took Elizabeth's arm. "Come. Father will want to greet them and make introductions to my family. Mr. Bingley will be pleased to see that you are in attendance."

Although Elizabeth wished to be introduced to the handsome Mr. Darcy, she declined. "I appreciate the offer, but I must go to Jane. If I am to be introduced to the group, it should be in partnership with my sister." The little group broke up so that each lady could find her respective family members. Elizabeth weaved her way through the crowd until she was beside her sister and aunt.

"There you are, Eliza. Jane mentioned you were here, but you are so short I could scarcely find you in the crowd." Elizabeth contained the frown that threatened on her lips. She was nearly the same height as Jane.

"I have been reacquainting myself with the young ladies of the community. They all went to find their families so they could be introduced to the new party."

Her aunt sniffed. "You are smart to seek out your sister. The gentlemen will recognize her beauty and wish to be introduced to her straight away. But I warn you not to get your hopes too high. Though you are better looking that I had anticipated, you still do not have your sister's fine looks."

"Then it is good for me that Jane is married, else I may never gain a gentleman's attention in her presence."

Her aunt looked as if she wished to say more, but she was interrupted by the arrival of her son-in-law. "My darling, you must come with me. And you, too, sister. I would have you meet our new neighbors. I, myself, have not yet met the gentleman, but I do not believe we should be made to wait for an introduction. As a fellow gentleman, I declare it is just as appropriate for me to introduce myself."

Mr. Collins pulled his wife along while Elizabeth and Mrs. Phillips followed in their wake. When they arrived to greet the Netherfield party, Mrs. Phillips pushed Elizabeth aside so that she stood just in front of her niece.

"Mr. Bingley, my good man, you must allow me to welcome you to Meryton. It is our humble pleasure to host you and your family and guests. I am Mr. Collins. My estate is Longbourn, and I am your nearest neighbor." Mr. Collins bent at the waist and offered a deep bow. Unfortunately, he had stopped too near to Mr. Bingley, which forced that gentleman to step back to avoid a collision. There was some scuffling, as Mr. Bingley jostled into Mr. Darcy who stood gaping in horror at the imbecilic gentleman who had eschewed decorum and introduced himself.

"Allow me to introduce my lovely wife, Mrs. Collins, my mother-in-law, Mrs. Phillips, and my sister, Miss — "

"Miss Elizabeth Gardiner!" Mr. Bingley's eyes lit with happiness to see a familiar face. "I would not have anticipated meeting you in Meryton, of all places, but I am glad to find you here. How is your father and mother?"

Elizabeth assured him her parents were well and encouraged him to make the introductions for his party. To his right stood his oldest sister, Mrs. Hurst, a plump woman who looked much like her brother. She was joined by her husband, a lethargic looking gentleman who eyed the punchbowl on the opposite side of the room. "This is my youngest sister, Miss Caroline Bingley. I believe you are the same age and will likely have many friends in common." Miss Bingley's mouth opened in horror at the thought of sharing any background with someone attending a public assembly. "And this is my good friend, Mr. Darcy." Mr. Bingley turned, indicating the tall man behind him. The air seemed to shift as he stepped forward and offered a polite bow. A sudden warmth spread through her, starting from the pit of her stomach and rising to her cheeks. His steady gaze met hers, and for a moment, she was certain he could sense the rapid flutter of her heart. Gathering her wits, Elizabeth dipped a curtsy to the group, which prompted Mrs. Phillips and Jane to follow suit.

"Miss Gardiner my first dance is promised to Miss Lucas, but I would be honored to dance the second with you." Elizabeth noted Jane's shocked look before accepting Mr. Bingley's offer.

"My dear, I believe we should dance, as well." Mr. Collins reached his hand out to Jane, but she did not accept it.

"I am sorry, Mr. Collins, but I have promised the first to Mr. Lucas. I did not expect you would wish to dance."

Mr. Collins' jowls shook as he answered her with some

animation. "No, of course. It would be unseemly for me to open the dance with my own wife. Though, for all those who live in tents and the porpoises, it is hardly any different to dance the second than the first." Elizabeth hid a smile when she saw Mr. Darcy's eyes widen at Mr. Collins' blunder. She must remember to share that with Suzy in her next letter.

∞∞∞

Elizabeth danced the first with Mr. John Goulding, the older brother of Miss Goulding. "My sister says you know the new gentleman from Netherfield." Elizabeth admitted that she did, though only through her father. From there, the two discussed travel. He had spent the summer months with a friend in Staffordshire, while she was planning to go to the neighboring county of Gloucestershire for the yuletide season. Their conversation was superficial but engaging.

Soon, Mr. Bingley found her for the next set. "I really cannot believe I have found you here, of all places, Miss Gardiner. But you must tell me, how is that you are sisters to Mrs. Collins?"

"Our parents were in a terrible carriage accident when Jane was but three and I was not yet out of my infancy. Unfortunately, they did not survive. My aunt, Mrs. Phillips, agreed to raise Jane, and my papa, who is by blood my uncle, raised me."

The movements of the dance took them apart for a while. When they reunited, Mr. Bingley asked. "Were you from here? Originally, I mean?"

Elizabeth skipped around her partner before answering. "Yes, my father owned Longbourn. Mr. Collins' father was his heir. My father passed away before he could father a son."

"Then your sister —"

"Yes, my sister married our cousin and has now returned

as mistress of our ancestral home."

Mr. Bingley looked down the line of dancers where Jane partnered her husband. Mr. Collins was sweating profusely and missed several steps of the dance, but it did not appear to affect his wife. She maintained a serene and sweet look on her face.

"They are very… different," Mr. Bingley finally said.

Elizabeth smiled. It was always like this. No matter how much her family insisted she was the spitting image of her sister, aside from her dark hair, she did not believe it. Men always found Jane enchanting and beautiful. And, though she felt unkind to think it, no one thought of Mr. Collins as handsome.

When the dance ended, Mr. Bingley offered his arm to Elizabeth. "You must let me introduce you properly to Darcy. I do not believe he made the connection when you were introduced before." Wearing a broad smile he walked to the corner where his friend stood, grim faced with his hands held firmly behind his back.

"Darcy, I need not have looked anywhere else. I knew you would be holding up a wall, and here I find you holding up two!" Mr. Darcy's frown deepened, but his eyes softened as they met Elizabeth's. "Allow me to properly introduce my companion. This is Miss Elizabeth Gardiner."

Mr. Darcy offered a small bow. "It is a pleasure to meet you again, Miss Gardiner." Elizabeth felt a slight flutter in her chest as she returned his gaze.

"No, no," Bingley laughed. "This is not a typical lady, desirous of your purse, Darcy. This is Miss Gardiner, as in Gardiner Imports and G & E Shipping."

Mr. Darcy's eyes widened. "Truly? I met with your father only last week. My father invested in Gardiner Imports some fourteen years ago. The profits have been staggering, to put it mildly. I decided to invest further into the newer venture."

Elizabeth nodded her head in acknowledgement. "Yes,

Papa's businesses have done very well, though the newer venture is no longer so new. I believe Papa and Uncle Paul began G & E at least eight years ago.

Mr. Darcy nodded his understanding but said nothing further. Finally, the silence was interrupted by the clearing of Mr. Bingley's throat. Mr. Darcy scowled at his friend. "You are not taking ill, I hope."

Mr. Bingley easily dismissed his friend's comment and then dramatically rolled his eyes toward Elizabeth. It took three attempts before Mr. Darcy got the hint. "Miss Gardiner, would you honor me with the next dance?"

Elizabeth pretended not to have witnessed Mr. Bingley's embarrassing display and accepted the offer. A shock of something unexpected ran from her fingers to her elbow when Mr. Darcy offered her his hand. She took a deep breath. The music began and they silently went through the steps. After several minutes with no conversation, Elizabeth spoke. "Is this your normal style of dance, sir?"

A look of confusion crossed her partner's face. "I do not understand your question."

She suppressed a smile. "Are you normally so austere at a ball? We must have some conversation." Then she smiled broadly before floating away to the next formation.

When she returned to him, he spoke. "You must forgive me madam. I did not arrive until late this afternoon. Evening really. There was a carriage—"

"A carriage in the road with a broken wheel! We must have been very near one another for I was also delayed today. I arrived so late that I did not have supper. I only just had time to prepare myself for the ball."

The dance took them apart again, but soon they rejoined and restarted their conversation. "How do you do it, Miss Gardiner? You and I had nearly identical days and yet you are bright and pleasant and do not seem displeased to be here, whereas I would much rather have spent the evening at Netherfield, chatting with my friend, and catching up on one another's lives."

"I would have also preferred to stay in tonight. I was tired and had many hopes to get to know my sister better. We were raised by two different family members and have had little opportunity to get to know one another. But it was not to be. Since I must be here, as it would have been rude to deny my host's wishes, I decided to be pleasant. It has turned out to be a nice night. The people are not much like what I am used to, but they are kind and friendly." Mr. Darcy looked around the room as if he saw the revelers in a different light.

Soon the dance ended and Mr. Darcy escorted Elizabeth to her group of friends. They had joined together once again and were tittering happily about some point of gossip. Mr. Darcy excused himself only a moment before Miss Goulding burst out, "Oh Elizabeth! I can call you Elizabeth?" Elizabeth nodded her consent prompting Miss Goulding to continue.

"Mr. Bingley's horrid sister, the younger one, loudly proclaimed to her sister that we are all provincial mushrooms. Then she said that the only good thing about being here is that our lack of fashion will juxtapose nicely against her superior understanding of how to dress. Mr. Darcy, she assured her sister, will soon fall at her feet and beg her to marry him."

Elizabeth looked toward the lady in question and then to Mr. Darcy's retreating back. "But that is not the funniest of it," Miss Goulding continued. "No sooner did she say it than Mr. Darcy led you to the dance floor. He has not even spoken with her all night!" At this, the ladies broke out into another round of happy giggles. And though Elizabeth did not credit there was anything more to her dance with Mr. Darcy's than an obligation to a business partner's daughter, she joined them in their merriment.

Chapter 4

Know Your Place

The next morning, Elizabeth, Jane, and Mr. Collins awaited the arrival of several ladies from town. The plan was to enjoy tea and discuss the happenings from the previous night's assembly, an event universal to women across the kingdom. Elizabeth and Suzy always met the morning after an event to laugh about silly moments or share thoughts about fashion. Why Mr. Collins was in attendance, Elizabeth could not say, but the odd man seemed quite thrilled to discuss every occurrence of the ball.

"Welcome, welcome," he called to the arriving Lucas family. Behind them a carriage followed, which included Mrs. Goulding, Miss Goulding, and Miss King. Finally, Mrs. Phillips arrived. Having no ready access to a carriage she had been forced to walk, which from the sour look on her face did not suit the lady.

"Jane, dear, you should have sent your man to collect me."

Jane blushed in a becoming manner. "I apologize, Mama. You should have mentioned it last night." The lady huffed her irritation, and then upon seeing Elizabeth, huffed once more.

Soon, everyone was settled in the drawing room. Elizabeth shared a settee with Charlotte, while Miss Goulding and Miss King sat on her left. "Tell me your thoughts of our newest neighbor. He was an agreeable sort, I dare say." Mr. Collins wore a smug expression. He clearly wished the ladies to ask him more about his interactions with Mr. Bingley.

"I believe we can ask Miss Gardiner her impressions of Mr. Bingley, as she appeared to be well acquainted with the gentleman. Tell us, dear, how is that you know him, and is he as agreeable as he appeared?" Lady Lucas' question did not please Mr. Collins or Mrs. Philips, and from the tight lines around Jane's mouth, perhaps not her, either.

"I have known Mr. Bingley for several years, but I had not met his sisters until the assembly. I can say little of them, but I will say that their brother is a very good-natured fellow. His father was good friends with my own papa. Since the father's passing, Mr. Bingley has been the one to discuss business with Papa. He has dined with us many times."

"He seemed to be pleased with your attendance. He spent many minutes speaking with you." Mrs. Goulding smiled at her daughter's new friend. "And his friend, Mr. Darcy, honored you as well. You were the only one he danced with the entire evening. He did not even ask his hostess!"

Elizabeth blushed. "Mr. Bingley introduced us. Mr. Darcy is also an investor in Papa's businesses, though I had never met him before. We did not speak much, but he did mention that he had arrived late and was very tired from travel. I believe he will be more amiable when he has had time to rest and settle in at Netherfield."

Mr. Collins cleared his throat. "I must warn you, sister, to not reach above your station. Mr. Darcy and Mr. Bingley are both gentlemen and you are naught but the daughter of a tradesman. Do not embarrass your hosts with your flirtations." Charlotte touched Elizabeth's hand to calm her after Mr. Collins' unseemly insinuations.

Recognizing the tension, Lady Lucas felt a need to defend her daughter's newest friend. "I must remind you, Mr. Collins, that Miss Gardiner is the daughter of a gentleman, she was only raised by a tradesman, same as your dear Jane."

"And for that matter," Mrs. Goulding added, "Mr. Bingley is not yet a gentleman. He is only leasing his estate. Until he settles, he is exactly as Miss Gardiner's father... a tradesman." Miss Goulding smiled approvingly at her mother's addition to the conversation.

"I only meant to warn my sister away from the gentlemen. I would not like to see her with a beating heart."

Miss King blinked in a confused manner until Miss Goulding leaned close and whispered, "Broken heart. He always confuses his words." Elizabeth's irritation fled in the wake of such a ridiculous comment.

"Let's change the subject," Jane suggested.

"Yes, let's. There is no point discussing my niece's prospects. She was not gifted the kind of looks that would interest gentlemen of Mr. Bingley's or Mr. Darcy's caliber, anyway."

Charlotte turned to Elizabeth. "The day is fine and I would like to walk. Would you like to join me? We can discuss the assembly while we do." She looked from Elizabeth to the two other young women. All agreed with alacrity and were soon removed from the frustrating conversation of Mr. Collins and Mrs. Phillips.

When they were safely out of earshot, Miss Goulding huffed. "I feel for you Elizabeth. Truly. To be stuck with such a family for the next eight weeks. I give you full permission to visit me at any time when you need an escape. And— " Her eyes widened, "Oh, I have called you Elizabeth, but I never granted you permission to call me Constance. You simply must, especially since you have allowed me to call you by your given name."

"And I am Mary," Miss King added in her quiet way. Soon all the ladies agreed to call one another by their first names.

Miss Goulding wished to continue her commentary on the 'odious Mr. Collins,' but Elizabeth deftly turned the conversation to the evening before. "I believe, Mary, that I saw you dance twice with Mr. Johnson." Miss King blushed at the observation, but after some prodding admitted the gentleman was 'very nice to talk to.' Soon, the irritations of the drawing room were forgotten, and the ladies laughed and tittered over remarks about the assembly.

∞∞∞

"I declare I have never met with nicer people or prettier girls as I did last night." Though Darcy paid little attention to the looks of the ladies, he could not disagree with Bingley's claims about the kindness of the attendees. Miss Elizabeth Gardiner had opened his eyes to that.

"Charles, you must be joking. I dare you to name one pretty girl from the entire assembly." Caroline Bingley had been in a mood since they entered the carriage for home last evening, and it appeared a full night's rest had done her little good.

"I can name several. Mrs. Collins is exceptionally beautiful."

"She is a handsome woman, I will grant you that, but she is also married. And her dress was so provincial." Miss Bingley raised her nose further in the air.

"Then I will mention her sister, Miss Elizabeth Gardiner. They are nearly identical, apart from their hair. And I doubt you can fault her clothing."

Miss Bingley sighed. "She is tolerable, I suppose, but hardly worth mentioning in this conversation. Besides, she is the daughter of a tradesman."

"Caroline, you are the daughter of a tradesman." Miss Bingley's face reddened, and she cast wary eyes toward Darcy.

"Besides, Miss Gardiner is a lovely girl. I have known her many years and have dined with her family more than a dozen times. Father also dined with them many times on Gracechurch Street."

"Gracechurch Street!" Miss Bingley physically cringed. "Why, that is all the way in Cheapside."

Ignoring Miss Bingley's screeching tones, Darcy addressed his friend. "She did seem a pleasant sort of lady. I enjoyed our conversation while we danced."

"Oh, but how dreadfully high-handed she was to solicit a dance from you, Mr. Darcy, when it was obvious you did not wish to participate." Miss Bingley fluttered her fan in what Darcy could only assume was intended to be seductive. It was not. "I was appalled by the way she stood and waited in front of you for such a long time."

"You are mistaken, Miss Bingley. I willingly offered to partner with her. It seems we were both stuck behind the broken carriage yesterday afternoon. She arrived in Meryton only a little before I did."

"No doubt she arrived by stage. I am surprised they did not make her walk the remainder of the way."

"I very much doubt it," Bingley said. "Mr. Gardiner is an exceedingly wealthy gentleman. He would have sent her in his own carriage. And likely with a footman and maid in tow. I know for a certainty that she came with her companion, as I spoke with the lady for a time."

"How wealthy could he be?" Caroline sneered. "I wager she has less than five thousand pounds in her dowry. I was told her sister came to her marriage with that much."

"I have heard it is fifty thousand. Her father has no other children yet, though he has been married many years. It is likely his business will also go to Miss Gardiner upon his death." Caroline gasped. Darcy schooled his features to pretend disinterest. Fifty thousand was a tremendous sum, and

Gardiner's business was likely valued at double that amount. She would make someone an exceptional wife. She was rich, mannerly, beautiful, and an excellent dancer. *It is too bad she is a tradesman's daughter.*

After many moments of silence, Darcy spoke. "How is that Miss Gardiner and Mrs. Collins are sisters, but were raised so differently?"

Mr. Bingley, having spoken with Elizabeth about that very topic the evening prior, answered. "When their parents passed away, they were left to their aunt, Mrs. Phillips to raise."

"In case you are wondering, that was the vulgar woman with the ridiculously small feathers in her cap," Caroline interrupted.

Darcy thought small feathers were no less ridiculous than large ones, but he chose to keep his opinion to himself. "Go on," he prompted.

Bingley cleared his throat. "Yes, as I was saying… Mrs. Phillips was to raise them both, but she did not have the ability to keep two young girls. That is how Mr. Gardiner came to adopt Miss Gardiner. Her mother was his sister, as well. He took Miss Gardiner and Mrs. Collins stayed in Meryton, with her aunt."

"But surely her aunt had room for both girls? Her husband appears to be a somewhat successful solicitor."

"I wondered the same thing last night, Darcy. But no one knows a family's true circumstances until they live them. Perhaps Mr. Phillips was not so well off at that time. Much can change about a person's finances over the span of twenty years."

Having recovered from learning of Elizabeth's family's great wealth, Miss Bingley once again raised her nose high. "If her family is so well off, then why have I not met her during the season? I cannot recall having set eyes on her one time in my life before last night."

Bingley smiled in such a way that Darcy wondered what

he was thinking. Hiding a smile, his friend answered. "I doubt you run in the same circles, Caroline."

Chapter 5

Oakham Mount

The next day, Elizabeth woke early and escaped the house before any of the residents awoke. She did not sneak away before the servants rose, but with the aid of good luck, she managed to slip out the door without being caught by her footman. Her mother and father would scold her if they were to learn that she willingly left Howes at Longbourn, but having grown up in London where it was neither proper nor safe for a lady to walk alone, she relished the opportunity to ramble without a care for whomever was forced to follow her.

Charlotte Lucas had mentioned Oakham Mount as the premier walking destination in the area. Elizabeth asked for exact directions and turned left when she reached the small road that connected to Longbourn's drive. "Walk east along the lane, and then cross into my father's land when you pass our house," Charlotte had explained.

Elizabeth found the path easily and began the ascent. The trail was well cut and only a few places required careful attention. It was not as rigorous as climbing hills in the Peak, an area Elizabeth had visited many times on her trips north to vacation with her mother's family. Despite the relative ease of this walk, she did find herself growing warm.

While she walked, she replayed the events of yesterday over in her head. The gathering of local ladies had not gone as desired. Elizabeth was disappointed by her aunt's disapprobation and her brother-in-law's rude comments. But she was more disheartened by her sister's unwillingness to refute her mother's or husband's comments. *I know she is a peacemaker, at heart, but I would have wished for her to stand up for me*, she thought.

Elizabeth was more pleased with her sister's company when their guests left and Mr. Collins returned to his study. "What shall we do today, Lizzy? I must sit for some time with Mrs. Hill to discuss the menus, but after that I can be available for anything you wish."

While Jane spoke with the housekeeper, Elizabeth explored the other public rooms of the house. The building had been well made, with solid stone exteriors and a well-worn maple staircase. But the interior had not been redone in some time. The primary salon had pretty colors, but everything was faded. The curtains had white spots where the sun had bleached them, and the print on the paper was difficult to discern in some areas. But age did not account for the very decided lack of comfort to be found in most of the furnishings. Elizabeth had felt a stab of sympathy when Lady Lucas perched delicately on an exceedingly lumpy side chair during yesterday's visit.

The remainder of the house was much the same, though older with more austere color choices. If Elizabeth was a betting woman, she would wager that the elder Mr. Collins had not allowed for any redecorating during his time. The paper in the other rooms appeared to be no less than forty years old. Only the east drawing room looked as though it had been remodeled during her lifetime. Elizabeth wondered if that was the only room her mother had redecorated before her untimely death.

In a mostly unused drawing room situated at the back of the house, Elizabeth found a walnut chessboard and a set of carved marble pieces. Only the bases of the pieces distinguished their set. For one set, the base was carved from matching marble;

for the other, it was carved from ebony. Elizabeth thought it the most beautiful set she had ever seen, and she longed to play, knowing her father, of whom she held no memories, had once held every piece.

That afternoon she asked Jane about it. "You are correct, it belonged to our father. I doubt anyone has played since he passed. Neither Mr. Collins or I play, and I seriously doubt Mr. Collins' father ever learned."

"If you wish it, I can teach you," Elizabeth offered, but Jane quickly refused.

"What use have I for such a thing? Chess is for the men." To Elizabeth's disappointment, Jane then took out a deck of cards and insisted her sister learn to play Piquet. Though cards held little appeal for the younger sister, she enjoyed her time alone with Jane.

Elizabeth was so caught up in her thoughts that she did not recall the last half of her climb. It was not until the view opened to reveal the town of Meryton that she regained her attention to her surroundings. "It is beautiful," she whispered to herself.

"It is indeed," a deep baritone voice replied.

∞∞∞

Elizabeth's hands went to her chest. "Mr. Darcy, I did not see you there." Darcy rose from where he sat on a small boulder.

"I apologize if I startled you, Miss Gardiner."

"Think nothing of it, sir. I was lost in my thoughts and failed to take in your presence. Although I must admit, I am surprised to find you here."

Darcy's lips quirked. "You assumed a gentleman such as myself should still be abed?"

Elizabeth stepped closer to the edge and looked down upon the town. "Not at all. I only meant that I would expect you to ride rather than walk in the morning."

Darcy held his hand toward the rock indicating that Elizabeth should sit. "I do prefer to ride, but I found a shoe was loose on my stallion, and I did not wish to take Bingley's without his permission. Since I was already up and ready, I chose to walk." *And I am glad I did*, Darcy mused, though his thoughts were more entangled than he cared to admit. The memory of their dance kept surfacing against his will—how natural it had felt to guide her, how every step seemed perfectly in sync. He had not wanted to dwell on it, yet here, in her presence, the recollection was unavoidable. The soft light of the sunrise cast Elizabeth's face in a becoming glow, and he could scarcely look away. Elizabeth smiled at him, before turning her eyes back to the scenery.

"Is this the highest peak you have climbed, Miss Gardiner?" Darcy sat on a neighboring boulder.

"Not at all. I have traveled to the Peak many times since my childhood. I enjoy the challenge of climbing those paths very much."

"The Peak District is very near my home," Darcy said. "I must admit that I am surprised to find that you have been there. Where else have you traveled?"

"I have had many opportunities to travel. We often spend the Christmas season with Uncle Paul and his family in Gloucestershire. For my tenth birthday we spent a month in Ramsgate." Darcy forced himself not to wince at the mention of that loathsome beach town. "But I must admit, the most adventurous trip I have taken was when we traveled to India."

"India!" Darcy exclaimed. "That is a very far distance, indeed. You must tell me everything about it." It delighted Elizabeth to share the details of her family's journey east. She spoke for some time about the exotic foods, animals, plants, and clothing she saw while there.

"It was a hardship to leave the place, and not just because I did not enjoy the confinement of the ship. The culture was lovely. I hope to return one day."

Elizabeth's lovely eyes shone with joy at the remembrances of her voyage. Darcy felt a warmth spread through his chest. *She is magnificent.*

"But that is enough about me. What travels have you made, sir?"

Darcy found his body had turned fully toward her of its own accord and he was surprised by how engaged he was in their conversation. "I have not traveled so far as India, but I did spend some time in Italy and Spain. I was unable to complete my tour, however, due to my father's illness. I returned home in time to spend two months with him before he passed."

"I am very sorry for your loss, Mr. Darcy." Darcy was used to such sentiments but was unaccustomed to hearing them said in such a way that he truly believed his loss pained the speaker.

Momentarily stunned by the sincerity of her words, Darcy took some time before replying, "Thank you." Wishing to change the subject, he asked, "Do you ride, Miss Gardiner?"

Elizabeth laughed. "You think me incapable, I suppose, because I live in London. But I must disappoint you, sir. I do ride. My father keeps several horses in the mews. I ride a small chestnut. Her name is Portia."

"I never did repent for doing good, nor shall not now."

"Bravo, sir. You guessed correctly her namesake. Or at least I tell people she is named in honor of my favorite character from *The Merchant of Venice*. She is, after all, very clever. But in truth, I simply liked the name. I was but nine when my papa purchased her, far too young to have read the Bard's work."

"Ah, but clearly you have read it since. I do not know many

women, men either, who would have recognized the quote so readily."

"I would chastise you for being harsh on the fairer sex, but since you were so moderate to include men in your censure, I can only bask in the praise." Darcy laughed at Elizabeth's good humor.

"Much as I have enjoyed this conversation, I must leave you. My sister and brother will be awake by now. It would be rude of me to arrive late to breakfast."

"May I escort you?"

Elizabeth thanked him for the offer, but politely declined. "I believe my sister's husband would be shocked to see you with me when I arrive at Longbourn. I would not wish for him to jump to the wrong conclusions." With a pert curtsy, Elizabeth said goodbye. Darcy watched her descend the hill until she was out of sight.

∞∞∞

As he walked the path back to Netherfield, Darcy pondered his conversation with Elizabeth. It was odd but not unheard of for a man of business to keep horses in London, but for him to have the space for at least two carriage horses, his own beast, and one for his daughter's pleasure — that was a rarity.

Darcy imagined her atop a horse. Would she approach riding with as much vigor as she did with walking and dancing? She would be resplendent in a dark red habit. Perhaps he would run into her after they both return to town, though he would likely have to go further afield to find her.

When in London, Hyde Park was Darcy's favorite riding haunt, but, at nearly an hour away, that would be too far from Gracechurch Street. Darcy was not certain of her home's location, having visited Mr. Gardiner at his warehouse on Bread

Street, but he assumed she still lived in or near the home Bingley mentioned. Finsbury Circus was not far from Cheapside, perhaps Elizabeth rode there. It was a small park, but lovely, and soon to be even nicer when the changes to the garden were made complete. Yes, that was the most likely place he would find her.

Darcy shook his head, the movement helping to rid his mind of tantalizing images of Miss Elizabeth Gardiner. *What are you doing, man?* He chastised himself. Elizabeth Gardiner was a beautiful, intriguing young woman, but that did not change the facts of the matter. He could no more pursue her than he could wed a house maid.

Though mannerly, kind, and educated, she was not from the background expected of him as the master of a large estate and grandson to an earl. Darcy could afford to speak with Miss Gardiner, but nothing more. Resolved, he pledged to do nothing that would raise her expectations.

Chapter 6

A Party at Lucas Lodge

"Here we are, my dear." Mr. Collins handed Jane out of the carriage, and quickly tucked her hand into the crook of his elbow. Neither spared a glance for the two ladies remaining in the vehicle. Elizabeth and Mrs. Annesley exchanged a look. Howes stepped forward and handed each lady out. After thanking the footman, Elizabeth took her companion's arm. "Never fear, Mrs. Annesley. I shall escort you." The elder lady chuckled and together they walked up the short flight of stairs to greet the Lucas family.

"Sir William, Lady Lucas, I thank you for inviting me to your party. I have looked forward to it the entire day." Elizabeth dipped a curtsy to her hosts.

Sir William patted his hands on his thick stomach. "Of course, my dear, of course. Your father was a good friend of mine. I could never ignore his precious daughter."

One thing Elizabeth had not expected from her visit to Meryton was the number of times her new acquaintances would refer to her father. Her mother was seldom discussed by the townsfolk, though if she resembled her sister in any way, it was understandable. But several had commented on Mr. Thomas Bennet. Though Elizabeth longed to hear everything she could about the man, she had to fight an unexpected bout of tears each time his name was spoken.

"You must tell me about him someday."

Her host patted her shoulder. "Certainly. Once our guests are settled, I will find you and share a few stories about the fellow. When I first met him, I was not yet Sir William, only Mr. Lucas. Your father did not care that I was naught but a shopkeeper. He treated me with great respect and kindness. I can see you have his nature."

Her heart soared at the unexpected compliment. "I look forward to learning more about him, but I must make way for your other guests." She and Mrs. Annesley made their way into the drawing room. Seeing her new friends gathered around a small coffee table, Elizabeth walked to them.

"There you are," Miss Goulding waved. "You have joined us just in time to take part in the wagering."

Elizabeth settled herself on a small chair to the left of Charlotte. "What are the terms?"

Miss Goulding laughed. "I knew I could count on you to be inquisitive rather than to shame me for my unladylike behavior." She cast a quelling look at Miss King until both ladies broke into merriment.

"I must assume from your behavior that Mary does not approve of your wicked ways."

Miss King laughed more. "It does not matter at all if I approve, Constance will do as she pleases. And I am not strong enough to fight her. I dare say, every ounce of trouble that finds me is because I go along with my friend's schemes."

Miss Goulding swatted Miss King's arm. "Nonsense. Besides, this is only for us. No one else need know about it."

When the two friends broke into another round of giggles, Elizabeth turned her eyes to Charlotte Lucas for answers. "Tonight there will be musical exhibitions, and Miss Goulding wagered that Mr. Collins would display."

"Does he play?" There was a small pianoforte at Longbourn, but in the two weeks since Elizabeth had arrived, Mr. Collins had not once played so much as a single note.

"He sings." Charlotte folded her hands primly in her lap.

"Tell her the full of it, Charlotte," Miss Goulding prompted. "He does more than simply sing."

A slight frown marred Charlotte's face. When she was slow to elucidate, Miss King leaned forward. "He writes his own lyrics to the tune of well-known songs."

"Pish," Miss Goulding scoffed. "He writes his own lyrics to the tune of exactly one well-known song. Greensleeves."

Deciding she wished to be a part of the conversation after all, Charlotte spoke. "He changes the words. We were wagering on who would be the subject of tonight's song."

Elizabeth was intrigued. Her brother-in-law had a high, nasal speaking voice. She did not think his singing voice would prove to be impressive. "Who has previously inspired his songs?"

Miss Goulding placed a finger on her chin. "Let me think. I believe there have been several songs written in Jane's honor, and at least two written as an ode to his mother-in-law." Elizabeth could only imagine how Mrs. Phillips must have crowed at the honor. "He wrote one to the ale master, and another to a great lady who lives in Kent, though he has never met her. Apparently, she sends him advice through letters."

Miss King leaned forward to explain. "Mr. Collins and the lady's rector are good friends, you see. The letters do not come from her but from his friend."

"So the wager is not if he will sing, it is on whom he will bestow his words?"

"Exactly," Charlotte nodded. "I believe he will sing another song for Jane."

"And I have bet on the baker. I saw Mr. Collins in his shop twice this week eating a sweet roll."

"And you, Mary? Who have you suggested?"

Miss King smiled at Elizabeth. "I have bet on you."

Elizabeth recoiled. "Then I greatly hope you do not win the bet."

Soon the conversation changed to other topics. Miss King recently received an invitation from her uncle to visit him in London after Yuletide and Elizabeth extended her own invitation for tea while Miss King was in town. Charlotte had convinced her father to purchase a new breed of chicken that lays blue eggs, and she was anxious for the hen to begin producing. And Miss Goulding had been fitted for a new dress that morning.

A commotion at the door drew their attention. Miss Lucas hid a frown. "It appears the Netherfield party has finally arrived." Elizabeth glanced at a clock that stood on the far wall. They were three-quarters of an hour late.

The four ladies watched as Sir William and Lady Lucas left their conversations and moved to greet their newest guests. "I apologize for our delayed arrival," Mr. Bingley told his host. "My sister had difficulty deciding on a dress." Miss Bingley looked not even a little embarrassed by her brother's admission.

Sir William assured his guests that everything was fine, and he encouraged them to find conversations. Mr. Bingley spotted Elizabeth and walked toward her. "Ladies, I am pleased to greet you this evening." He bowed.

While her three newest friends engaged in a conversation with the gentleman, Elizabeth found herself watching Mr. Darcy. Miss Bingley had clutched his arm tightly when the party arrived, but she was unsuccessful at keeping it. Mr. Darcy walked her to Jane, and while the ladies were conversing, he gently removed her hand from his person and walked away. Miss

Bingley turned to speak to him, but he did not stop to respond. Elizabeth hid a smile. *Well done, Mr. Darcy,* she thought.

He caught her eye as he escaped from Miss Bingley, and Elizabeth thought he might come join his friend. Her heart beat faster at the possibility. But he turned left and walked toward a window where he stood with his back to the guests.

When the conversation came to a natural pause, Elizabeth spoke. "I thought your friend might join us, but he has chosen to evaluate Lady Lucas' gardens, it seems."

Mr. Bingley turned to look. "That is Darcy's way. He is a good fellow, but uncomfortable around people he does not know well."

Elizabeth's emotions warred. On the one hand, Mr. Darcy's discomfort was to be pitied. On the other, he was a grown, well-educated man; he should force himself to engage at a party no matter how great his disquiet.

∞∞∞

Elizabeth sat with her friends for a while longer until she spotted Sir William Lucas approaching with a warm smile. His stout frame moved through the room with surprising grace, and when he reached her side, he bowed slightly.

"Miss Gardiner, I have not forgotten my promise. Would you still wish to hear more about your father?"

Elizabeth's heart fluttered at the mention of him. "Indeed, Sir William. I would be most grateful."

"Come, then. Let us move to a quieter corner. Such tales are best shared without the distractions of company."

They walked together, Sir William leading her to a small alcove near the windows, away from the liveliness of the party. He gestured to a seat, and she sat, folding her hands in her lap.

Sir William took a deep breath, his gaze far away as if recalling a distant memory.

"I first met your father when I was but Mr. Lucas, a humble shopkeeper with no grand title to my name. I owned a haberdashery, though I believe you already knew that." She nodded.

"It was long before I had the honor of being knighted by His Majesty. At that time, I was very much a part of the tradesman class, but your father—Thomas Bennet—he treated me as an equal, never once looking down upon my station. That is to be expected, though. He was always such good friends with your papa, who was, himself, born to a solicitor."

Elizabeth felt a warm pride swell in her chest, though the familiar ache of loss remained just beneath it.

"One day, he entered my shop, not long after he had become engaged to Miss Fanny Gardiner, your dear mother. He was in fine spirits, you understand, and he had Mr. Gardiner with him—your adopted father, of course, though then he was simply her brother and Mr. Bennet's friend. The two men were in a merry mood, teasing one another. Mr. Bennet wished to purchase a gift for Miss Gardiner, something special. He was clearly smitten, though Mr. Gardiner laughed and confessed that he could not possibly advise on what his sister would appreciate."

Elizabeth smiled softly, imagining the scene as it unfolded. Her father, young and in love, seeking a perfect gift for her mother. "What did he choose for her?"

"Your father eventually chose a fine ribbon, as I recall, and he took great pleasure in the selection. Mr. Gardiner, on the other hand, seemed utterly relieved when the ordeal was over. He said, 'I know not how you endure the expectations of women, Bennet, but I daresay I am not built for such matters.' The two of them laughed heartily as they left my shop."

Elizabeth giggled. "Papa has eaten his words, I think. He regularly purchases gifts for my mother."

"I suspect he does. Love does such things to a man." Sir William paused, his expression softening as the memory shifted. "A few months later, I was knighted. A great honor, to be sure, though I confess I felt somewhat out of place among the gentlemen. It was your father who first offered his congratulations, and more than that, he made it his mission to introduce me to society, ensuring I was included in gatherings. He was the kind of man who never forgot a kindness, nor allowed another to feel alone in their success."

Elizabeth blinked back a sudden rush of emotion. She had always known her father was a good man as her papa had told her many stories, but to hear these stories of him through the eyes of another brought him to life in a way she had not experienced.

"He spoke of you often, even though you were just a babe in arms," Sir William continued, his voice taking on a gentle, almost wistful tone. "You were the light of his eye, Miss Gardiner. He saw so much of himself in you, even then. Your love of laughter, your quick wit—it is though I am seeing him before me again — though you are much prettier."

Her chest tightened at the mention of her father's pride. Her papa ensured that she knew of her birth father's love for her, but to hear it spoken aloud by someone else was a balm to the wounds left by his absence.

"Does Jane also remind you of my father?"

Sir William hesitated for a moment before clearing his throat. "Perhaps if your father had lived, I might see more of him in her. Unfortunately…"

He looked to where Mr. Collins stood next to his wife. "If your father had lived, I do not believe he would have allowed your sister to marry Mr. Collins."

Elizabeth stiffened at the mention of her brother-in-law, but she held her tongue, waiting for him to continue.

"I have no doubt that Mr. Gardiner will ensure you are properly matched, as you deserve," he said, his voice heavy with meaning. "But Mr. and Mrs. Phillips… they did not do so for Jane. It pains me to say it, but your father—he would not have permitted such a match, I am certain."

Elizabeth pressed her lips together, her thoughts swirling. Her papa had said as much when Jane announced her engagement, but to hear someone else speak it… it was unsettling.

Both Elizabeth and Sir William settled into a moment of reverie, thinking of what was and what might have been. Finally, after some time had passed, he sighed.

"That was not what I wished to say, and I beg your pardon. It was rude of me." Elizabeth made no reply.

The gentleman continued. "But rest assured, your father's legacy lives on in you, Elizabeth. And I have no doubt that Mr. Gardiner will see to it that you are wed to a man who is worthy of your hand."

Elizabeth smiled faintly. "I thank you, Sir William. Your words have brought me great comfort."

He bowed his head, his expression kind. "It is my honor, my dear. Your father was a fine man, and I count myself fortunate to have known him."

∞∞∞

Darcy stood at the window for what he knew was an impolite amount of time, but he could not force himself to turn around. If he did, his eyes would gravitate toward Elizabeth, and that would not do. He had almost walked to her when he saw her sitting with Bingley and her friends. It would have been so easy to take the open chair to her left and wait until her fine eyes turned to him. It would not do. Miss Gardiner was a beautiful and engaging lady, but she was not for him.

"Tell me, Colonel, does your regiment plan to host any events while you are stationed in Meryton?" Against his will, Darcy turned from the window and Elizabeth. She stood less than five feet away speaking to Colonel Forster who had recently led his militia regiment to Meryton.

Before the colonel could respond, Darcy's own voice added to the conversation. "As much as the local populace would enjoy the society of such events, I think England's army has more to concern itself with during a time of war."

Elizabeth's eyes danced. "Mr. Darcy, I had quite convinced myself that you would stand by the window in a taciturn manner the entire evening. And here you are interrupting my conversation with logic. It is not fair to prove me wrong with such ease."

Darcy thrilled at her teasing speech. "My apologies, Miss Gardiner. If it helps, I will share that Bingley plans to host an event or two. If Colonel Forster cannot promise to do so, you at least have the Netherfield events to look forward to."

Colonel Forster was a jovial man who agreed it was beyond him to host parties for the gentlefolk of Meryton. "My men are much in need of training. I am afraid I must refrain from committing myself to hosting duties and focus on their drills, instead."

The three spoke of general topics until Colonel Forster excused himself to speak with Mr. Lane. Elizabeth and Darcy stood awkwardly in his absence until Miss Lucas joined them. "Elizabeth, we would like to start the music. Jane plans to open for us. Would you go next? I heard you play at your sister's wedding and would very much like to have that honor again."

Although she did not appear to be excited about the opportunity, Elizabeth relented without too many arguments against it. The three of them stood and listened to Mrs. Collins' halting attempts at the instrument. When the song ended, there was a collective sigh of relief from Darcy and his companions.

"Jane would have been a great proficient at the instrument, if she had practiced more," Mrs. Phillips boasted. "I would not allow her to spend too much time at it, though. She has such pretty hands, and I was afraid they would grow knotted and cramped from hours at the piano. My Jane is the prettiest in the county, and I could not afford to lessen her beauty with music practice."

Darcy frowned at the woman's illogical speech. *This is more evidence of why you must put Miss Elizabeth Gardiner from your mind. Her family is ridiculous.* Mrs. Collins glowed at her mother's nonsensical praise, oblivious to how the lady shamed her.

"If you will excuse me, Mr. Darcy. It seems that my meager skills on the pianoforte are needed."

Darcy's attention snapped back to the lady who stood next to him. "I look forward to hearing your performance." He bowed and then watched Elizabeth's pleasing form walk away.

When Elizabeth's song began, Darcy was mesmerized. Never before had he heard anyone play with such sweet emotion. And when her voice added to her beautiful playing, his feet moved forward of their own accord. He stood at the corner of the instrument and watched as her fingers ran lightly across the keyboard. Too soon, her song ended to much applause by all who attended.

"Elizabeth, you have such great talent," Mrs. Collins clapped from the other side of the pianoforte. Elizabeth face beamed at her sister's praise. Darcy had not been impressed by Mrs. Collins' attitude toward her sister, but his opinion softened upon hearing her words and upon seeing how happy they made

Elizabeth.

Having witnessed Darcy's attention to Elizabeth, Miss Bingley stepped forward and stole all of Darcy's hope for a second performance. "I will play next, Eliza."

Elizabeth stood from the bench. "The high C key sticks a little," she warned. Miss Bingley rolled her eyes at the advice. Then her eyes searched for Mr. Darcy but found he had stepped away from the instrument. With flared nostrils, she began a fast and loud rendition of one of Beethoven's *Eroica* variations.

Elizabeth found Darcy once again. "Miss Bingley plays with great precision," she said.

Darcy's relished the humor he saw in Elizabeth's sparkling eyes. "If one cannot find joy in the music, then it is imperative to play precisely and with great volume." To his great delight she laughed.

When Miss Bingley's song finally ended, Mr. Collins moved toward the pianoforte. "If you will permit it, I would like to perform an original composition." Lady Lucas' smile faltered, if only for a second, before nodding in approval.

"Ahem." Mr. Collins loudly cleared his throat, in a bid for everyone's attention. When the group quieted again, he spoke. "I have had the great pleasure of coming to know more of my wife's sister. She has impressed me as a polite and friendly guest. And in her honor, I give you my song."

Darcy looked down at Elizabeth who stood in shocked silence, her face heated to a bright crimson.

"La, La, Laaaa," Mr. Collins warmed his vocals with a series of warbling notes.

"Oh, dear," Elizabeth muttered from beside him.

Too soon, the song began.

> *Elizabeth, my sister, dear,*
> *You walk the fields to exercise.*

My wife's sister but reared in town,

Despite that you seem so mannerly.

"It does not even rhyme," she whispered to herself. Before Darcy had time to think of how to respond, Mr. Collins belted out the chorus.

Elizabeth, Elizabeth!

You are as lovely as your name.

Elizabeth, Elizabeth,

But not so lovely as my Jane!

Mr. Collins paused to view the strained looks upon people's faces. Misinterpreting the pleased expressions on the countenances of his wife and mother-in-law as broad approbation, he soon began his second verse.

Your father is a man of trade,

Your mother was from Derbyshire.

Their humble beginnings should be lauded,

For you have a sizable dowry.

Darcy winced at the man's poor comportment and terrible rhymes. His singing would have been forgiven had he not injured Elizabeth's pride in such a public manner.

"Shall I interrupt him, Miss Gardiner?"

"Thank you, sir, but I fear it is best to allow these things to play out. Your gentlemanly offer has not gone unnoticed, however."

Seeing the hurt in her eyes, Darcy was tempted to disregard her advice and force the man to be quiet. Instead, he stood stalwartly by her side, wishing to throttle Mr. Collins but doing nothing more than offering her his silent support.

Unfortunately, the song continued for three additional verses. Verse three referred to Elizabeth's preference for plain dishes. Verse four made mention of her brown hair and suggested it should have been blonde. And verse five, the worst of them all, implied she was a bluestocking due to her excessive love of reading. By the time the song ended, Elizabeth's eyes glistened with unshed tears. Darcy wanted to shake the idiotic man for disturbing the lady's equanimity. But her courage rose when her friends joined the group.

Laughing at their sympathetic looks, she said, "I suppose you have come to gloat, Mary. You wagered the song would be in my honor and you have been proven correct."

Miss King grimaced. "I wish I were not. I hope Mr. Collins has not occasioned you too much discomfort."

"Oh that was nothing," Miss Goulding said. "At least he got most of his words correct this time!"

This made Elizabeth laugh. "Indeed. The only mistake I heard was when he said I did not prefer a 'racket'. I believe he meant 'ragout'."

The ladies giggled, and even Darcy cracked a smile.

Mr. and Miss Bingley made their way to the little group. "Eliza, I must compliment you on your performance, but you are not to steal all the glory. It appears you come from a very musical family." Miss Bingley smirked as she slid her eyes to where Mr. Collins stood talking with his wife.

"Thank you, Miss Bingley. I enjoyed your song, as well. You play with such command of the keyboard." Darcy hid a smile by looking at his feet.

"I have had the pleasure of many great masters. Who was your teacher? I admit to being surprised by your skill. It must have been difficult to attract a competent master to visit you in Cheapside."

"My mother taught me the basics, and when I advanced my papa hired Monsieur Chambert." Elizabeth's voice was steady but, in her eyes, there were daggers.

"Chambert!" Miss Bingley gasped at the name of the most famous, and expensive, pianoforte master in England. "I know you jest, Eliza. He is very selective in his choice of students."

Elizabeth shrugged. "As you say, Miss Bingley."

"Oh, come now. You cannot think we will fall for your stories. Monsieur Chambert would never lower himself to give lessons so far from Mayfair."

"You are correct. He would not wish to come so far. If you will excuse me." Elizabeth curtsied to the group and moved toward her sister.

Darcy watched as Elizabeth gracefully stepped to Mrs. Collins' side. It took much effort to tear his gaze from her person. When he finally gained control over his eyes, Miss Bingley quietly cleared her throat. "That girl will do anything to make herself look like a good catch for you, Mr. Darcy. You must remember that she is a nobody from Cheapside. It does not matter how great her portion, she is not for you."

Darcy nodded. Elizabeth Gardiner was not for him. Pity.

Chapter 7

Netherfield in the Rain

The next two weeks were mostly pleasant for Elizabeth. Never one to linger on her disappointments, she quickly forgave Mr. Collins for his indecorous song. The man was certainly an imbecile, but not one with ill intent in his heart. She found his ballad embarrassing, improper, offensive, and poorly constructed, but it was not written with malice. After a month in her brother-in-law's presence, she firmly believed he was a decent fellow. He could be easily managed, if only Jane was strong enough to do it.

As for her sister, Elizabeth feelings were more inconsistent. Though Jane disliked conflict and wished to keep everyone happy, she was not as sweet natured as Elizabeth had once believed. For the most part, the two sisters got along. Jane was a good hostess and wished to please Elizabeth, but there were times when she would say something careless. It was those casual insults that led Elizabeth to trust her mother's and friend's cautions. It wounded her to admit it, but Jane's goodness was only on the surface, just as Suzy had said. Although her sister had not been mean-spirited or intentionally cruel, her comments were thoughtless at times, and often hurtful. Jane gave every impression of being overly spoiled by her adopted mother and too reliant on her good looks.

After some effort, Elizabeth convinced her sister to attempt chess. Jane quickly learned the rules of the game, and after three matches, became somewhat adept at strategy. Unfortunately, that was to be the last time the two played.

"Jane, why are you sitting in this dreary old room?" Mrs. Phillips wrinkled her nose at the décor in the unused drawing room.

"Elizabeth is teaching me to play chess. She believes I will become a proficient with enough practice." Mrs. Phillips eyes squinted at her least favorite niece. Elizabeth sat straighter in her chair. She refused to be intimidated by her aunt.

"Chess may be well and fine for a girl like Elizabeth. You, my Jane, are a beautiful woman who had the good sense to marry a landed gentleman. You have moved up in the world and need not spoil your mind or your posture hunched over a chessboard."

Choosing to ignore the intended gibe about her beauty and posture, Elizabeth remained silent. But, oh, how she wished to bite back. It was especially difficult to overlook the comment about "moving up". Jane and Elizabeth may have been raised by tradesmen, but they were born to the gentle class. Marrying a gentleman was Jane's due. For herself, Elizabeth did not care about her husband's status as long as she loved him.

Jane picked up her queen and stroked its smooth surface, before gently placing it back on the board. Elizabeth said a silent prayer that her sister would not relent, but her resolve crumbled. "You are correct, of course. I should not wish to give Mr. Collins any reason to be displeased with my figure or my pastimes."

Elizabeth attempted to persuade Jane to play many times after that day, but it was not to be. Her sister held firm to her decision, though she was as polite and sweet in her refusal as ever. When not visiting with neighbors or walking to Meryton, the sisters spent time working in the still room and playing Piquet, Jane's favorite two-person card game.

Elizabeth had never been fond of card games. If she was

forced to sit still for so long, she preferred it to be for something useful, like sewing, or for something mentally challenging, like reading and chess. But for her sister, she would make the sacrifice.

One day, on a walk to Meryton, Elizabeth asked a question that had haunted her since she was a very young girl. "Jane, what do you think our lives would have been like if our parents had not died?"

Jane's mouth tugged slightly downward. "I do not like to think about it. It gives me such pain to know that we never truly knew our mother and father."

"I also feel pain when I think of what we missed. However, I cannot help but wonder how our personalities would have been affected had we been raised as the gently bred ladies that we are."

Jane stopped and placed her hand on Elizabeth's forearm. "I do not wish to distress you, but I cannot but think that your life has turned out better for it. You have been well loved by my uncle and have a hefty dowry, too."

Elizabeth nodded in agreement. "I am fortunate to have Papa's love and affection. Although I am not his daughter by blood, he has always treated me as if I were his own. I could not have asked for a better father. But that is not what I mean, and you know it."

"I know you wonder how our lives might have been had we grown up as true sisters, but I do not think our relationship would be so different than it is now. Mama has told me that our mother did not wish for another daughter and was very angry upon your birth. Then, when you turned out to be so brown she pushed you from her chest. Your own mother refused to care for you. Our father had to pay both a nurse and a wetnurse."

"But many children have a wetnurse."

Jane huffed a sigh. "Elizabeth, our mother would not

have been kind to you. You were not a son, and you are not as attractive as I am. You are better off in London." Having nothing more to say, Jane plastered a pleasant look on her face and continued down the path toward Meryton. Elizabeth was stunned by the sentiment, and it took her some time before she resumed her walk.

By the next morning, Elizabeth had made peace with her sister's comments. While Milly fastened the last buttons her dress, Elizabeth studied her appearance in the mirror. It was true, Jane was the more stunning of the sisters, at least according to the latest preferences in London. Neither lady reached the height that was considered fashionable, yet Jane's fair hair easily established her as the beauty of the two. Their eyes were nearly the same shade of blue, but the dark navy ring around Elizabeth's gave them a striking intensity. She may not have been the one to command attention, but she appreciated the way her pale eyes stood out against her dark hair and brows.

"You look very well, Miss Gardiner. Prettiest lady in Meryton."

Elizabeth smiled at her maid. "Thank you, Milly, but I must disagree. I look very well, but Jane is the prettiest lady in town."

"Not to all of us," Milly said as she folded Elizabeth's nightgown. Not knowing how to properly respond, Elizabeth left the room and went in search of her sister. She found her in the breakfast room reading a note alongside Mrs. Annesley.

"Oh, Elizabeth, it is the greatest thing. I have been invited to tea with Miss Bingley and Mrs. Hurst. It seems the gentlemen will be away from the house for a visit with the militia, and they wish me to come keep them company."

Jane had made her admiration of the Netherfield ladies very clear. She respected their position in society and wished to emulate their fashion. Elizabeth found them both to be the epitome of everything that was wrong with the ton. They were shallow, mean spirited, and spent too much money on fashion that was meant to impress with its cost but not its style. Their position in society was also dubious. By nature of being Suzy's best friend and the goddaughter of the Earl of Effington, Elizabeth knew many of the young ladies in the first circles. Never once had she been introduced to Miss Bingley or Mrs. Hurst. She would not share these thoughts with Jane, however.

"Jane, dear Jane!" Mr. Collins swept into the room waving a sheet of paper. "I have the most exciting news."

Jane gently placed her own missive on the table before responding. "What is it, dear?"

"My friend, Mr. Greene has agreed to visit us. His most venereal patroness has agreed that he can leave his post and join us for a time." Elizabeth bit the inside of her cheek to keep from laughing at Mr. Collins' unintentional insult of the lady. She would need to add that to her letter to Suzy.

Elizabeth mastered her countenance before speaking. "Who is Mr. Greene?"

Happy to talk about his friend, Mr. Collins pulled out a seat for his sister-in-law and urged her to sit. Mr. Collins loved nothing more than a captive audience. "He has been my greatest friend since university. When we graduated, he went on to be ordained and I, of course, came back here to prepare for my role as a landowner. You will like him. We are so much alike in looks and personality, everyone says we are practically twins!"

Jane asked, "When should we expect him?" For her part, Elizabeth hoped his visit would not overlap her own. One Mr. Collins was more than enough.

"That is the best part, my dear. He will arrive tomorrow!"

Elizabeth was appalled that her sister had received so little notice of a houseguest, but it did not appear to rattle Jane. "Very well, I will ask Mrs. Hill to have a room made up for him."

Turning to Elizabeth, Mr. Collins continued. "You will

enjoy his visit, Elizabeth. He has a very good position in Hunsford but is heir to a small estate in Suffolk." Mr. Collins stopped for a dramatic inhalation, only to begin again. "He would be a very good match for you, assuming you catch his interest."

Elizabeth did not know how to respond to that, so she remained quiet. That was to Mr. Collins' satisfaction, as he was not done with his commentary.

"His patroness is Lady Catherine de Bourgh. She is the sister to an earl and has been so kind to extend her condescension to me. Mr. Greene often includes small pieces of advice that she has shared for my benefit." Mr. Collins waved his letter. "Even today he wrote of her suggestion for closets. Jane, there is not time now, but we must consider adding shelves to all our closets. Lady Catherine says it is a superior way to maximize space."

"But rather poor for hanging clothes." Elizabeth's joke earned herself a stern look from her brother-in-law.

Jane's placid smile soothed her husband's irritated feelings. "I am very pleased your friend will join us. I know you have wished for his presence often." Picking up her own missive she continued. "Today I received a note from Miss Bingley. She has asked me to attend tea this afternoon. May I use the carriage?"

Mr. Collins' eyes widened. "Today? Of course not! I must be away. There is so much to do before Mr. Greene arrives." Realizing his wife was disappointed, he added, "Jane, I am very pleased they invited you, which is as it should be. You are so beautiful and gentle. And, of course, you are the wife of the area's premier landowner. But you must realize that I must have the carriage. I need to stop by Lucas' and Goulding's to share my good news and I cannot be expected to walk that far. You can take the horse. I dare say the exercise will be good for your circulation."

Elizabeth could not help but look at Mr. Collins' soft physique. The exercise would do him more good than it would Jane. "Perhaps you could delay your trip to town. You can drop Jane and me off at Netherfield and then proceed with your visits." To her shock, both Jane and Mr. Collins were affronted by her suggestion. They responded at the same time.

"Delay? I cannot delay. This is the most exciting thing to happen in Hertfordshire in years." Mr. Collins emphatically shook his head at the idea, causing his neck to jiggle.

"Elizabeth, your name was not on the invitation. It would be bad manners for me to show up with my uninvited sister in tow."

Elizabeth chose to ignore her brother-in-law's comment and responded to Jane. "It would also be poor manners to invite one lady of the house and not the other. I am certain Miss Bingley meant the note for both of us. What do you believe, Mrs. Annesley?"

Elizabeth's companion had been sitting quietly while the others spoke, but Elizabeth could tell by the set of her mouth that she was bothered by the conversation. "I believe you are correct, Miss Gardiner. It is in poor manners to leave you off the invitation. However, I suspect that is as Miss Bingley intended."

Jane's lips tightened. "Be that as it may, in this I must have my way. You were not mentioned on the invitation, and I will not embarrass Longbourn by bringing along my unwanted sister."

Jane's words struck Elizabeth like a physical blow. Her throat tightened, a painful ache spreading as she battled to keep her tears at bay. Elizabeth forced herself to nod along as Mr. Collins droned on about his friend, the words barely registering; her mind was too consumed by her sister's callous comments. When she could no longer bear it, she excused herself and retreated to her room.

After an hour of quiet contemplation, Elizabeth dusted off her injured feelings and sat at her desk to begin her newest letter to Suzy. *There is no need to be gloomy,* she told herself. *It is only a visit to Netherfield. It is not as though Jane will spend the afternoon with ladies I like.* But no matter how much she endeavored to talk herself into being pleased that she did not have to attend with her sister, her heart knew the truth.

My dearest friend,

Longbourn is to be invaded by a Mr. Collins replica. I am unsure if I should stay for the enjoyment of two such ludicrous men or ask papa to send the carriage posthaste.

Elizabeth sat in one position for many hours. After finishing her letter to Suzy, she wrote additional ones to her mother, father, and her grandmother in Lambton. So engrossing were her efforts that she did not look up until a rumble of thunder rattled the windowpane. Consulting her watch, she reasoned that Jane should be close to Netherfield at that time. But when a steady rain began to fall, Elizabeth could not help but wring her hands in worry.

Chapter 8

In Aid of a Sick Sister

When Mr. Collins returned from his visits in the neighborhood, Elizabeth met him at the door. "You must send the carriage to check on Jane. She has not yet returned, and I worry that she was caught in the rain."

Mr. Collins patted her arm. "She is probably staying with Miss Bingley until the rain ends. Such fine people would not think to put my wife out in this weather."

"But what if she is injured?"

Mr. Collins waved away her concern. "You are a good sister to my dear Jane, but she is an adequate rider."

Elizabeth was not convinced of that and spent the rest of the evening worrying about her sister's health. Before breakfast the next morning, Mr. Collins received a note from Netherfield. Jane had been thrown from her horse after a particularly violent crash of thunder. In her fall, she twisted her knee and was now bound to her bed. "You see, Elizabeth, Jane is well. It is only a twisted knee that hampers her. She will be as good as new in a matter of days."

"We must go check on her."

Mr. Collins added three thick slices of bacon to his plate. "No, my dear. I cannot leave Longbourn. You have forgotten that my friend will arrive today."

Elizabeth's mouth flew open in shock. "But she is your wife!"

"She will be well. I will write to her and check on her tomorrow," he mumbled around a mouthful of bacon.

Elizabeth was not satisfied with this answer. "I plan to walk to Netherfield to check on Jane," she told Mrs. Annesley. Her companion had some concern about the long walk, but Elizabeth insisted. "I am fit to walk it. 'Tis only three miles."

Mrs. Annesley tutted but she did not forbid the trek. "Take Howes with you. I do not like you walking so far alone."

Elizabeth and her footman set out for Netherfield. Although she attempted to dodge puddles, there were too many to avoid and by the time she arrived at the Bingley's residence, her skirt was heavy with mud. Mr. Bingley's butler could not hide his distaste when he looked upon her bedraggled state, but he did not forbid her entrance.

"Miss Elizabeth Gardiner," he announced to the members of the household. They were seated around the breakfast table. Mr. Bingley and Mr. Darcy quickly stood upon her entrance. Mr. Hurst nodded but did not stop from enjoying his eggs.

A lock of hair had come loose from its pins and Elizabeth tucked it behind her ear. "I apologize for my intrusion, but I wished to see my sister."

Miss Bingley's eyes widened at the state of Elizabeth's dress. "Eliza Gardiner, did you walk here?"

Elizabeth winced at Miss Bingley's address. She had not given the lady permission to call her by her first name, and certainly not a shortened version that she abhorred. Tucking her irritation away, she answered. "I did. It is not so far, and the air is fresh after last night's rain."

"Your dedication to your sister shows to your advantage, Miss Gardiner." Mr. Bingley held out a chair for Elizabeth to join them, but Elizabeth demurred.

"I insist," he said. "You have just missed the apothecary. Mr. Jones gave Mrs. Collins something for the pain which has put her to sleep. He insisted your sister remain abed for a day or two. Her leg should not be jostled in a carriage." With no little reluctance, Elizabeth took the offered chair. There was little use rushing to Jane's bedside if she was sleeping peacefully.

"Miss Gardiner, may I get you a plate?" Mr. Darcy's serious, dark eyes temporarily held her in silence. She nodded her head. Soon, a plate of bacon, eggs, and toast were placed in front of her.

Conversation around the table was stilted. Her presence had upset Miss Bingley and Mr. Darcy's silence was deafening. Clearing his throat, Mr. Bingley spoke. "I think your sister would like to have you here while she recovers. Can I send to Longbourn for your things? Caroline can have a room made up for you."

Elizabeth smiled at Mr. Bingley's kindness. She would feel better about Jane's recovery if she were there to assist her. "Thank you, Mr. Bingley. Can my companion take my room? I can stay with Jane."

Miss Bingley took affront to the question. "Do not be ridiculous, Eliza. We have enough rooms for all of you. I will have Mrs. Nichols take care of everything."

Elizabeth thanked the lady and then excused herself to check on Jane. She did not like that her sister was injured, but she was happy that she could be of some assistance while Jane recovered.

∞∞∞

After four hours of sleep, Jane awoke to find Elizabeth reading near her bedside. "What are you doing here?" She struggled to sit up in her bed, and Elizabeth hurried to help her.

"You must be careful with your knee. Mr. Jones said it was very badly sprained." Jane winced before settling back into the pillows that her sister had plumped for her.

"He said it should be well enough to hold my weight within a few days, but I will likely hobble for at least a week, possibly two."

Elizabeth nodded. "Yes, I pulled back the covers to look at it. You are very badly bruised and swollen. It must hurt a great deal."

Elizabeth offered a glass of cool water and Jane took a deep drink. "Mr. Jones' tonic helps to ease the pain, but it makes me very tired." She took another drink and then handed the glass back to her sister. "But you have not answered me. Why are you here?"

"I came to check on you. I was very concerned when you did not arrive last night. I came right away when the note was sent this morning about your accident."

"That is very sweet of you, but you were not invited. We discussed this yesterday."

Elizabeth counted to five before answering. Pasting a sweet smile on her face she said, "Actually, Mr. Bingley suggested that I stay until you are recovered. He thought you would prefer my company, and I certainly do not wish to be separated from you. We see one another so little."

Jane's face showed her skepticism, but she accepted Elizabeth's statement as truth. Elizabeth read aloud for a while, but soon Jane's leg grew achy, and she was forced to take another dose of tonic.

While Jane slept, Elizabeth met with Mrs. Annesley who had arrived with a tote for each of them. Elizabeth was pleased to change out of her dirty skirt. The maid Miss Bingley assigned to her was not as competent as Milly, and Elizabeth was forced to fix her own hair. But once she was presentable, she made her way downstairs for tea.

"Miss Gardiner, welcome. I am glad you were able to steal

away from your sister and join us for a while." Elizabeth greeted Mr. Bingley with a smile and a curtsy and then took her place across from Miss Bingley.

"Mr. Darcy, do come join us. You will grow faint from hunger." Miss Bingley addressed the words just over Elizabeth's shoulder. She turned and saw him standing at the window, his eyes fixed on the view outside.

"Is that a garden you look at, sir? My legs are quite worn out from my walk this morning, but if the weather holds, I will wish for a place to exercise tomorrow morning."

Mr. Darcy turned from the window. "It is. Just beyond the rose garden, you will find a maze. I think it may suit your need for exercise, and if I guess correctly, for adventure."

Elizabeth was pleased by his response. "You have caught me out. I do enjoy a bit of adventure, and a labyrinth sounds just the thing."

To Miss Bingley's displeasure, Mr. Darcy smiled at Elizabeth. To her further irritation, he then took a seat on the other side of Mr. Bingley, as far from his hostess as possible. "How terrible it must be, Eliza, to spend all your time in town. Your garden must be very small. I know you dearly love to walk."

Elizabeth accepted her cup of tea before answering. "Our garden is rather large for town, though not as large as some. My godfather's garden is much bigger, for instance. I often walk there with his daughter."

Miss Bingley sniffed. "I suppose size is a matter of perspective. What you may call very large I should likely call miniature."

Mrs. Hurst agreed with enthusiasm. "Caroline, do you recall the tea we attended at the Earl of Effington's house? His daughter was not yet officially out as she was waiting for a friend to return from a trip, but her father allowed her to hold a series of tea parties that spring. That garden was the grandest one I have seen in London."

"Indeed," Miss Bingley agreed. "With your tendency to roam, I fear you may get lost in that garden, Eliza."

Elizabeth allowed the steam from the tea to warm her face. "Do you refer to Lady Susan Corwell?"

Miss Bingley's eyes widened. "Silly me. Of course you have heard of her. Her name is often in the papers." Elizabeth would never share that she was the E.G. often listed beside Suzy's initials.

"I know her, and I, too, have taken tea there." Mrs. Hurst looked suitably impressed, but Miss Bingley's squinted in disbelief. That Suzy's father was the godfather she had mentioned earlier would also go unsaid. Those two could not be trusted with that information. They would see it as an opportunity for their own aspirations.

Though Miss Bingley wished to continue discussing various prominent persons from London, Mr. Darcy managed to turn the conversation to the attractions of town. He, Elizabeth, and Mr. Bingley talked for many minutes about the theatre, opera, and the various museums.

"Have you had a chance to visit the Roman artifacts exhibit?" Mr. Bingley hitched his thumb toward his friend. "Darcy is an even bigger history enthusiast than you are."

Mr. Darcy leaned forward to better see around his friend. "Do you enjoy history, Miss Gardiner?"

"I do, though I would not go so far as to call myself a connoisseur. I am simply an admirer." She turned to Mr. Bingley. "And to answer your question, Papa took me to see that exhibit only a week before I arrived here. He was especially interested in the weaponry, but I enjoyed looking at the jewelry the most. There was an ivory hairpin that I thought was especially lovely."

"Oh Eliza, how sweet you are. I would never wear anything less than gold in my own hair." Elizabeth imagined Miss

Bingley's many feathers covered in gold. The image caused her to smile.

"Gold would look very nice against your copper hair." Seeing that her hostess was well pleased with the compliment, Elizabeth thanked her for the meal and excused herself. She did not come back down for supper, choosing to stay with Jane the rest of the day.

Chapter 9

Past Remembrances

The next morning bloomed bright and all evidence of the storm two days prior faded. Elizabeth stopped in Jane's room before going down for breakfast. "How are you feeling this morning." Jane huffed, making Elizabeth laugh. "That well?"

"My knee is aching, my stomach is weary of the tonic, and my hair is a mess."

"Let me brush your hair for you." Elizabeth attempted to unsnarl some tangles, but Jane slapped at her hands.

"I want a maid to do it. You only know how to fix your own unruly hair."

Elizabeth's mouth tightened but she did not voice her annoyance. "I will ask for Sally to be sent for you." Then, before she could rethink her decision, she sailed from the room.

On her way to breakfast, she passed Mrs. Nichols and asked her to send the maid to assist Jane with refreshing herself. When the housekeeper walked away, Elizabeth took three deep breaths, her ire ebbing with each. Equanimity restored, she entered the room.

"Good morning, Miss Gardiner," Mr. Bingley called from the buffet. He was happily loading sausages onto his plate. Mr. Darcy gave a brief nod, his gaze never leaving hers as he subtly motioned toward a seat. Elizabeth felt warmth rise in her cheeks under the heat of his dark eyes.

"Allow me to prepare your plate. Do you prefer bacon or sausage?"

Elizabeth sat next to Mrs. Annesley, the only other person in the room, before answering. "Neither, actually. Just eggs and toast. And some coffee if it is available." Mr. Darcy signaled to the footman who immediately fetched the pot.

"How does Mrs. Collins fare, this morning?" Mr. Bingley looked up from his heaping pile of sausages. "Is her leg better?"

"She is well enough to be cranky. My papa always said that is how he knew I was recovering from an injury or illness."

Mr. Bingley was shocked. "Surely not. Mrs. Collins always appears so sweet and composed."

"I assure you, sir, all ladies may become cranky at times. Jane does not like that she is tied to the bed, but she will be more herself soon." Elizabeth added a healthy amount of cream in her coffee and stirred it before continuing. "If I guess correctly, I predict she will join the party tonight for supper."

The breakfast conversation was enjoyable for Elizabeth. Mr. Bingley shared exploits of his youth prompting Mr. Darcy to share his own. "My cousin, Richard, bet me that I could not swim across River Derwent. It was March and the water was exceptionally cold, but I did not want to be proven unmanly."

"How old were you?"

"I was at the very grown age of eight." Mr. Darcy smiled causing a previously unseen dimple to appear in his right cheek.

Elizabeth's pulse sped. She had thought him attractive before, but this Mr. Darcy was a true thing of beauty. She swallowed and reminded herself to speak. "Oh dear. You did not attempt it did you."

He nodded gravely. "I did, but I was unprepared for the

intensity of the freezing water or for how it caused my lungs to seize. I flailed around until my oldest cousin jumped in to rescue me. He was very cross about ruining his boots."

Mrs. Annesley chuckled. "Miss Gardiner knows the River Derwent well."

"How so?" Elizabeth groaned, knowing that Mr. Darcy's question would soon be answered.

Mrs. Annesley smirked. "My charge had a love for climbing trees. Her family was picnicking when she spotted a tree that appeared to her eyes a 'fantastic challenge'. That is exactly what she told me afterward." Mr. Darcy leaned forward, interested to hear the rest of the story.

"Unfortunately, that fantastic challenge bested her. Her parents did not know she had even attempted the climb until they heard the splash. Her father had to dive in to rescue her as she was caught up in her skirts."

"Did your father punish you, Miss Gardiner?" Mr. Bingley had become so engrossed in the various stories that he forgot all about his sausages.

"He did. I was made to stay inside for a solid week without a walk, a ride, and certainly without climbing a tree."

"And have you climbed any trees since?" The mirth in Mr. Darcy's eyes told her he knew the truth.

"A lady is allowed to keep some facts about herself private, sir."

Mrs. Annesley rolled her eyes. "Miss Gardiner may choose not to answer, but I will tell you that she has broken her arm and sprained her ankle since then. I shall let you determine how each occurred." He laughed heartily at the lady's response.

Elizabeth and Mrs. Annesley soon excused themselves to check on Jane. The maid had done her work and Jane sat up in bed wearing a fresh nightgown. Her hair had been brushed to a shine and plaited to hang over her shoulder. "I hope you are feeling better now that you have been refreshed."

"I do. Thank you for sending Sally. She was kind enough to bring a deck of cards."

Elizabeth settled next to the bed, preparing for Jane to deal. "Another game of Piquet?"

"Not today. I plan to play vingt-et-un for a while and then take a nap."

Elizabeth was disappointed. Though she did not care for cards, she did enjoy spending time with her sister. A one-person card game was not the way to accomplish it. Searching for a way to stay near her sister's side she asked, "Would you like for me to read while you play?"

Jane dealt the cards on the lap desk that had been provided. "No thank you. You and Mrs. Annesley can do as you please. I will see you after my nap." It was not the response Elizabeth had hoped for, but she refused to demonstrate her discontent.

"If you are certain you wish to be alone, I will go downstairs." Jane nodded as she continued to deal her cards.

With false cheer, Elizabeth said, "It appears I will have a chance to walk in the labyrinth today." Mrs. Annesley laid her hand on Elizabeth's shoulder as they walked down the hall.

After leaving Mrs. Annesley in the morning room to chat with Mrs. Hurst, Elizabeth made her way outside. The weather was fine, and the air was crisp. She breathed deeply. Mornings in the country were one of her favorite things. She had always enjoyed her trips to Gloucestershire to Uncle Paul's estate. Netherfield was not as fine as Meadow Haven, but it promised a fine garden, and the fresh air was not to be discounted.

As she ambled toward the maze, Elizabeth found Mr. Darcy and Miss Bingley walking the path. "Miss Gardiner," Mr. Darcy startled to see her.

Miss Bingley drew her body closer to her escort's. "Eliza, I am surprised to see you here. You are such a great walker, I would have thought you would prefer the muddy fields to our well-kept paths." Mr. Darcy's lips tightened at Miss Bingley's comment, and Elizabeth liked him even better for it.

"I do enjoy a romp across a field, Miss Bingley, but today I have chosen to stay close to the house in case Jane has need of me."

Guiding a reluctant Miss Bingley toward Elizabeth, Mr. Darcy offered his arm. "Would you care to join us? Miss Bingley and I had planned to explore the maze for a while."

"Mr. Darcy, you are ever the gentleman, but there is hardly enough room for the three of us. Besides, Eliza wishes to stretch her legs. She will not want to move at our more sedate pace."

Elizabeth did wish to walk with more swiftness than Miss Bingley would prefer, but the temptation to be near Darcy was too great. If she could also annoy the lady, then so much the better. With her sweetest smile, she took Mr. Darcy's arm. "Thank you for the kind offer. I will join you for a while." Miss Bingley's nostrils flared, but she did not speak against it.

The three walked in silence for a while, but one lady was displeased with this and soon broke the quiet. "I do love this maze, but it is nothing compared to the gardens at Pemberley. I have told Charles that he must give up the lease here and find a more suitable estate. One in Derbyshire would be preferable, I think."

"Derbyshire is very far north. Your brother is often needed in London to deal with his business interests. I think for that reason, Netherfield is a better location for him. He would not enjoy staying so long at his estate. Here he is a half-day's distance from the attractions of town." Though Mr. Darcy addressed Miss Bingley, he kept his eyes on the path.

"My brother is ready to be a steady estate owner, Mr. Darcy.

I think a place in Derbyshire would be perfect for him. There is no more beautiful county in all the kingdom." Miss Bingley leaned slightly forward so that she could see Elizabeth. "If you are ever able to pull yourself from London, I recommend you visit The Peak District. Given your great love for walking, you will find it perfect for you."

"I have visited Derbyshire many times and climbed many of the peaks in that area. We were there only a few months ago, though our stay was cut short by my father's business. I did not do as much exploring as I would have liked."

Mr. Darcy was intrigued. The story of her dunking in the River Derwent indicated that her family had visited the area once when she was a child, but to have come to his home county many times invited his curiosity. "How is that you have found yourself in Derbyshire so many times? While I agree with Miss Bingley about the county's beauty, it is not often a location people visit without having family in the area."

"You have caught me out, sir. I do have family in Derbyshire. My mother hails from near a small village called Lambton. Perhaps you know it?"

"Lambton! But that is only five miles from Pemberley. I have been there many times. But who are your mother's people?"

Feeling left out, Miss Bingley interjected. "It is unlikely you will know them. Eliza's family are far below the notice of a Darcy."

Both Elizabeth and Mr. Darcy chose to ignore the lady. "My mother was a Brown. Madelyn Brown."

"Miss Brown! I have met her many times at her father's estate. I visited him, myself, just this summer. We probably just missed one another." After a moment, he asked, "How often do you visit?"

"We try to visit at least once a year, though there are years we go more often and years when we go less. Mama married my papa in the year seventeen ninety-seven. That was my first trip to the area. I was six years old and wished for nothing more than to finally have a mother to love me. Perhaps that is why I love the area so well. It is less about the area and more about what the county gave to me."

Darcy looked at her in thoughtful contemplation until Elizabeth grew warm and Miss Bingley grew irritated. "The sun is simply too bright. If I stay outside any longer, I shall grow as brown as Eliza."

Confused by the look on Mr. Darcy's face, Elizabeth chose this moment to disengage her arm from his. "You should escort Miss Bingley back to the house while I continue to enjoy the outdoors for a while longer. I thank you for the escort and the pleasure of your company." She dipped a quick curtsy to her two companions and then walked quickly down the path.

∞∞∞

Elizabeth disappeared around the bend in the path before Darcy had a chance to argue his desire to stay outside with her. Miss Bingley was certainly capable of finding her way back to the house without his help. He looked down at the lady still grasping tightly to his right arm. Perhaps it was for the best. Though she strove for his attention, Miss Bingley did not present one-tenth the level of temptation that Elizabeth garnered with so little effort.

On the walk back, he allowed himself to dream of a life unencumbered by duty and responsibility. If he were a different man and not Mr. Darcy of Pemberley, he would give in to his desires for Elizabeth Gardiner. But he was not a different man, and no amount of wishing would change that. His heart had soared upon learning that her mother was the daughter of a gentleman. *Perhaps,* he thought. But reality soon stomped his hope. Elizabeth was born to a tradesman and raised by another.

It was better to keep his distance from the beautiful brunette, no matter how much he would like to do the opposite.

He helped Miss Bingley find her sister before excusing himself to the library. He had several letters from his steward to attend to, and that could not be accomplished with Miss Bingley's constant effusions. He settled himself at the desk he had made his own for the duration of his stay and opened the first letter. His attention could not be captured by the tallies of the year's harvest. Instead, his mind wandered to more fulfilling remembrances of a pair of fine eyes amid a pretty face.

Seventeen ninety-seven. The year his mother died and Elizabeth's first visit to Lambton. It was also the first year of his father's investment in Gardiner Imports, which could not be a coincidence. That had been such a painful year for Darcy. At the age of thirteen, his life should have been filled with boyish adventures and studies, but that was not the case. Thinking about those difficult months, a memory pulled itself forward from the depths of his mind.

"Father, I will stay here while you attend to your business." Darcy sat on a bench comfortably placed in the shade of a large oak tree. His father had business with a guest of Mr. Brown, but Darcy did not wish to go inside. The weather was too nice. Besides, there would be ladies inside, and ladies always asked him how he fared since his mother's death. He did not wish to fight back the tears that always threatened when someone mentioned her. He rubbed the ache that had bloomed in his chest.

"Who are you?" A small girl, covered in dust, jumped down from the fence behind him. "Are you here for the wedding?" She offered a broad smile. She had recently lost her front two teeth. A new tooth had recently pushed through in one spot, but the other remained bare. He could not help but smile back at her as he wondered what Georgiana would look like when she was this age.

"My father has business here."

"But are you staying for the wedding? My papa is getting

married tomorrow." Uninvited, the girl climbed onto the bench and sat next to him. Darcy moved over a little to give her space.

"I do not believe my father will attend the wedding."

She looked disappointed by this news. "That is a shame. My new mama said we will have cake and punch. Do you like cake?"

Darcy did like cake, but some obstinance prevented him from admitting it. "I prefer tartes, but cake is tolerable."

"Oh, I love strawberry tarte! But that does not mean I cannot also love cake. It is the same with mamas. My first mama died when I was a baby, and I love her even though I do not remember her. But my new mama said that a person can love two people at once. So I love my new mama, as well." She kicked her legs. "Do you have a mama?"

The question stabbed Darcy's already tender chest. He rubbed the spot again. "My… my mother died last winter." She placed her small hand on his arm but said nothing. They sat that way for many minutes.

"Elizabeth," a lady called from the side of the house.

"I must go. I was not supposed to leave the garden area." She hopped from the bench and waved cheerfully as she ran down the path toward the house.

That exchange had lingered in Darcy's mind for years. The girl, now known to him as Elizabeth Gardiner, had effortlessly achieved what so few adults could. She had offered him comfort without uttering a word, without demanding conversation.

Chapter 10

Humiliations

That afternoon, Jane informed Elizabeth that she wished to go downstairs for the evening conversations. Elizabeth thought that if Jane could stand to be carried down a flight of stairs that she could handle the carriage ride to Longbourn, but she did not say as much. "Howes and I will return to retrieve you after supper."

"Will you call Sally? She will need to assist me with dressing." Elizabeth pulled the cord and left to meet the other houseguests in the drawing room.

Miss Bingley had ordered three courses for supper. By the time the meal was complete, Elizabeth was too full and wishing for nothing more than quiet, but it was not to be. She had promised Jane an evening with the others.

Elizabeth and her footman climbed the stairs and found Jane sitting with her foot propped on a small footstool near the fire. Her knee was still swollen and sore. Howes lifted Jane with ease. Elizabeth picked up the stool and followed behind.

"Mrs. Collins, it is good to see that you are well enough to leave your room, though I wish you could do so without a footman's assistance." Knowing her sister's love of cards, Mr. Bingley saved a seat at the table for Jane. Miss Bingley and Mr. Hurst joined them, and Hurst began to shuffle the deck. Howes gently lowered Jane to the ground and then helped her hop a short distance to the seat. Elizabeth placed the footstool near and assisted her sister in raising her foot without showing her ankles.

Mr. Bingley hovered nearby, and Jane smiled sweetly at him. "Would you like to partner your sister, Miss Gardiner?" Jane's mouth tugged into a frown. Elizabeth knew that look. Jane wished to partner with her attentive and attractive host. Happy for the chance to avoid cards, Elizabeth demurred, claiming instead that she preferred to read.

"Eliza Gardiner is a great reader and prefers it above all things." Miss Bingley rolled her eyes and Jane stifled a giggle.

Mr. Darcy sat reading near the fire, and Elizabeth chose a seat near him. He smiled as she sat down. "Is that true, Miss Gardiner? Are books your only source of joy?"

"I admit that I do enjoy reading, but I take pleasure in many things."

"She does not enjoy cards. I must beg her to play," Jane called from the card table.

"If you recall, I offered to play this morning, but you refused." Jane shrugged and studied her cards.

"Tell us Eliza, what other hobbies do you have? Aside from being a great walker." Miss Bingley smirked at her partner.

"I do enjoy walking, but I also like to ride."

Darcy closed his book. "You told me as much once before. Do you have any other pastimes?"

"My friend, Suzy, and I volunteer at a girl's school in town, which is not so much a hobby, but I do enjoy spending time with the girls. I also like to play the piano and sing, and, of course, I love to dance."

Darcy chuckled. "I assumed as much. You appeared to be very pleased with the activity on the evening we first met."

"I also enjoy chess, though I have not had the opportunity

to play much on my trip here. Suzy and I play a few times a week. And of course I play my papa and Uncle Paul."

He set the book on his lap. "Would you like to play now? Bingley is not a fan, but I enjoy a game when I have time for it."

Before Elizabeth could answer Miss Bingley called out. "Eliza, I insist that you take my place at the table. This group would benefit from some music."

Mrs. Hurst did not understand her sister's ploy and suggested that she should take the abandoned chair. A frustrated Miss Bingley took her place at the piano where she began a complicated song. As she had at Lucas Lodge, she demonstrated her technical proficiency but failed to impart any feeling into the music. Elizabeth and Darcy listened for a while before both lost interest.

Elizabeth was pleased when Darcy abandoned his seat and chose one closer to her. "I have walked and ridden out many mornings since we met on Oakum Mount. I had thought I might run into you at least once."

She cautioned herself to not read too much into his words, but it was difficult to do. "I am afraid I was heavily reprimanded when Mrs. Annesley awoke to find me from the house without a maid or footman. I have chosen to remain inside until a more appropriate hour. I do not like to force Howes from his bed so early. He should not be punished with lack of sleep simply because I arise early and enjoy a ramble before the sun comes up."

∞∞∞

Darcy sat in quiet conversation with Elizabeth for many minutes. Never before had he found a woman half as interesting or kind as she was. *And beautiful, too,* he thought. It would be no hardship to spend evenings in such a way. For a moment, he allowed himself the luxury of imagining nights with her. They could share a chess game, she would play and sing, he would read aloud, and then they would end the evening in fascinating conversation. When the hour was late, he would escort her to their suite of rooms, which would lead to a different type of pleasure altogether. Yes, a lifetime with Elizabeth Gardiner would be a joy for some lucky man, but not for Darcy. *Why could she not at least be born to a gentleman? Even someone as low as Mr. Collins would be acceptable.*

Frustrated with this line of thinking, Darcy changed the topic. "Our conversation this morning gave me reason to think. I believe we met once before. I was a lad of thirteen and you could not have been older than six." Darcy then conveyed the story of a small, snaggletooth girl who invited him to her mama and papa's wedding. "You were very sad that I would not attend because there was to be cake."

Elizabeth wiped a tear of mirth from her eye. "I am very fond of cake, sir. You are lucky that I was in a mood to share."

Their laughter caught the attention of Miss Bingley. She left the piano and joined them. "What are you two speaking about? I must have my share."

"It seems Mr. Darcy and I met once when I was a girl of only six years."

"Shocking! Why would Mr. Darcy have met a shopkeeper's daughter?"

"Miss Gardiner is not a shopkeeper's daughter," Bingley called from the table. "Her father is a successful tradesman, just like our own." Miss Bingley's face heated.

"My father had a meeting with her father to discuss business. Miss Gardiner was dusty and missing her two front teeth, but even then, I thought she was a charming girl. Though I must say, I am glad your teeth have grown back." All but Miss Bingley and Jane giggled at Darcy's jest.

"Miss Gardiner is certainly a beautiful woman," Bingley said. "Though I, too, am glad that she is in possession of all her teeth."

Mrs. Collins laid her cards on the table. "That is kind of you to compliment my sister, Mr. Darcy. But you must know that Elizabeth was not a pretty child. In fact, that is why my mother refused to raise her. She insisted there was only room for one of us, and she wished to keep the prettier of the two. Elizabeth was bound for the orphanage, but my uncle rescued her."

Darcy looked to where Elizabeth sat. Her face had paled, and her eyes glistened with unshed tears. He longed to say something, but how could one respond to such a comment? *I am sorry your aunt is such a terrible person. I am sorry your sister is a conceited fool.* Neither of those were proper, though both were true.

"It has been a long day. If you will excuse me." Elizabeth gave a half-smile, but it did not reach her eyes. Those beautiful, alluring eyes. He longed to punish her thoughtless sister.

"Jane, I will send Howes to collect you." Darcy winced at the tightness of Elizabeth's words.

Her sister waved her away. "No need. Mr. Bingley will lend a footman to assist me. I wish to finish this round." Elizabeth nodded.

∞∞∞

The next morning, Elizabeth was called down to greet Mr. Collins. Jane's husband had arrived with his friend. "I am here, of course, to introduce my oldest friend, Mr. James Greene. And, of course, to check on my dear wife."

Mr. Bingley welcomed the gentlemen and asked them to sit. "Mr. Collins said you were a man of the cloth. Where do you serve?"

Mr. Collins had not misspoken when he said that he and Mr. Greene were much alike. Both men were tall but soft, though the rector's chin did not wobble overmuch when he spoke. Like her brother-in-law's, his hair was coated in too much grease. In this, Mr. Collins was the more fortunate of the two, as Mr. Greene's sparse hair, despite the generous use of product, stuck up at odd angles around his head. More importantly, both gentlemen were fond of talking about themselves.

Mr. Greene went on with enthusiasm, hands waving and spittle flying from his mouth. He spoke about his grand position in Hunsford and the generosity of his patroness, the venerable Lady Catherine de Bourgh — or, as Mr. Collins had once called her, the "venereal" lady. Elizabeth bit back a laugh at the memory.

"Darcy, is that not your aunt?" Mr. Darcy grimaced at his friend's question.

Mr. Greene's eyes widened in shock only a second before he bolted to his feet. "Are you Mr. Darcy of Pemberley?" When Mr. Darcy nodded that he was, the minister continued. "Oh my! Oh my, oh my, oh my! I knew that I would be among great men here at Netherfield, but I never expected to meet Lady Catherine's favorite nephew." In a sudden and jerky motion he bowed deeply. "Before I go on further, I must tell you that your aunt and betrothed were very well when I left." Elizabeth could not justify the stab of jealousy she felt upon hearing this.

"I must correct you. I am not engaged, though I am happy to know my aunt and cousin are well." Elizabeth released a pent-up breath.

Mr. Greene gave a vigorous nod. "Of course, of course. Your aunt has mentioned that your engagement is of a peculiar nature." Perspiration dotted his forehead. He mopped it with a cloth made gray from too many washings. "Things are not yet official, though you will certainly marry Miss de Bourgh. She is the jewel of Kent, after all. But until you sign the papers, you may call yourself unspoken for."

"I assure you, sir, I have no plans to marry my cousin." His tone was serious enough that even Mr. Greene, who appeared to be of mean understanding, was able to comprehend the implication.

Uncomfortable with the silence, Mr. Collins spoke. "I have heard many good things about your intended, Mr. Darcy. I have, of course, never had the pleasure of her company but my friend has written much about her. She must be very beautiful, despite her sickly nature. And, of course, she would have been a great proficient at many things, had she the opportunity to learn." Elizabeth was mortified by her brother-in-law's rambling.

"Sir, are you here to see Jane? I can escort you."

Mr. Collins frowned. "Elizabeth, can you not see that the gentlemen are speaking?" Elizabeth's face heated at the reprimand. After a moment of awkward silence, he stood. "You have interrogated our conversation and now I forget what I was saying. You may as well take me to see Jane." Embarrassed further by what Suzy called a *Collinsism*, Elizabeth hurried the man from the room.

She waited in the hall, while Jane sat with her husband. After ten minutes, he emerged. "No need to escort me back. I can find the way." Elizabeth was torn. She knew Mr. Collins and his friend would stay longer than was polite. If she returned with him, she might be able to persuade him to leave without wearing out his welcome. If she did not, she would avoid the first-hand embarrassment that was a certainty in any conversation in which the man participated. Deciding that she had endured enough humiliation in the past twenty-four hours, she said her goodbyes and went in to speak with her sister.

As she had done the day prior, Jane sat in bed playing vingt-et-un on a lap desk. "If you have come to remind me of my duty to Mr. Collins and our guest, then you need not speak."

Elizabeth had not planned to speak on the topic but did not say so. "Are you desirous of leaving? Your knee is less swollen, and you could probably withstand the discomfort of the carriage ride if the driver goes forward with caution."

"I do not wish to go home today." The pout that marred Jane's face was out of place given her normally serene expressions. "Mr. Greene will be well entertained by my husband while I am here. Besides, I am having fun at Netherfield. Miss Bingley and Mrs. Hurst stop in every afternoon to chat with me. And I had such a good time playing cards last night. Longbourn is excessively boring."

Elizabeth took her sister's hand. Even though she did not enjoy the ladies' presence, she could comprehend Jane's feelings. "I understand, but we cannot continue to trespass on Mr. Bingley's kindness."

A single tear ran down Jane's cheek. "You do not understand. You have been given so many opportunities and have the wealth to stay single if you wish it."

"I thought you wanted to marry Mr. Collins. Papa would have introduced you to several gentlemen in London had you expressed interest."

"To tradesmen. I wished to be a lady."

Elizabeth did not understand her sister's reasoning and did not try to, for it mattered not. Jane had made her choice, and now as unpalatable as it was to return to Mr. Collins' home, it was her duty as his wife. "Tomorrow then." Jane gave a curt nod before flipping over a card. Taking the cue, Elizabeth left. She might as well write Suzy about how she "interrogated" the men's discussion.

∞∞∞

That night, Mrs. Collins joined the party for supper. Her

knee appeared to be less tender. Darcy watched as she hobbled to the dining room, though with great assistance from Mr. Bingley.

Darcy dared not turn his head to where Elizabeth walked on Hurst's arm. His own appendages had been claimed by Miss Bingley's clawing fingers on the right, and Mrs. Hurst's lighter grip on his left.

"My dear Mrs. Collins, it has been such a pleasure hosting you and Eliza while you convalesced, but I dare say you will return to your own home tomorrow. Your leg is much better."

Mrs. Collins offered her hostess a placid smile. Bingley had claimed her the most beautiful lady of his acquaintance, but Darcy found her face to be rather lackluster, especially when compared with the vibrancy her younger sister's countenance held.

"Yes, I told my sister that very thing this afternoon," Mrs. Collins replied.

Darcy could not help but wonder if Elizabeth had been disappointed by Mrs. Collins' decision to leave. His own emotions were unclear. He would miss her bright eyes and beautiful smile, but he would not miss the roiling feelings of confusion and frustration she created within him. He wanted her and he could no longer deny it, which was the very thing that made her dangerous. Yes, it would be better for her to leave now before his heart became engaged.

Supper consisted of four courses, much to Darcy's irritation. Miss Bingley missed no opportunity to showcase her hostess skills or her brother's wealth. *Does she think this is an appealing demonstration? Her menus are too heavy and would bankrupt many a gentleman's coffers.* The fish soup was the only light item offered that evening, and Darcy savored every bite, while sampling only the barest amounts of the other items.

"Are you unwell, sir?" Darcy looked up to see Elizabeth looking at him from across the table.

"Mr. Darcy is not one to make a glutton of himself, Eliza. You are used to dining with tradesmen and are unaccustomed to the table manners of the first circles."

Elizabeth's eyes lit with humor and Darcy wished to know the joke. "I am sure that is exactly it," she replied.

Miss Bingley nodded before turning to Mrs. Collins. "Tell me, again, the story of how you came to live with your aunt and poor Eliza was sent to live with your uncle? I have never laughed so hard as I did last night when you told it the first time. I was so diverted I wrote about it to my friend."

Darcy was as ashamed of Miss Bingley as he was of Mrs. Collins' willingness to humiliate her own sister. Elizabeth deserved to be cherished. Not only was she engaging and talented, but she was also quite beautiful. He could not imagine an aunt refusing her based on looks. Even if she had been an unattractive child, which Darcy could not imagine, the idea was appalling. Once again, he allowed his eyes to find her. Her head was bent over her plate, and she moved food around without eating. Disgusted, he placed his own silverware down. He could no longer pretend to enjoy the meal.

Chapter 11

Return to Longbourn

Mr. Greene's presence at Longbourn quickly soured Elizabeth's enjoyment of her visit. If she had to endure the phrase, "My exalted patroness, Lady Catherine de Bourgh," one more time, she was certain she would scream. In the last half hour alone, the man had invoked the lady's name no less than eleven times—a number Elizabeth knew precisely, having kept meticulous count in her growing frustration. To his credit, at least he got the wording right. Mr. Collins, in his usual blundering manner, had once referred to her as Mr. Greene's exhausting patroness—a description Elizabeth found likely accurate, considering the poor lady's frequent dealings with such an insufferable bore.

Jane's hurtful comments at Netherfield had gone a long way toward reducing the possibility of a sisterly relationship between the two ladies, but her insistence that Elizabeth accept Mr. Greene's attention eliminated all hope. After two days in the man's overbearing and detestable presence, she could take no more. "Jane, I have decided to walk to Meryton."

"Take Mr. Greene with you. He will enjoy seeing town."

Elizabeth attempted to hide a cringe. "I had planned to stop and see Charlotte on the way."

"Mr. Greene will not mind." Jane smiled at the gentleman who hovered too near Elizabeth.

"Indeed, I will be pleased to escort you, Miss Gardiner, and I will not mind giving you time to chat with your friend. Ladies do require their moments of gossip. And I must admit that I also enjoy hearing the latest on dit. Why, Lady Catherine always says, 'Mr. Greene, you are an excellent listener.' And it is true. I hope I do not sound too enamored with myself when I say—"

"Let me call for Howes." Elizabeth could take no more of the man's prattle.

"Nonsense," Jane interjected. "You will be out in the open. No need to take your footman."

Elizabeth responded with a tight smile. "I do not think Papa, Mama, or my companion would agree." All three looked toward Mrs. Annesley who sat with a sewing basket in the corner. The lady shook her head in the negative.

"See there. I must include Howes in my excursion."

"Take your maid, as well," Mrs. Annesley advised. Elizabeth offered a saucy wink to her companion and then hurried from the room. Howes and Milly arrived before she had donned her pelisse and boots, but they were forced to wait while Mr. Greene struggled to put on his own outerwear.

The walk to Charlotte's was long and excruciating. "Although I am quite pleased with my position in Hunsford, you will be happy to know that I have also a sizable inheritance coming to me when my cousin, Mr. Gerald Gilbert passes on. Of course, I do not wish for such a thing, but when he does, what a terrible time his wife and daughters will have."

"Yes, it is difficult when a beloved father and husband passes."

"To be sure, to be sure. But that is not all. I visited the family last spring when Lady Catherine urged me to find a wife. 'Go to your family in Suffolk,' she said. 'Marry a cousin. Someone who is sensible and able to economize. Then when the girl's father passes on and you take your place at the head of the table, your wife's family will have a place to live and will not be forced from their home'."

No lady with half a thought in her head would accept the man. Given that he was still single she could only assume the Gilbert daughters had done as she would do and refused him.

"My cousin had the bad luck to father five daughters and no sons. Terrible decision on his part."

"I doubt he planned it, sir. Babies have a habit of being born as they are."

Mr. Greene pondered this. "I believe you are correct. My patroness has only a single daughter. I am sure she would have preferred a son. But Rosings is not entailed to male heirs. Mr. Gilbert should have considered this when he chose his wife."

"Perhaps he was in love with the lady."

"Yes, love. Ladies do enjoy the idea of such things." His face brightened as an idea formed. "Will you take my arm, Elizabeth?" He leaned in, so close their bodies nearly collided.

Her already frayed nerves snapped. Elizabeth took a deliberate step away, her voice cold as steel. "Sir, I have not given you permission to address me with such informality. We have barely known one another for a week, and, even if that time were longer, we are not engaged. You must address me as Miss Gardiner."

Mr. Greene's mouth fell open in shock. "My apologies. I believed we had gone beyond such conventions."

"We have not, nor shall we ever." She lengthened her stride, but to her dismay, Mr. Greene's long legs easily closed the distance between them.

"You are a coy one, Miss Gardiner, but do not worry. I am not offended by your comments. It is my understanding that this is the normal attitude of refined ladies who wish to be courted properly. Do not fear, I am of a mind to woo you just as you should be."

For twenty long seconds, Elizabeth did not say a word. When her mouth caught up with her mind, however, she gave him a piece of it. "Sir, you are mistaken. I do not wish to be wooed by you. We would be perfectly dissatisfied with one another. I am convinced that we cannot make one another happy."

"Silly girl. Of course we can. I am a very eligible fellow, you know. And you, as lovely as you are, are only the daughter of a tradesman. Marriage to me would bring you up in the world." Frustrated, Elizabeth quickened her pace to a near run. Mr. Greene, unaccustomed to such vigorous exercise, was forced to be quiet since all his breath was spent on loud huffing and puffing.

After several minutes, she risked looking back. Howes and Milly, long accustomed to her fast-paced rambles, easily followed behind. Further back, Mr. Greene bent with his hands on his knees taking in great gulps of air.

That will show him. To think that he is worthy of me, the great imbecile. And to think, Jane pushed his presence upon me! Elizabeth would have seethed further, but her thoughts were interrupted by the sound of approaching horses.

"Ho there, Miss Gardiner. What brings you out on this fine day?" Mr. Bingley greeted her with a broad smile, oblivious to the tension in the air, as he and Mr. Darcy approached atop two large stallions.

Elizabeth quickly composed herself. "Good day, Mr. Bingley. Mr. Darcy."

While Mr. Bingley remained cheerful and unaware, Mr. Darcy's expression darkened with concern. He nodded in greeting, but his eyes flicked between Elizabeth and the still panting Mr. Greene, clearly sensing something amiss.

∞∞∞

Darcy and Bingley dismounted. "We were just on our way to visit you at Longbourn. I had planned to personally extend an invitation to my ball."

"A ball!" Mr. Greene gasped. He patted at the sweat on his brow.

"Unfortunately, I believe you will have returned to Hunsford before the event." Darcy stepped a little closer to Elizabeth, effectively blocking the oafish parson's path. He could not explain why, but the thought of such a senseless man sharing space with her caused his hands to clinch.

"Darcy is correct. I believe you said you would remain in Hertfordshire through the twenty-second. I am afraid the ball will be held on the twenty-sixth." Bingley appeared to be genuinely disappointed. Darcy had to refrain from rolling his eyes.

Mr. Greene's chest puffed. "Yes, yes, I thank you for considering me. Four days is not so much. I believe Lady Catherine will be kind enough to grant me an extension on my stay at Longbourn, especially since my business here is incomplete." The waggled his eyebrows at Elizabeth.

Darcy forced his hand open. *It is not the done thing to beat a minister*, he reminded himself. Elizabeth's menacing glare told Darcy that she, too, was having a similar internal conversation.

"If you remain in the area, you are welcome to attend. And you..." Bingley turned, once again to Elizabeth. "You must agree to open the ball with me."

Mr. Greene stepped closer to Elizabeth. "And I — "

"And I would ask for your supper set," Darcy broke in. He smiled at the lady before turning a menacing eye to the parson.

Elizabeth happily agreed to each dance.

"Ahem." Mr. Greene puffed his chest. "And I would honor you with the final set." *Hardly an honor! Do you even know how to dance?* Darcy, once again, found his hands clenched at his sides.

"Thank you, Mr. Greene. I will write your name down for that spot."

"And if may be so bold, perhaps you might save —"

"Miss Gardiner, were you planning to visit your friend, Miss Lucas? If so, may we escort you there?"

Elizabeth smiled so sweetly up at him, Darcy's toes curled. "Yes, thank you. I would love the company."

Calm yourself, he silently advised himself, but his disloyal heart would not listen. It beat twice its normal pace the entire walk to Lucas Lodge.

While there, Bingley extended his invitation to the ball. As expected, it was accepted with great joy by Lady Lucas and her daughters. "Sir William will be exceedingly pleased, Mr. Bingley. I am only sorry he was not here to greet you, today."

Bingley made the usual comments and then turned to Miss Lucas. "Miss Lucas, may I have your second dance?" A beatific smile spread across the lady's face rendering her almost pretty. With ladylike poise she promised to hold the dance for Bingley.

Mr. Greene puffed out his chest. "And I, Miss Lucas, am in need of a partner for the first. I assume you will dance with me?" Though Mr. Greene's request was less eloquently worded, Miss Lucas graciously accepted his offer as well.

Darcy, unused to dancing at all, sat in silence until Elizabeth's assessing gaze caught his attention. When she had his notice, she slyly looked at Miss Lucas. Chastened, Darcy cleared his throat. "Miss Lucas, I would also like to request a dance. If you are available, will the third suit?"

Miss Lucas looked first to Elizabeth, whose wide smile filled him with an inexplicable sense of pride, before turning her eyes on the speaker. "I will be pleased to save that set for you, Mr. Darcy." Her response did not fill him with dread as many others had. Darcy would never enjoy dancing, but Elizabeth had opened his eyes to the goodness of the people around him.

When the appropriate amount of time had passed, the party bid farewell to the members of Lucas Lodge and made their way back to Longbourn. Darcy offered to escort Elizabeth and Bingley, having finally caught on to the lady's discomfort, crowded her other side before Mr. Greene had an opportunity to importune her. The rector was further excluded by the form of two large stallions that trailed their masters.

Out of mutual, unspoken agreement, the trio set a rapid pace. By the time they reached their destination, Mr. Greene was once again trailing far behind, sweat pouring from his forehead.

Mr. and Mrs. Collins greeted the party with sincere happiness. "How good of you to come, gentlemen. Are you here to check on my beloved? Her knee is greatly improved."

Bingley bowed. "Mrs. Collins, I hope you are well recovered from your accident." The lady blushed and quietly indicated that she was healing well.

"Excellent. Then you will likely be in the pink of health by November twenty-sixth, for that is the night I plan to host a ball."

"A ball!" Mr. Collins' squeal was nearly identical to the one his dearest friend gave upon hearing the same news. "Oh, Jane, what will I wear?"

After some moments, Mrs. Collins managed to calm her husband. By then, Mr. Greene had arrived. "Mr. Darcy, you will be more comfortable here." He indicated the seat nearest Mr. Collins. "Allow me to change places with you."

Though they were not touching, Darcy sat near enough to

feel the tension radiating from Elizabeth. "I thank you for the offer, but my chair is acceptable." It was not actually acceptable; never had he sat in such a lumpy seat. If he could not allow himself to love the lady, he would at least protect her in this small way from such an odious suitor.

Once settled, Mr. Collins secured a set from his wife and another from Elizabeth. "And I would like to ask for a second set, Miss Gardiner."

"Are you sure you wish to do so, Mr. Greene? I have oft heard my aunt say that no man should dance twice with a lady who is not his wife, even if they are engaged." A muffled snicker from Bingley drifted to him from Elizabeth's other side.

The gentleman's eyes widened, and his hands went to his chest. "Oh dear, she had never said so much to me. Do you truly believe she will be disappointed? Especially since I have every hope that Miss — "

"She will be very upset, I assure you. She was quite adamant each time I heard her say it."

Bingley stifled another laugh. Had Darcy been less displeased with Mr. Greene, he would have spared one, as well.

"You must be correct. You are, after all, her most esteemed and favorite nephew. Thank you. Oh, thank you, sir, for guiding me in this." Darcy inclined his head.

∞∞∞

The visit continued for an additional quarter hour before the gentlemen bid everyone goodbye. Messrs. Collins and Greene walked them out, while Elizabeth stayed behind with Jane.

"Are you in pain, Jane? Would you like for me to find a different pillow for your knee?"

"I am well." Jane's mouth bowed into a frown.

Elizabeth was tempted to ignore her, but a niggling curiosity drove her to press. "Then what is that has you so stern-faced?"

Jane fixed Elizabeth with an exasperated glare, her usual sweetness evaporating. "You do not know? And here I thought you were the intelligent sister."

"I assure you, I would not have asked if I understood your mood."

Jane leaned forward, her voice sharp and cutting. "Then I will tell you, sister. I am ashamed of you. Mr. Greene has been nothing but agreeable to you. He has waited on you, entertained you with stories of his home, and to what end? You have treated him abominably. And to have allowed Mr. Darcy to perpetrate such a farce—it is utterly unconscionable."

Elizabeth recalled her father's advice to stay calm during a dispute, knowing it would only unsettle her opponent further. Taking his wisdom to heart, she took two deep breaths before responding. "Unconscionable would be to encourage the man to persist. He is everything abhorrent to me, and I cannot fathom why you insist on pushing him upon me."

Jane crossed her arms, her tone dripping with disdain. "You are ridiculous. He is a very eligible man, with a home and a future estate at his disposal once his cousin dies. You may have an enormous dowry, but you are still only the daughter of a tradesman."

"I am not ashamed of Papa's status. I will marry for love or not at all. And as you say, I have a very large portion and can do as I please."

As she walked away, Elizabeth heard her sister's final, biting remark. "Being friends with an earl's daughter does not make you part of the peerage."

Chapter 12

The Ball

With the help of her friends, Elizabeth managed to avoid both Jane and Mr. Greene for most of the next ten days. The weather cooperated, allowing Elizabeth to take many walks and to visit Miss Lucas, Miss Goulding, and Miss King in turns. Of course, she was forced to spend some time with her sister and the minister. Breakfasts and suppers were a trial. Jane would smile sweetly when Mr. Greene seated himself too close to Elizabeth's chair. "How good you are to my sister, sir," she said night after night. It was such a predictable comment, as was Mrs. Annesley's moue of distaste, that Elizabeth set wagers with herself on how quickly it would come at each meal.

One evening, Mr. Greene declared, "I believe, I shall write to Lady Catherine. I seek to learn her opinions of a second dance with one's intended."

Elizabeth nearly choked on the piece of juicy quail in her mouth. "Intended? Are you engaged, sir?"

Mr. Greene offered her a toothy smile. "Not yet, my dear, but soon." He patted her arm and Elizabeth repressed her desire to stab his fat fingers with her fork. "I have thought further about Mr. Darcy's advice. And thought I do not doubt the veracity of his comments, I believe Lady Catherine would not be opposed to a gentleman dancing twice with his intended. I plan to write her to confirm."

Thinking quickly, Elizabeth asked, "What if she is averse to the idea? Would your letter not expose you as wishing to thwart her wishes?

"Elizabeth has a good point, my friend. You must not write to the lady about this. I would not like to see you on the receiving end of Lady Catherine's displeasure." Mr. Collins spoke around a mouthful of quail. Normally Elizabeth would have been appalled, but on this occasion, she was only glad for his support.

Mr. Greene's continued presence at Longbourn was particularly hard to endure during the four days after the twenty-second, the date he had originally planned to depart. Any irritation that drags on past its due date only intensifies. But even as the days seemed to stretch endlessly, the twenty-sixth of November eventually arrived.

"How well you look, Elizabeth." Jane reached out and fingered the plaited silk on Elizabeth's sleeve, silently assessing the cost of the material.

Elizabeth had come to know Jane better in the past four weeks. Though she was not a terrible person, she was spoiled and disliked anyone receiving attention that she felt was her due. Her sister could be unkind when she felt she was not in the spotlight. Elizabeth had prepared herself for a difficult evening. She knew her dress was of a finer quality than Jane could afford, and being a single lady, she would receive more offers to dance than her sister would. She waited for Jane's commentary to turn sour, as it often did in moments like this.

"Although anyone dressed so fine would look so well."

There it is. But Elizabeth could not say so aloud. Her mother would be appalled if Elizabeth were to break etiquette, even with a mean-mouthed sister.

Schooling her face, Elizabeth replied. "Thank you, Jane.

You also look well. That is a perfect color for you." Jane wore a soft blue gown that perfectly matched the lightness of her eyes. Elizabeth's own gown was a deeper hue of the same color. It did not perfectly match the navy that rimmed her own blue eyes, but it was as close as a young maiden could wear.

The ladies waited in silence for the gentlemen to join them. Both Mr. Collins and his friend had clearly invested considerable time in their appearance, though the results were far from impressive. Each man had liberally applied hair grease, creating a slick, oily sheen that only accentuated their rumpled appearance. Their efforts did little to improve their look, with their ill-fitting, slightly outdated clothes adding to the overall lackluster effect. Elizabeth could not help but worry that, under the heat of the crowded ballroom, the grease might begin to run into each man's eyes.

"My dear, we must hurry, else we will be late," Mr. Collins called as he rushed down the stairs. Jane's demeanor remained unperturbed.

"As you say, husband." Taking his arm, she added, "I look forward to our dance this evening." Mr. Collins strutted as he escorted his wife to the waiting carriage.

When the party finally arrived at Netherfield, the ballroom was already full, and the musicians were beginning the first strains of music. "I had worried you abandoned me." Mr. Bingley held his arm aloft. Elizabeth gently placed her hand in the crook of his arm and allowed him to escort her to the head of the line. When the dance ended, he escorted her back to her friends who stood with Miss Bingley.

"You look quite fine, tonight." Miss Goulding pulled Elizabeth into the circle of ladies. Elizabeth thanked her friend and greeted everyone else.

Miss Bingley eyed the cut of Elizabeth's dress. "Your gown is quite nice. Pray tell, which Cheapside seamstress do you use? I believe her talents are wasted in that part of town."

Elizabeth hid a smile. "Madame Etienne created this one."

"Madame Etienne! You do love to tease, Eliza." Miss Bingley's eyes traveled down the length of Elizabeth's gown and up again.

"I do enjoy teasing, Miss Bingley, but in this I am completely serious. Madame Etienne made most of my gowns this past year. My friend, Suzy, introduced us." Miss Bingley's mouth tightened in displeasure, but she said no more.

Soon the party was joined by Miss Lucas' younger brother, Mr. John Lucas, who collected Elizabeth for their dance. The steps were fast-paced, allowing little time for discussion. Skipping down the line, Elizabeth caught sight of Mr. Darcy. He partnered Miss Bingley and looked quite miserable by the situation.

Elizabeth was thankful for the many repetitions her dance master had required, for it was only her superior knowledge of the steps that allowed her to continue without bumping into anyone. She was captivated by the gentleman five spaces up the line. The bright white of his cravat and shirt accentuated the subtle tan on his cheeks. His long, lean build and broad shoulders were emphasized by the cut of his jacket. She had long wished to touch his shoulders and find out if they were padded, though she suspected they were not. Elizabeth had always found him to be handsome, but in his formal wear, he was nearly irresistible. She very much looked forward to their dance.

Do not be a dunderhead, Lizzy. Mr. Darcy may flirt and dance with you, but you cannot expect to marry such a man, no matter how grand your portion. Though she disagreed with Jane on the type of gentleman she could attract, Elizabeth was not unaware of her status among the ton. Her father may have moved the family to Brook Street, but that did not change the fact that he was a tradesman. She was welcome to visit the finest parlors in London, but that did not mean she would be welcomed into the family rooms of those same homes.

During the season, several gentlemen had paid court to her. A baron had called on her, as well. But all had pockets to let, and her papa had chased each man away. Darcy was reputed to be among the wealthiest men in England. That fact, combined with his connections to the Earl of Matlock meant he would likely offer for a society lady. *Someone like Suzy.* Elizabeth was discomfited by the thought.

∞∞∞

"I believe this is our dance." Darcy had endured the entire evening with barely concealed impatience, his gaze never straying far from Elizabeth. At last, it was his turn to stand across from her, to bask in the light of her bright eyes and the charm of her playful smiles.

As she took his arm, a thrill ran through him, the softness of her touch a stark contrast to the clawing grip of Miss Bingley. He could not help but savor the difference, every moment in her presence heightening his longing.

The dance began, and as the movement drew her toward him, Elizabeth's teasing voice reached his ears. "I hope, sir, that you have thought of at least three topics to discuss during our dance. I have warned you before about staying silent."

She moved away with the flow of the dance, and Darcy's heart nearly propelled him to follow her. *I love her.* The realization struck him with the force of inevitability. He had fought and denied it, but there was no use anymore. He could do nothing about it, but even admitting it to himself brought a bittersweet relief.

The dance brought them together again. "Would you like to discuss horses?"

She laughed, a light melodic sound that paired perfectly with the orchestra. "Horses? At a ball? No, no, sir. I know you can do better."

He chuckled. "I suppose it is a poor choice of conversation for a dance. What about books?"

Her eyes sparkled. "I would not normally wish to discuss books while dancing, but it is better than talking about horseflesh."

Though it was difficult to carry on a conversation while moving together and apart, Darcy thought it the most pleasant partnering he had ever experienced. The topic continued through supper until everyone assembled was disturbed by the tapping of a knife upon the crystal. Mr. Collins stood to address the room and Elizabeth groaned.

"I would like to thank Mr. Bingley for hosting this ball, and for serving such excellent food. It has been many years since I have tasted such a fine meal." Mr. Bingley graciously accepted the praise. Mr. Collins continued. "As many of you know, tomorrow my friend, Mr. Greene, will return to his home in Hunsford. In honor of him, I would like to sing a song I prepared for the occasion."

"No, no, no." Elizabeth's voice barely registered.

Mr. Collins took a moment to warm up his voice with a series of trills. He then loudly began his newest song, which to the surprise of no one in the room, was set to the tune of Greensleeves.

My friend, Greene, you leave too soon,

We'll resort to letters from one another.

But I am consoled in knowing that,

We'll soon be as close as brothers.

"At least it rhymes," Darcy said under his breath.

"Yes, that is something, at least."

You will marry Elizabeth,

And she will be happy as my Jane.

She will make you a splendid bride,

And you will honor her Bennet name.

Before Mr. Collins could begin his second verse, an embarrassed Bingley stood and began to clap. The rest of the party tentatively joined in. "Excellent rhyming, sir, but I believe I hear the musicians starting up."

Darcy turned to look at Elizabeth. Her cheeks were pink with humiliation, but her eyes were dry. Any other lady would have crumbled at such an embarrassing scene, but not his Elizabeth. When had he begun to think of her as *his* Elizabeth? He dismissed the worrisome thought. *I can contemplate that later,* he silently told himself.

Standing, he helped pull her seat out from the table. "It seems we are to begin dancing sooner than I anticipated. I have enjoyed our time together."

"Thank you, Mr. Darcy. I, too, have appreciated our dance and conversation." He led her back to the ballroom and helped her find her friends. Miss Goulding pulled her tight. "You poor thing," he heard the lady murmur as he walked away.

∞∞∞

Darcy was too disturbed by his feelings for Elizabeth and his irritation with Mr. Collins to consider finding a dance partner. He had taken to the floor four times already. Surely Bingley would be pleased with his participation and not harangue him further. Seeking a moment of privacy to collect himself, he stepped behind a large plant.

"Your song was excellent, my friend."

"I write what I see, and any fool can tell that you and Elizabeth are meant for one another." The voices of Messrs.

Greene and Collins rang out from the other side of the plant. Darcy cocked his head to better hear their conversation.

"I plan to ask her tonight while we are dancing. I have thought about it, and I believe it will be the most romantic possibility."

"She will say no," a lighter, more feminine voice added. "She has told me so herself."

"Nonsense, Jane. She would be a fool to refuse my friend."

She would be a fool to accept him, Darcy thought.

"It would be foolish, but that will not stop my sister. My mother has always insisted she was obstinate, and she is correct. Elizabeth will tell him no."

"Then he will simply have to force her. It will be in her best interest." Darcy's hand clenched upon hearing Mr. Collins' appalling words.

"Force her? I do not understand?" Mr. Greene's whiny voice rang out. They had moved closer to the plant and Darcy held his breath, fearing they might find him lurking.

"Compromise her." Mr. Collins said with dramatic flair. "During the dance, you will stumble forward. Knock her down, if you must. Just make sure that the event is witnessed. I do not like to cause gossip, but this is Elizabeth's only chance to wed a gentleman."

Darcy had heard enough. He was about to step out and strangle both men when Mrs. Collins' voice stopped him. "I do not like to do this to her, but she is my sister. As the elder, I must have her best interests at heart. Therefore, I must tell you, sir, you must not simply trip onto her. You must thoroughly ruin her. If you pull at her gown, just so, it should rip apart. She will be angry at first, but she will thank you for it later."

The strains of music began, forcing the trio apart as they went to seek their dance partners. Darcy left his hiding spot and headed straight for Elizabeth. She stood alone and smiled as she saw him draw near.

"Pretend I have stepped on your foot and fall backwards. Trust me." His voice was urgent, laced with an intensity that left no room for doubt. Darcy then stepped forward and gently, but firmly, pushed her backwards. Her eyes widened in confusion, but she obeyed, trusting him despite her uncertainty.

"Oh!" she gasped as she landed softly on the floor, the sound of her surprise cutting through the murmur of the crowd.

"Miss Gardiner!" Darcy quickly crouched in front of her, his expression one of genuine concern as the crowd's attention shifted toward them. "I apologize, madame, for my clumsiness." He leaned in closer, his breath warm against her ear as he whispered, "Pretend as though I have injured your ankle."

"My ankle," she whimpered softly, playing her part.

"May I?" he asked, his voice thick with concern, though he didn't wait for her answer. His hand closed gently around her ankle, the warmth of her skin through the fabric sending a jolt through him. The small gasp she let out at his touch resonated deep within him, stirring something raw and unexpected. He pretended to check for a break, but his focus was entirely on her—the soft rise and fall of her chest, the way her eyes met his. He mentally shook himself from his trance.

Remembering himself, Darcy leaned in closer, his voice barely above a whisper. "I have just overheard your sister, Collins, and Greene in conversation. They have conspired together. Mr. Greene intends to compromise you during your dance. Your sister told him you would not accept his offer and suggested this was his only chance."

"Jane?" Elizabeth's voice trembled, and real tears welled in her eyes. Darcy's heart twisted at the sight, wishing fervently that those tears were from a simple injury. That pain would heal quickly, unlike the deeper wound she now bore.

"I am sorry to disappoint you," Darcy murmured, his voice filled with regret, "but you must not dance with him this evening. In fact, you should not even return with them to Longbourn." Elizabeth nodded, her face a mixture of sorrow and determination.

Several revelers had started to move closer. Sir William Lucas called out, "Miss Gardiner, are you injured?"

Raising his voice so that others nearby could hear, Darcy said, "She has turned her ankle." Turning back to Elizabeth, he said, "Allow me to take you to a room. I will have Bingley call for the apothecary." Before she could respond, he scooped her into his arms with a firm yet gentle resolve, carrying her from the room. The sweet scent of flowers, jasmine he believed, reached his nose, stirring something deep within him. Though he told himself his actions were purely protective, the knowing glances from others suggested otherwise.

"Mr. Darcy, a footman can carry her." Miss Bingley called from behind them, but Darcy ignored her, his focus entirely on Elizabeth.

"Sir, if you wait, I will have the carriage called round. There is no need for her to stay here."

At the sound of Mrs. Collins' voice, he instinctively held Elizabeth more firmly to his chest. To his surprise, she leaned her head into the crook of his neck, as though seeking comfort in his embrace. The gesture, so intimate and trusting, nearly made him falter.

"Mrs. Collins, I seem to recall that you stayed here for four nights with a wounded knee. Would you deny the same for your injured sister?"

Mrs. Phillips stood beside her daughter. "That is hardly the same, sir. My Jane has a very delicate constitution, as all gentlemen's wives do. Elizabeth is naught but a tradesman's daughter. She is accustomed to more practical solutions."

Seeing the sour looks directed at her from the people who had spilled out into the hall, Mrs. Collins paled. "Mother, Mr. Darcy is correct. I wish only for Elizabeth to be well." Darcy gave a curt nod and then continued to carry Elizabeth up the stairs. Bingley and Mrs. Annesley followed behind. When they were alone, Darcy shared what he had heard in the ballroom.

Mrs. Annesley placed a comforting hand on her charge's shoulder. "That settles it, you must stay here tonight, Miss Gardiner. I will send Howes to Longbourn to inform Milly. She will pack your things." Turning to Bingley, she continued. "May I request that we stay here until her father can be reached to send a carriage for her."

"Nonsense, we will take her to London ourselves. Darcy wishes to see his sister, and my own sister misses the thrills of town. We can be prepared to leave before noon tomorrow, if that will suit." Mrs. Annesley agreed that it did.

Chapter 13

Return to London

The carriage pulled to a stop in front of Longbourn, and Elizabeth's heart pounded in her chest. She took a deep breath, trying to steady herself as she prepared for what she knew would be a difficult encounter. Mr. Darcy and Mrs. Annesley accompanied her, but their presence did little to ease the storm brewing inside her. She was relieved that Mr. Bingley's carriage had not followed, sparing her the humiliation of Caroline Bingley witnessing another of her family's uncomfortable moments.

As they stepped out of the carriage, Jane appeared at the door, her face alight with a bright, seemingly genuine smile. To Elizabeth's relief, neither Messrs. Collins or Greene were with her.

"Elizabeth, you can walk. I am so happy your injury was slight!" Jane's voice was as sweet as honey, but Elizabeth was no longer fooled by her sister's superficial kindness. Jane descended the steps quickly, her arms outstretched as though she intended to embrace her sister.

Elizabeth stiffened, fighting back the tears that threatened to spill over. She could hardly believe the cruelty that lay beneath Jane's perfect facade. The contrast between her sister's outward sweetness and the bitterness Elizabeth now felt in her heart was almost unbearable.

"Jane," Elizabeth said, her voice tight with emotion as she stepped back, avoiding her sister's outstretched arms. "I need to speak with you."

Jane paused, her smile faltering slightly, but she quickly recovered, tilting her head with that same practiced sweetness. "Of course. What is it, dear sister?"

Elizabeth's throat tightened as she searched for the right words, but her emotions got the better of her. "How could you?" she whispered, her voice trembling. "How could you plot against me with Mr. Collins and Mr. Greene?"

Jane's eyes widened slightly, but she did not feign innocence. Instead, she sighed softly and looked down for a moment, as if gathering her thoughts. When she looked up again, her expression was one of quiet resolve. "I will not deny it," she admitted calmly. "Yes, I did speak with them. But I did it for your own good."

"For my own good?" Elizabeth's voice rose with incredulity. "How can you possibly say that? How could trapping me in a marriage to Mr. Greene be for my good?"

Jane's expression hardened, the sweetness in her eyes replaced by something cold and calculating. "Because if I must suffer a marriage to Mr. Collins," she said, her voice edged with bitterness, "then it is only fair that you should share a similar fate. Mr. Greene is an eligible man, and you would be well provided for. I am doing this because I care for you. You may not see it now, but you will thank me one day."

Elizabeth's breath caught in her throat, the hurt and betrayal cutting deeper than she ever imagined. "Thank you?" she echoed, her voice filled with disbelief. "You expect me to thank you for your attempt to condemn me to a life of misery?"

Jane shrugged, her demeanor unyielding. "We must all do our duty, Elizabeth. Sometimes that means making difficult choices for the greater good. It is not always about happiness.

You would have security if you were married to Mr. Greene, and our social situations would be similar. I would be able to see you more if you were the wife of a gentleman. As the daughter of a tradesman, your position in society is an embarrassment to Mr. Collins and me."

Elizabeth shook her head, feeling as though the ground beneath her was slipping away. "I cannot believe what I'm hearing," she said, her voice barely more than a whisper.

Jane looked from Elizabeth to Mr. Darcy, who still stood near the carriage. "I cannot fault you for your aspirations to reach a higher sphere. Your efforts with Mr. Darcy will fail, however, and then where will you be? Unmarried in London."

"You are not the Jane I thought I knew… or rather the Jane I *hoped* to know."

Jane's expression softened slightly, but there was no true remorse in her eyes. "I am sorry you feel that way, but I stand by what I have done."

Elizabeth felt Mr. Darcy's presence draw nearer, a silent pillar of support, and it gave her the strength she needed to turn away from Jane. "Howes," Elizabeth called, her voice steadying, "please help Milly bring my things. I have no desire to linger here any longer than necessary."

Her footman nodded before stepping into the house. Mr. Darcy moved closer and silently offered his arm. She hesitated for only a moment before taking it, grateful for his support.

As they turned to leave, Jane called after her. "Elizabeth, please, you must understand—" But Elizabeth did not turn back. She had heard enough.

∞∞∞

As the carriage rumbled along the road, the soft hum of

the wheels on the gravel provided a steady rhythm to Darcy's thoughts. He stole a glance at Elizabeth, seated across from him, her profile lit gently by the light filtering through the carriage window. The events at Longbourn still weighed heavily on his mind, but now, with the countryside gradually giving way to the outskirts of London, his thoughts shifted to their arrival in London.

Finally, Darcy broke the silence, his voice measured. "Miss Gardiner, might I inquire as to your address? I will need to share it with my driver at our next stop."

Elizabeth looked up. "Of course, Mr. Darcy. We reside on Brook Street."

Darcy felt a jolt of surprise. "Brook Street?" he repeated, barely able to conceal his astonishment. "That is quite near my own home on Grosvenor."

Elizabeth's eyes held a hint of amusement. "Yes, Papa purchased Bledsoe House five years past. Uncle Paul learned of the opportunity and suggested that we become neighbors. It has certainly made it easier for me to see my dearest friend."

Darcy blinked, momentarily at a loss for words. Brook Street was a highly desirable location, and it struck him as incredible that he could have been so close to Elizabeth's family without ever realizing it. He cleared his throat, trying to mask his surprise. "It is… quite a surprise that we have never met before now," he managed to say.

Elizabeth's expression softened, a touch of wistfulness in her gaze. "I have only been out for one season," she explained. "The year prior, I was in India. My father's business interests required our presence there, and so I was a year delayed in my come-out."

Darcy nodded, absorbing this information. Her explanation made sense, though it still seemed extraordinary that their paths had not crossed sooner. "I see," he said slowly. "I missed much of the past season due to business at Pemberley. It seems our paths were not destined to cross until recently."

For a moment, silence settled between them, the clatter of the carriage the only sound. Darcy found himself imagining what it might have been like if he had come to town the past spring instead of working tirelessly at Pemberley—if he had seen Elizabeth at the many balls and gatherings he had attended in London. He could picture her, radiant and lively, moving gracefully through the dance, her laughter echoing in the grand halls.

A pang of something he could not quite identify — regret? longing? — stabbed at him as he wondered what it might have been like to court her properly, to have asked her for every dance, to have been the one to draw out those enchanting smiles. Perhaps if they had met under different circumstances — she as a gentlewoman or he with less responsibilities toward his sister and family name — things might have been different between them.

But as tantalizing as these thoughts were, Darcy forced himself to remember the reality of their situation. No matter how close their homes might be, no matter how easy it was to imagine a different fate, Elizabeth Gardiner was still the daughter of a tradesman. And he was the grandson of an earl, with all the expectations and responsibilities that came with his lineage.

He stole another glance at Elizabeth, who was now gazing out the window, lost in her own thoughts. Even in the throes of disappointment there was a warmth and ease about her that made it so tempting to forget the boundaries that society had placed between them. But Darcy was nothing if not a man of duty and restraint. He could not afford to indulge in idle fantasies, not when so much was at stake.

Clearing his throat again, Darcy sought to steer the conversation back to safer ground. "You have told me so little of India. It must have been a fascinating place to visit," he remarked, his tone deliberately neutral. "I have heard it is a land of great beauty and diversity."

Elizabeth turned her attention back to him, her eyes brightening at the mention of her travels. "Indeed, it is," she agreed, her voice laced with genuine fondness. "The landscapes are unlike anything I have seen elsewhere, and the people we met were incredibly hospitable. It was a wonderful experience, though I am glad to be back in England now."

Darcy nodded politely, though his thoughts remained elsewhere. Even as Elizabeth spoke of her adventures, his mind kept circling back to that fleeting image of what might have been—the vision of the two of them, side by side, navigating the intricate dance of London society.

But it was no use dwelling on such thoughts. He had responsibilities, a family name to uphold, and a future that did not allow for such indulgences. No matter how compelling the idea of a life shared with Elizabeth might seem, Darcy knew better than to entertain it.

With an inward sigh, he settled back against the carriage seat, determined to put these distracting thoughts aside. There was still much to be done, and he could not afford to let his emotions cloud his judgment. Yet, as they continued their journey toward London, the thought of what could have been lingered stubbornly in the back of his mind, refusing to be entirely dismissed.

∞∞∞

As the carriage rolled to a stop in front of Bledsoe House on Brook Street, Darcy could not help but be impressed by the stately facade that greeted them. The house was a testament to taste and refinement, its elegant lines and grand proportions rivaling those of his own residence on Grosvenor Street. He mentally noted the shining glass windows, the polished stone steps leading to the front door, and the overall air of understated opulence. This was no ordinary home, but rather one that spoke of quiet wealth and a discerning eye for beauty.

Darcy was aware that the home had once belonged to Viscount Bledsoe, a man who had squandered his fortune at the card table, losing nearly everything in the process. The irony of such a house now belonging to a family of tradesmen was not lost on him, but he could not deny that the Gardiners had restored the property to its former glory. It was nearly as large and imposing as his own, a fact that Darcy found both surprising and oddly reassuring.

When the carriage door opened, Darcy stepped down first, then turned to offer his hand to Elizabeth. She accepted his assistance, her earlier strength seeming to waver as she looked up at the familiar sight of her home. Alerted to their arrival, the front door opened, and an elegant couple emerged. He knew Mr. Gardiner from their business dealings but had not seen his wife in many years. Mrs. Gardiner was a woman about ten years his elder, her features still possessing a youthful charm. Darcy recognized her immediately.

"Elizabeth!" Mrs. Gardiner called out, her voice a mixture of happiness and concern as she hurried down the steps. "What has happened? Why are you home so early?" Her eyes darted between her daughter and Mrs. Annesley, clearly searching for answers.

Elizabeth had remained composed throughout the journey, but now, at the sight of her family's familiar faces, her resolve crumbled. The tears she had fought so valiantly to hold back finally broke free, spilling down her cheeks as she let out a soft sob. Mrs. Gardiner tucked her daughter close and hurried her into the house.

Mr. Gardiner looked to Darcy for answers. "Miss Gardiner

has had a disappointment in Meryton, sir. I am certain she will tell you all about it." Mr. Gardiner gave a curt nod, before turning to follow his daughter and wife inside. Darcy and Mrs. Annesley trailed behind.

"There now, my dear," Mrs. Gardiner murmured, her tone soothing as she stroked Elizabeth's hair. "It's all right. You are home now. Whatever it is, we will sort it out together."

When Elizabeth did not reply, Mrs. Annesley, who had stood quietly to the side, exchanged a glance with Darcy. Her eyes asked the question she did not voice aloud, and Darcy understood immediately. He stepped forward, clearing his throat before addressing Elizabeth's parents.

"Mr. and Mrs. Gardiner," he began, his voice carefully controlled, "there has been... an incident. I am afraid your daughter has been the target of some rather unpleasant scheming by certain individuals, with the intention of compromising her. Fortunately, the situation was averted before any harm could be done."

Mr. Gardiner's fist clenched. "I see," he said slowly, his expression a mixture of gratitude and fury. "Thank you, Mr. Darcy, for looking after my girl. I shudder to think what might have happened had you not been there."

Darcy inclined his head. "It was my duty," he replied simply. "I am just relieved that we were able to bring her home safely."

Mrs. Gardiner pulled back from Elizabeth and wiped a tear from her cheek. "There now, darling. You will give yourself a terrible headache if you continue to cry so." Elizabeth sniffled, but the worst of her weeping had subsided.

Turning to Darcy, Mrs. Gardiner's eyes softened. "It is lovely to see you again, sir. It has been many years, has it not? Though, you were only a child when I last laid eyes upon you."

"I was unsure if you would recognize me."

"You look too much like your father for that." She hugged Elizabeth once more before turning back to him.

Darcy nodded, feeling a mix of emotions he rarely experienced. "The pleasure is mine, Mrs. Gardiner. I remember you well from years past. It is good to see you again, though I wish it were under better circumstances."

Mrs. Gardiner smiled, though it was tinged with sadness. "Yes, well, life rarely affords us such luxuries, does it?" She sighed, giving Elizabeth another comforting squeeze. "Let's get you upstairs, my dear. We will send for some tea, and you can rest. There is nothing more to worry about now."

Elizabeth nodded, her tears beginning to subside as she allowed herself to be led toward the stairs. Darcy watched them go, feeling an odd sense of loss. Mrs. Annesley followed.

Mr. Gardiner watched his wife and daughter ascend the stairs. When they were out of sight, he spoke. "Will you tell me more about the incident?"

Darcy shared the story about Mr. and Mrs. Collins' plans to tie Elizabeth to Mr. Greene, even if it meant through compromise. Mr. Gardiner irritation grew as he learned of the perfidy one sister plotted against another.

"I should have taken both girls from Harriet when they were young. I should have known that she would spoil Jane and ruin any goodness that was in the child. At a minimum, I should have insisted that Jane spend more time in London with us." Darcy rather thought Mrs. Collins too old to blame her raising for her poor choices and mean-spirited ways, but he said nothing.

The two gentlemen stood in silence for a while. Mr. Gardiner ran an agitated hand through his hair and sighed. "Thank you, Mr. Darcy. I know this was not an easy situation."

Darcy offered him a small, weary smile. "It was the least I could do," he said. But as he turned to leave, the weight of the day's events pressed heavily on his shoulders. The image of

Elizabeth's tears lingered in Darcy's mind. He had brought her back to the arms of her loving family, where she belonged, and there was a sense of rightness in that. Yet, as the carriage pulled away from Bledsoe House, Darcy could not shake the ache that settled in his chest.

He stared out the window, his thoughts troubled and his heart heavier than he expected. He had done his duty, fulfilling his role as a gentleman and protector. But the encounter had left him with more questions than answers. Chief among them was the unsettling realization that, despite his best efforts to maintain distance, Elizabeth Gardiner had begun to matter to him in ways he had not anticipated. The question was, what would he do about it?

Chapter 14

Invitations

Darcy assisted his sister up the steps to Matlock House. The house was only three doors from his own, but a cold rain required the use of a carriage, else he and Georgiana would both be soaked and frozen. The heat from inside welcomed him as Godsey, the Matlock's butler, opened the door and ushered them in. "Lady Matlock is in the yellow salon with her guests." Darcy dipped his head in wordless acknowledgement before offering his sister his arm.

"Do you think they will like me?"

He looked down at his sister. She had come so far since the near calamity of last summer, when a former friend of Darcy attempted to take advantage of Georgiana's youth and innocence in order to steal her dowery of thirty-thousand pounds. Thankfully, Darcy got to her in time to prevent George Wickham's schemes. He promptly fired Mrs. Young, Georgiana's companion who had an alliance with the so-called gentleman. Unfortunately, he had not yet replaced the lady.

Perhaps it is time to find a new companion for my sister, he thought. Georgiana's shyness around new people hindered her from making friends. Darcy's business requirements prevented him from spending significant time with her, and he could not help but wonder if an excellent companion would draw her out. *I must find time to ask Miss Gardiner. Perhaps she will know of someone as fitting as Mrs. Annesley.* He ignored the other thoughts that followed; the ones that told him that marrying Elizabeth would mean Mrs. Annesley would be free to serve Georgiana. *She is not for you,* he reminded himself for the thousandth time since parting from her two weeks prior.

He patted Georgiana's hand. "They will love you."

She took a bracing breath. Both he and his sister had a sense of cautious optimism about today's event. His aunt, Lady Matlock, was hosting a few volunteers from the local girl's charity she supported. Each of her guests, she had assured him, were young and friendly. "Perfect friends for our dear girl." Darcy hoped that was true. He shuddered at the thought of another Miss Bingley.

He prepared himself for just such an unpleasant lady, but the sight that greeted him as they stepped into the room was far from what he had anticipated. Seated comfortably on a brocade settee, with her dark curls framing her beautiful face, was Elizabeth Gardiner. Darcy's heart thudded in his chest. Beside her, in animated conversation, sat Lady Susan Corwell, younger sister to his friend Viscount Chryston. She was laughing at something Elizabeth had just said.

For a moment, the world seemed right—Elizabeth was here, in his aunt's parlor, looking as if she belonged. But Darcy's relief quickly turned to unease as he took in the entire scene. Three other ladies sat on another sofa, all of whom looked entirely too pleased by his entrance.

Lady Matlock greeted them with her usual warmth. "Fitzwilliam, Georgiana, how lovely to see you both. Please, come in and take your seats."

As they moved further into the room, Darcy's sharp eyes caught the calculated way his aunt directed the seating arrangements. She ushered Georgiana to a chair near the three unknown young ladies. But then, with a subtle smile, Lady Matlock guided him to a chair beside Lady Susan. Darcy's cousin,

Colonel Richard Fitzwilliam sat on the other side of Elizabeth

"Lady Susan, I believe you have met my nephew before. He is, I think, friends with your brother." Lady Matlock remarked as she settled into her own chair. "You must have much to discuss."

Lady Susan's eyes sparkled with humor as she turned to Darcy. "Indeed, Lady Matlock, it has been far too long since we last spoke, Mr. Darcy. My friend said the two of you met in Hertfordshire. Can you tell me your thoughts of the place? She mentioned that the people were warm and welcoming, though I know at least three for whom that was not the case."

The sound of Elizabeth's laugher, light and unguarded, distracted Darcy. What had Richard possibly said to please her so? Darcy could not prevent a glance in her direction. His unease grew. What was Lady Matlock playing at?

"Of course, Lady Susan," he replied, forcing his attention back to the lady by his side. She was his friend's sister, after all, and he owed her the courtesy of his full attention. Yet even as they exchanged pleasantries, Darcy's thoughts remained with Elizabeth.

Lady Susan noticed his distraction. Leaning closer, she whispered, "You seem troubled, Mr. Darcy. Do the proceedings not meet your expectations?"

Darcy's jaw tightened. "I am merely surprised to see Miss Gardiner here today. I had not expected her company."

"Lizzy and I volunteer at the girl's school. We do everything together, actually. She is my greatest friend, you know?"

Darcy had not known. Elizabeth had mentioned a friend named Suzy once or twice, but he had hardly made the connection. How could he?

"I am sure she will chat with you soon, but for now, your aunt has placed her near your cousin for reasons that I can only surmise."

"And what reasons might those be?" Darcy asked, though he feared he already knew the answer.

Lady Susan's lips curled into a half-smile. "Oh, I could not possibly speculate. But I do believe that whatever the outcome, it will be most entertaining."

Darcy did not share her amusement. As the tea service began and the conversation flowed around them, he found himself unable to fully engage. His eyes kept straying to Elizabeth, who seemed completely at ease in Richard's company. Richard, who was charming and attentive, and who—Darcy was loath to admit—had always had a certain way with ladies. He had no right to feel possessive, and yet... the very idea of his cousin winning Elizabeth's favor twisted in his gut.

Darcy's mind was a whirl of confusion. He did not wish for Richard to win Elizabeth, but Darcy could not have her, either. The barriers between them seemed insurmountable—her being the daughter of a tradesman, and his family's expectations to marry someone with higher status. His own father and grandfather had married daughters of earls, and his great-grandfather called a marquess his father-in-law. Could Darcy do any less?

Elizabeth's laughter rang out again, and his mood darkened further. His eyes drifted once more to the settee where Elizabeth sat with Richard. His cousin's easy charm was on full display, and Elizabeth, ever gracious, responded with warmth and bright smiles. Darcy's chest tightened at the sight.

The tea service provided a blessed distraction. Elizabeth turned from Richard and focused on the others around the room, which pleased Darcy greatly. "Miss Darcy, I am pleased to make your acquaintance. Your brother has told me a little about you, but I would like to learn more." It was true. Darcy had shared a few stories of his youngest sister with Elizabeth when she stayed at Netherfield. He had often wondered how Georgiana would fare with someone like Elizabeth in her life.

Georgiana studied the pattern on her teacup. Her shy nature often made such social gatherings a trial, but she was determined to make a good impression. Gathering her courage, she leaned forward slightly, her soft voice carrying across the space between them.

"Miss Gardiner," she began, "I... I hope you do not find it too forward of me to say, but my brother has written of you often in his letters."

Elizabeth's eyebrows lifted in surprise, and a small, pleased smile played at her lips. "Truly? I hope he has not spoken ill of me," she replied, her tone was light, but it did not hide her curiosity.

"Oh no, not at all," Georgiana hastened to reassure her. "On the contrary, his words were always in praise of your... your intelligence and wit. And he had great admiration for your ability on the pianoforte. He wrote that your songs gave him much pleasure."

Darcy, who had been straining to catch their conversation, felt a flush of warmth creep up his neck. He had not realized how often he had mentioned Elizabeth in his letters to Georgiana. His sister's innocent revelation seemed to catch Elizabeth off guard as well, though she recovered quickly.

"Thank you, Miss Darcy. I am pleased to know that Mr. Darcy wrote kindly of me, though I must admit that he has exaggerated my prowess with the instrument. I am not so technically proficient as some others I know." Darcy's lips quirked at the remembrance of their shared conversation about Miss Bingley's playing.

"My brother never exaggerates. I am certain your playing is everything he said it would be." Georgiana, emboldened by Elizabeth's kindness, ventured a suggestion that took even Darcy by surprise. "I wonder if you might do me the honor of playing a duet with me. I find I am always more confident with someone by my side."

Elizabeth's eyes lit up with genuine surprise. Thankfully, she did not object to his sister's request. "I should be most happy to, Miss Darcy. Music is one of my great pleasures."

"Excellent," exclaimed Lady Matlock. "I should love to hear you play, as well."

Elizabeth and Georgiana rose and made their way to the instrument in the corner of the room. Darcy watched them with a mixture of pleasure and apprehension. Georgiana, usually so reticent, had immediately found comfort in Elizabeth's company. She smiled and appeared to giggle as they searched through the music. The sight of their heads bent together over the sheets of paper gave him sincere pleasure.

Soon, there song began. The notes filled the room, and everyone stopped speaking to listen for a while. God, how he loved her. The agony of never having her tore through him. He stole a glance at his cousin, who sat in rapt attention. *If my aunt believes Elizabeth is good enough for Richard, then why would she not be suitable for me?*

∞∞∞

Suzy observed Mr. Darcy's distraction. With a teasing smile she leaned forward and whispered. "Are you so fond of music, Mr. Darcy? Or is it the performer that has caught your attention?"

Mr. Darcy tore his gaze away from the piano, attempting to mask his discomposure. "Music has always been a pleasure of mine," he replied evenly. Suzy attempted to hide a smirk.

When the song ended, the room broke out into applause. "Brava, ladies," Colonel Fitzwilliam exclaimed. Mr. Darcy clearly felt himself drawn toward the piano, but first he needed to extricate himself from Suzy's side.

"Lady Susan," he began, turning to her with a courteous

bow, "you have been a most gracious companion this afternoon. However, I find myself compelled to offer my congratulations to Miss Gardiner and my sister for their splendid performance."

"Of course, Mr. Darcy. It would be remiss of you not to acknowledge such talent. Please, do not let me keep you."

With a slight nod, Darcy moved away from her, his heart quickening as he made his way to where Elizabeth and Georgiana were standing, still basking in the glow of their duet.

Colonel Fitzwilliam waited for Mr. Darcy to cross the room before he seized the opportunity and slipped into the seat his cousin had just vacated.

"You seem to have a sudden interest in this side of the room, Colonel. What brings you here?"

With a playful grin, he quietly replied. "I could not help but notice that my mother's matchmaking plans might not be proceeding as smoothly as she hoped. It is quite obvious she intended to pair me with Miss Gardiner and Darcy with you."

Suzy chuckled. "I had surmised as much myself. Unfortunately for your mother, it seems Mr. Darcy has other plans."

The Colonel's grin widened. "I noticed that, as well. I have never known Darcy to mention a lady — in speaking or writing — to his sister. That he wrote about Miss Gardiner to Georgiana must mean that he she has captured his interest."

"But will he be strong enough to act upon it? I do not wish for my friend to be trifled with."

Colonel Fitzwilliam looked from where Darcy stood at the pianoforte back to the lady beside him. "Darcy would never act dishonorably."

Suzy let out a relieved breath, before leaning forward. "Then what say you to a little mischief?" she whispered.

He leaned in as well. "You hardly know me, but I assure

you that I am always up for a bit of mischief. What do you have in mind?"

Suzy smiled. "Perhaps we should turn the tables on your mother and ensure that Mr. Darcy and Lizzy spend more time together instead."

Colonel Fitzwilliam chuckled. "It is perfect. I can, perhaps, see my favorite cousin settled with an admirable lady, and I can thwart my mother's well-intentioned but poorly executed plans."

"Excellent," Suzy replied. "Then let us see what we can do to make this Christmas a bit more interesting."

∞∞∞

When the tea ended, Georgiana said goodbye to Misses Harris, Rudolph, and Hammonds and promised to visit the school with her aunt on a day when they volunteered. Disappointed that they had no conversation with Darcy, each lady sent him a look of longing before they departed. Normally such obvious maneuvers would have repulsed him, but on this day, he paid them no attention. Elizabeth was the only person his eyes saw.

Too soon, the Effington carriage pulled to the front of the house. Lady Susan gave a conspiratorial wink to Richard. "Before I leave, I must invite you to spend yuletide with my family. Lizzy's family always joins us at Meadow Haven. It would be so much fun to have a larger party this year. Your eldest son and his family are, of course, also welcome."

Lady Matlock, pleased to have another opportunity to throw the young ladies together with her youngest son and favorite nephew, agreed readily. "Unfortunately, my eldest and his family will visit with his wife's mother and father during the season, but the earl and I would love to travel with you to Meadow Haven." She stopped to look at her youngest son. "Richard, will you come with us?" When he acknowledged that he would, she turned to her nephew. "Darcy, please say that you can come, too."

Christmas with Elizabeth. Darcy's heart raced at the idea.

"Oh, Brother, can we?" Georgiana's face lit with hope.

Darcy smiled at his sister but then turned his eyes to Elizabeth. "Of course. I would not miss it." Suzy and Richard exchanged a knowing smile.

Darcy and Richard escorted the ladies to their carriage. Richard talked quietly with Lady Susan, and Darcy took advantage of his time alone with Elizabeth. "I hope your heart has recovered from your disappointment."

The smile on her face faltered. "I... I believe being around good friends and loving family has a restorative effect. But..."

"But it is no easy thing to realize your hopes for sisterly affections have been shattered." Her head bobbed in a jerky nod. He longed to pull her to him. To comfort her in the ways a man comforts the woman he loves.

A moment passed before either spoke. "Next time we meet, I would like to ask your opinion about companions. My sister is in need of someone, and I know you respect and admire Mrs. Annesley very well. I had hoped that one of you might act as a reference to another respectable companion."

"Perhaps we can discuss it during our holiday. Mrs. Annesley will be visiting her sister during that time, but I can ask her opinion before we travel."

"That would be appreciated." He bowed deeply. "I look forward to spending Christmas with you at Meadow Haven, Miss Gardiner."

Elizabeth looked up at him, her expression unreadable but tinged with something that made Darcy's heart skip a beat. "And

I you, Mr. Darcy."

Chapter 15

Meadow Haven

Three days later, the Effington carriage made its way northeast toward Gloucestershire carrying Elizabeth, Suzy, and Mrs. Gardiner. The gentlemen were scheduled to arrive the following day after completing business in London.

Elizabeth felt a sense of anticipation as the vehicle made its way along the tree-lined lane. She had visited the estate many times before, but she thought the sprawling grounds looked especially enchanting under a dusting of heavy frost. It had not yet snowed in this part of the country, but the weather had turned particularly cold, and the sky was gray. She anticipated a white Christmas.

Beside her, Suzy leaned forward eagerly, her breath fogging the carriage window. "There it is, Lizzy! Meadow Haven, just as beautiful as ever. I cannot wait to show you the new renovations Papa has made to the west wing. You will hardly recognize it!"

Mrs. Gardiner, seated opposite the two young women, observed them with a fond smile. She had always been impressed by the close bond between her daughter and Suzy. "I do hope we are not arriving too early. I should hate to inconvenience your household by coming before the other guests."

"Nonsense, Mrs. Gardiner," Suzy replied with a wave of

her hand. "You know you and Lizzy are always welcome here, and besides, we will need every moment to ensure everything is perfect for the festivities. This is my first time acting as hostess for a house party. Your assistance is very appreciated."

The carriage came to a halt in front of the grand entrance, and a footman assisted the ladies out. Howes, the Gardiner's own footman, directed others to remove the luggage. Suzy took Elizabeth's hand and rushed her inside out of the cold. They were greeted by the housekeeper, Mrs. Billings, a stout woman with smile lines around her eyes. Elizabeth had always liked the earl's jolly retainer.

"Lady Susan, Mrs. Gardiner, Miss Gardiner." She dipped into a deep curtsy. "It is a pleasure to greet you. We have prepared your rooms, and I have taken the liberty of arranging a light luncheon, if you are hungry."

"Thank you, Mrs. Billings," Suzy replied. "But first, I think we should like to refresh ourselves." She turned to her companions. "Will a half hour be sufficient?" The ladies agreed that it would, and each made her way to her set of rooms.

The ladies sat down for a light luncheon of cold meats, cheese, and sliced apples. "What is first on your list?"

Suzy swallowed a bite of ham before answering. "I am glad you ask, Lizzy. I believe we should begin by setting menus for the next weeks. I feel positive Mrs. Billings has stocked all the essentials, but there are a few specialty dishes I would like to serve."

"Mama can assist you with that task. What shall I do?"

Suzy thought a moment. "I wish for our decorations to be grander than ever, this year. Could you make a list of all the items we will need to decorate for Christmas? Perhaps even sketch your ideas for garlands and wreaths for the main rooms?" Elizabeth assured her that she would do her best. She was not particularly adept at drawing, but she could manage a simple sketch.

The ladies separated after the meal, with Mrs. Gardiner and Suzy heading toward the housekeeper's office, and Elizabeth making her way to the blue parlor to find paper and pencil. She began her sketches in that room before moving on to the library. She had gotten no further than sketching the dimensions of that room before Suzy found her.

"Here you are."

"You have found me." Elizabeth patted the seat next to her. "I am only now beginning my plans for this room, but I have sketched ideas for the blue parlor." She handed her friend the drawing.

Suzy studied it. "I see what you are hoping to achieve, and I like it, but I think there should be more." She walked across the room and obtained her own pencil from the desk and sat back down near her friend. "If we add small wreathes to these windows…" She drew small circles in the middle of each rectangle. "And…. Oh! You have not included mistletoe. There must be a sprig in every room."

Elizabeth rolled her eyes. "I will add it to the sketch for this room. Then I will hand my design to you and you can add or remove as you please." Suzy agreed this was the best way to go about the task and set to work redesigning her friend's sketch.

As they worked, Suzy's lively chatter filled the air, her thoughts never straying far from the topic of the approaching house party. "Lizzy, I must ask—of all the gentlemen who will be joining us, which do you find the most agreeable? I hear Colonel Fitzwilliam has quite the reputation with the ladies."

Elizabeth looked up from drawing swags of holly on the mantel, her expression one of mild amusement. "The Colonel is a charming man, to be sure, but I cannot say that I have given the matter much thought"

Suzy's eyes sparkled with mischief as she leaned closer.

"Not even for a certain tall, dark, and brooding gentleman? I must admit, Lizzy, I was surprised to see how well you and Mr. Darcy got on at Lady Matlock's tea. He is not usually so... attentive to young ladies. At least that is what Nicholas said when I discussed it with him."

Elizabeth's heart gave a small, traitorous leap at the mention of Mr. Darcy, though she quickly masked it with a light laugh. "Mr. Darcy and I are merely acquaintances. There is nothing more to it. And I do wish you would refrain from discussing my dealings with the gentleman, especially with your brother."

"Merely acquaintances?" Suzy echoed, raising an eyebrow. "Well, I suppose that is as it should be, considering that Lady Matlock has set her sights on him for me."

Elizabeth's hands stilled on the page, her mind racing. "Has she indeed? And what do you think of that?"

Suzy shrugged nonchalantly. "I think Lady Matlock believes as many others do—that Darcy would be a good match for someone of my standing. He is wealthy, well-connected, and despite his aloofness, I find him rather intriguing. But I am not so sure I wish to be the next Mrs. Darcy, if you take my meaning."

Elizabeth forced herself to resume her task. "I can understand why she would think so. Mr. Darcy would certainly be a prize for any young lady."

"Any young lady, including you?" Suzy's tone was playful, but Elizabeth could sense the genuine curiosity beneath it.

"I have no designs on Mr. Darcy," Elizabeth replied, more firmly than she intended. "Besides, I am certain he would be much better suited to someone like you—someone of rank and high connections."

Suzy's eyes narrowed slightly as she studied her friend. "You speak as if you know him well enough to make such a judgment. Perhaps there is more to this acquaintance than you let on?"

Elizabeth felt a rush of heat rise in her chest and cheeks. "I assure you, Mr. Darcy is merely an acquaintance. I have enjoyed his company, but there is nothing more to our relationship."

Sensing her friend's agitation, Suzy did not press the matter further. She allowed the conversation to drift to other topics, and soon they were immersed in sketching designs for the dining room, discussing the proper arrangement of the table settings and the placement of candles.

As they worked, Elizabeth found herself increasingly distracted by thoughts of Darcy. She had tried to dismiss her feelings, to convince herself that his attentions were nothing more than polite interest, but the idea of him being intended for Suzy unsettled her more than she cared to admit. After all, society would deem him a far better match for Lady Susan Corwell, the daughter of an earl, than for the adopted niece of a tradesman, no matter how wealthy her family had become.

But try as she might, Elizabeth could not push the thoughts of Darcy from her mind. His kindness, his steady, intense gaze, the way he had spoken to her at Lady Matlock's tea—all of it lingered in her thoughts, despite her attempts to remain indifferent.

"Lizzy," Suzy's voice broke into her reverie, drawing her attention back to the present. "You have been very quiet. Are you sure there's nothing on your mind?"

Elizabeth forced a smile, shaking her head. "Just thinking of all the work still to be done."

Suzy gave her a long, considering look but did not push further. "Well, we are nearly finished here. Shall we move on to the grand hall? It is the last room to be decorated, and I want it to be perfect."

With a nod, Elizabeth followed Suzy out of the dining room, determined to focus on the task at hand. But as they began stringing garlands and arranging the holly wreaths, Suzy's probing questions and her own conflicted feelings continued to swirl in her mind, leaving Elizabeth more uncertain than ever about what—if anything—she truly wanted from Mr. Darcy.

∞∞∞

Three days later, the sound of approaching carriages echoed through the courtyard of Meadow Haven, signaling the arrival of the awaited guests. A dusting of snow covered the ground causing everything to look clean and fresh for the newcomers. The grand double doors were flung open, and Suzy, radiant with excitement, stood ready to greet her guests.

The first carriage came to a stop, and the footman swiftly opened the door. Mr. Darcy was the first to step out, his tall, imposing figure cutting a striking silhouette against the winter landscape. He glanced around, his gaze sharp and discerning, until it landed on Elizabeth, who stood beside her friend. For a moment, the world seemed to narrow to just the two of them. Elizabeth's heart gave a small, involuntary leap as their eyes met. She managed a polite nod and a warm smile.

Behind him, his sister Georgiana alighted from the carriage, her features softened by a shy smile. Colonel Richard Fitzwilliam stepped from the second carriage, his eyes aglow with his usual good humor, before turning to assist his mother and father down.

Suzy stepped forward. "Welcome to Meadow Haven! We are so delighted you could join us for the holidays."

Mr. Darcy offered a polite bow, his expression as composed as ever. "Thank you, Lady Susan. It is a pleasure to be here."

Georgiana, standing slightly behind her brother, was visibly more reserved. Suzy's warmth, however, quickly put her at ease. "Miss Darcy, it is such a pleasure to see you again. I trust you had a pleasant journey?"

Georgiana smiled softly. "It was very pleasant, thank you, Lady Susan. I am looking forward to spending time here."

While Mr. Darcy and Georgiana moved on to greet Mr. Gardiner, Lord Effington, and his son, Viscount Chryston, Colonel Fitzwilliam stepped forward with a grin. "Ah, Lady Susan, I see you have the place in perfect order. I hope you have left some room for a bit of holiday mischief?"

Suzy laughed, her eyes twinkling with delight. "For you, Colonel, I might allow a little mischief—for a good purpose, of course."

Their playful exchange did not go unnoticed by Lady Matlock, who observed them with interest. A small smile tugged at her lips as she considered the possibilities. Elizabeth, however, scrutinized them with curiosity. *What mischief could these two be up to?* She wondered.

As the guests made their way inside, the grand hall of Meadow Haven came alive with activity. Mrs. Gardiner, standing a few steps behind Suzy and Elizabeth, moved forward to greet the Darcys. Mr. Darcy quickly introduced his sister to Elizabeth's mother.

"Miss Darcy, it is a pleasure to meet you. My daughter, Elizabeth, has spoken very highly of you."

Miss Darcy, though still shy, was clearly pleased to be introduced so warmly. "Thank you, Mrs. Gardiner. I am very glad to be here and to see Miss Gardiner again."

Elizabeth, recalling their previous musical connection, smiled at the girl. "I hope we might play together again during your stay, Miss Darcy."

A shy blush colored the girl's cheeks, but she nodded eagerly. "I would like that very much."

∞∞∞

Darcy stood near the entrance of the grand salon, waiting for the ladies to make their entrance. Richard and Nicholas stood near the fire, enjoying a glass of brandy and talking horseflesh. But his thoughts were far from horses; they lingered instead on the woman who had occupied his mind since his arrival—Elizabeth Gardiner. He had seen her only in passing since the guests had arrived.

Finally she arrived arm-in-arm with Lady Susan. She wore a violet silk gown that perfectly drew out the blue in her eyes and the pink in her lips. Oh, how he wished to kiss those delectable lips.

Once all the guests had arrived, Lady Susan suggested it was time for the meal. She approached Darcy with a playful smile. "Mr. Darcy, may I have the pleasure of your arm?" she asked, her tone light and teasing.

Darcy offered his arm with a nod, careful to hide his disappointment. Lady Susan directed him to the hostess' seat and released his arm with a smile. "Oh dear." She picked up the place cards on each side of her. "It seems you have been reassigned, Mr. Darcy. I hope you do not mind."

"Not at all," he replied, his voice carefully controlled. After a moment of searching, he took his seat beside Elizabeth, noting the faint flush that rose to her cheeks as he settled in.

"Miss Gardiner," he said, inclining his head slightly, "it seems we are to be dining partners this evening."

Elizabeth returned his greeting with a polite smile. "Indeed, Mr. Darcy. I hope you find the arrangements to your liking."

Their words were simple, but the atmosphere between

them was charged with a tension that neither could ignore. Darcy could feel the weight of Lady Matlock's gaze from across the table, and he knew Elizabeth was aware of it as well. He knew his aunt had different intentions for him—intentions that did not involve Elizabeth. The knowledge of it made him uncomfortable, but not nearly as much as the realization that he did not care what his aunt thought.

Suddenly resolved to act in a manner that ensure his own happiness, Darcy relaxed. "How have you found your stay at Meadow Haven so far, Miss Gardiner?" he asked.

"It has been lovely," Elizabeth replied, her voice steady, though her eyes flickered briefly to Lady Matlock before returning to him. "We have spent every Christmas here since I was six. Except, of course, the year we traveled to India."

"Does the earl's family often host others, or is it generally just your family that attends?"

"Normally it is only our family. I was surprised when she offered an invitation to your aunt and you, though I suppose it makes sense given that you are an old friend of Nicholas."

"You were not disappointed, I hope?" His dark eyes held hers captive. To his delight, she blushed. He followed the pink in her cheeks, down her neck. He dared not look any further.

"No, I was very pleased to know your family would also attend."

From across the table, Richard interrupted. "Miss Gardiner, I told my father on the ride here how much I enjoyed your duet with my cousin. Perhaps we might be treated to another during our stay?"

Earl Matlock looked over from his conversation with Mrs. Gardiner. "Yes, my son said your playing was very pleasing. I hope to hear for myself."

Georgiana, who had been quietly observing her dinner companions spoke up. "I...I would very much like to play with you again, Miss Gardiner. I enjoyed our duet so much last time."

"Then we shall have to arrange something, Miss Darcy. I look forward to it." Georgiana's face glowed with pleasure and Darcy's heart fell a little more in love with Elizabeth.

∞∞∞

As the dinner wore on, Elizabeth found it increasingly difficult to maintain her composure. She glanced at Mr. Darcy, who was now engaged in conversation with Lord Matlock, his expression as controlled and unreadable as ever. Yet, there had been moments during the meal—fleeting glances, a quiet word—when she felt certain there was something more beneath his composed exterior, something that mirrored the turmoil within her.

Georgiana's shy admiration and Darcy's fleeting glances gave her confidence. But with every glance at Lady Matlock, Elizabeth's hopes wavered. She could feel the older woman's gaze on her, assessing, calculating. Perhaps her friend was correct—Lady Matlock saw Darcy as a match for Suzy, not for a woman of Elizabeth's standing. Certainly, society would deem such a union more suitable, given Suzy's rank and connections. The idea that Lady Matlock might actively push Darcy toward her friend sent a pang of unease through Elizabeth's chest.

Chapter 16

Snow Games

The party settled into something of a routine. Mornings were reserved for individual interests. Usually Elizabeth and Georgiana, as the girl had asked Elizabeth to address her, would meet for piano practice. In the afternoon, the younger generation would gather in the parlor for games. Each day, Suzy managed to partner Elizabeth with Mr. Darcy. Against all good judgment, she relished her time with him. Elizabeth warned herself not to fall further head over heels for the man, but it was a lost cause. She was thoroughly smitten with the gentleman, even though nothing good could come of it.

After three days of indoor activities, the weather finally turned. Overnight, a significant snowfall had transformed the world outside Meadow Haven into a winter wonderland. The trees and fields were draped in a thick blanket of white. The air was still, the only sound the occasional click of ice flowing down a nearby creek.

Elizabeth stood at the window of her room, gazing out at the scene with a mixture of awe and anticipation. Suzy would plan outdoor games today. A tingle of anticipation ran through her as she imagined Mr. Darcy helping her with her coat and scarf. But the thrill soon evaporated. Elizabeth resolved to find a way to impede Suzy's efforts to push her into Mr. Darcy's notice. It would only lead to heartbreak for Elizabeth. She was determined to spend the entire day with Suzy, and if she must share time with a gentleman, she would ensure it was with Nicholas.

There was a knock at her door, and before Elizabeth could respond, Suzy burst in, her eyes sparkling with excitement. "Lizzy! Have you seen the snow? 'Tis perfect—just what we needed for our plans today!"

Elizabeth turned to her friend, smiling at her enthusiasm. "And what would that be?"

"A sleigh ride, of course! Colonel Fitzwilliam and I have arranged everything. We will go out after breakfast." She paused, a mischievous glint in her eye. "I will ensure that you and Mr. Darcy share a sleigh."

Elizabeth's smile faltered slightly, but she quickly recovered. "I pray you do not."

Suzy laughed, waving off Elizabeth's entreaty. "Nonsense. It is the perfect opportunity for you two to…" She gave Elizabeth a saucy wink before adding, "become better acquainted."

Before Elizabeth could respond, Suzy raced out the door. "I must be on my way. I cannot allow my guests to sit in the breakfast parlor alone." Sighing, Elizabeth followed.

The group of young people were pleased with the diversion the snow provided. After breakfast each donned their warmest gloves and coats before braving the cold. Mr. Darcy's tall figure waited at the bottom of the steps. When he saw her, he bowed. "Miss Gardiner, are you prepared for a frigid ride?"

Elizabeth swallowed. The possibility of spending time with Mr. Darcy, even in the confines of a sleigh, filled her with a mix of dread and anticipation. "I am looking forward to it," she finally replied.

The groomsmen brought around two sleighs. The first seated four people comfortably, though all six people could have easily fit. The second was much smaller. The horses pawed the snow as they waited.

"Nicholas, will you drive us?" Suzy did not wait for her brother's agreement before directing the others. "Miss Darcy, you will sit up front with my brother. Colonel, you will sit in the back with me." Then, with a sweet smile she turned to the two remaining members of the party. "Mr. Darcy, if you would be so good to drive my friend."

Mr. Darcy bowed to his hostess. "It will be my pleasure." Then he turned to Elizabeth. "Are you ready?"

Elizabeth offered a tentative smile, noting the way his eyes softened as he spoke to her. "As ready as one can be."

"I shall do my best to ensure you have a pleasant experience," he replied, offering her his arm as they approached their sleigh. Mr. Darcy helped Elizabeth into the seat, ensuring she was comfortably settled before climbing in beside her. Elizabeth's breath caught when, for one delicious moment, his thigh brushed against her own. He settled himself and moved a respectable distance away before taking the reins in hand. He gave them a quick flick, and the horses began to move, the sleigh gliding smoothly over the snow.

The ride was both exhilarating and nerve-wracking. The crisp air stung Elizabeth's cheeks, but the warmth of Mr. Darcy's presence beside her was enough to keep the chill at bay. At one point, the sleigh hit a bump causing her to slide into his side. He was so warm, so solid. She wished to snuggle closer, but propriety demanded she move back to original spot on the bench.

Elizabeth stole a glance at Mr. Darcy, her heart skipping a beat when she found him watching her. "It's beautiful, is it not?" she said, gesturing to the snow-covered fields.

"Very much so," he agreed, though his gaze remained on her rather than the scenery. "I find that winter, despite its cold, has a certain charm."

Elizabeth's lips curved into a smile. "You do not prefer the warmth of summer?"

"I have come to appreciate the beauty in all seasons," Mr. Darcy replied, his voice low. "And in the unexpected joys they bring." His deep baritone sent a shiver across her.

They rode on in silence for a few moments longer. Elizabeth could feel her earlier apprehensions melting away, replaced by a warmth that had nothing to do with the layers of clothing she wore.

Mr. Darcy pulled them to a stop overlooking a creek. Snow rested on the rocks along the bank, and ice had formed in the slower, more shallow waters. It was amazing what one snowfall could do to change the desolate appearance of winter. She was about to say so when a sudden shout from Colonel Fitzwilliam interrupted her thoughts.

"Snowball fight!" He called out from his own sleigh, which had pulled up alongside theirs. Suzy, seated beside him, giggled as he helped her from her seat.

Mr. Darcy and Elizabeth barely had time to react before the first snowball sailed through the air, narrowly missing Mr. Darcy's shoulder. "It seems we have been challenged," he said, a smile playing at his lips. "Shall we defend ourselves, Miss Gardiner?"

Elizabeth laughed, her spirits lifting as she gathered a handful of snow. "I suppose we must, Mr. Darcy. It would be a shame to let them win so easily."

"Over here, Miss Darcy," Nicholas called. The three pairs took their positions, and the battle began in truth.

"Oh!" Miss Darcy cried when Colonel Fitzwilliam launched a snowball into her chest. He laughed heartily, until another one splattered across his own broad form.

"That will teach you to accost my sleigh partner!" Nicholas wore a smirk.

The battle quickly descended into chaos. Mr. Darcy proved to be adept at the game, his precision and speed making him a formidable opponent. Elizabeth, though less skilled, managed to hold her own, her laughter ringing out as she dodged and returned fire.

The cold was forgotten in the flurry of snowballs and the rush of adrenaline. Mr. Darcy and Elizabeth found themselves working together, their movements synchronized as they shielded themselves against the onslaught from the other participants.

Their four foes went on the attack, forcing them to retreat. Stepping backwards, Elizabeth lost her footing when a well-aimed snowball caught her on the shoulder. With a startled cry, she tumbled down the bank into the shallow creek below. The icy water soaked through her clothes instantly, and a sharp gasp escaped her lips as the cold bit into her skin.

"Elizabeth!" Mr. Darcy scrambled down the bank to reach her. "Are you hurt?"

"N-no, I am well," Elizabeth stammered, though her teeth were chattering from the cold. "It is just... v-very cold."

"We must get you back to the house immediately." With haste, he removed his gloves and worked at the buttons at the front of her coat.

"Wh...what are you do...doing?"

"You must be out of this coat." He pulled the offending garment from her and then quickly slipped out of his own thick coat. "Here, take mine."

Elizabeth wished to refuse his offer, but she was so cold. She allowed him to wrap her in the warm folds and guide her back to the sleigh.

Suzy's eyes were full of fright. "We must get you warmed up right away, Lizzy. You will catch your death out here."

Darcy hugged Elizabeth's shivering body to his side as he guided the sleigh back to the house. "It will not be long, now," he assured her.

∞∞∞

The warmth of the library was a welcome contrast to the biting cold that still lingered in Darcy's bones. He hardly felt it as he rushed Elizabeth back to the house, but after her mother took her away for a warm bath and a rest, the freezing temperatures began to penetrate. It had been hours, but he had not yet escaped the chill.

The fire crackled softly in the hearth, drawing Darcy closer. He had sought refuge here, hoping for a moment alone to collect his thoughts. The day was not over and already his emotions had run the gamut between exhilaration and terror. Suffice it to say, he wished to never experience such again, but it was nothing compared to the frustration felt when her mother guided her up the stairs. He wanted to be the one to care for her.

He crossed the room and moved toward the fire, eager to shake off the remnants of the cold. As he neared the hearth, he caught a movement out of the corner of his eye. Startled, he turned to find Elizabeth seated in one of the armchairs, her feet tucked beneath her and a book resting in her lap.

"Miss Gardiner," Darcy began, struggling to find his composure. "I did not realize anyone else was here."

Elizabeth offered him a small, hesitant smile. "It is a public room."

Darcy hesitated. "May I join you?" he asked, his voice quieter than usual.

"Of course," Elizabeth replied, her smile widening slightly. "There is plenty of room by the fire."

Darcy took the seat opposite her. For a moment, neither of them spoke. It was Elizabeth who broke the silence first. "Thank you for your kindness today, Mr. Darcy. I am afraid I was rather foolish to have fallen into the creek."

"You were not foolish," Darcy replied quickly, his tone earnest. "It was an accident, nothing more. I only regret that you suffered from the cold."

Elizabeth's fingers traced the edges of the pages absently. "My mother was beside herself with worry. I am afraid she will never let me hear the end of it."

Darcy smiled slightly at that. "Your mother cares for you very much. I can understand her concern. But I am relieved to see that you seem to have recovered."

Elizabeth nodded, lifting her gaze to meet his. "I have, thanks to the warmth of the fire—and to your help. I am grateful, sir."

Darcy shifted slightly in his seat. Her words made him feel both proud and uncomfortable. There was so much he wanted to say.

"Miss Gardiner," he began, his voice low and careful. "I have… "

Elizabeth looked up. Her blue eyes, so bright in the light of day looked dark by the light of the fire. "Yes?"

Darcy cleared his throat. "I have come to admire you… greatly."

Elizabeth's lips pulled upward. "I admire you, as well," she whispered.

Darcy could feel his control slipping, the desire to reach out to her, to take her hand, nearly overwhelming. The fire crackled softly, the only sound in the room as they sat there, staring at one another.

Finally, Elizabeth looked away, breaking the spell. "I

should return to my room. My mother will worry if she finds me gone."

Darcy stood as well, his heart aching with the loss of the moment. "Of course," he murmured, his voice tight.

As Elizabeth made her way to the door, she paused, glancing back at him. "Thank you, again, Mr. Darcy." And then she was gone, leaving him alone in the library.

∞∞∞

Richard made his way down the dimly lit corridor of Meadow Haven. The evening had settled in, and most of the guests had retired to their rooms. He had too much energy for sleep, however, and decided to play a round of billiards. With any luck, Darcy or Nicholas would be found there.

As he approached the billiards room, he heard the unmistakable sound of balls clattering together. A small smile tugged at his lips. He pushed open the door and was greeted by a surprising sight. The very un-Darcy figure of Lady Susan Corwell was draped across the table as she lined up a shot.

Startled, Lady Susan looked up, her expression quickly shifting from surprise to playful defiance. "Come to challenge me, have you?"

Richard grinned. "I did not expect to find you here, Lady Susan, but I suppose I could be persuaded to join you."

She straightened, her eyes gleaming with mischief as she stepped back from the table. "I should warn you; I am very good at this game. Father will no longer play me."

Richard chuckled, taking up a cue and examining the table. "I would not expect anything less, but I will not go easy on you simply because you are a lady."

Her laughter rang out. "Good."

They played for a while, exchanging playful banter with each shot. Lady Susan's skill was evident—she was precise and confident, her movements fluid and graceful. Richard found himself genuinely impressed, but more than that, he was captivated.

"How do you think our plan is progressing?" he asked, leaning against the table after missing a shot.

She paused, her cue in hand. "With Darcy and Elizabeth, you mean?"

"Yes," Richard nodded, watching her closely. "They have been spending more time together, and I think they are beginning to understand each other better."

Lady Susan sighed. "Today's proceedings gave me hope. Although I would never wish for my friend to be dunked in freezing water, I was quite pleased with how your cousin responded."

"Should we continue as we have been or allow things to unfold as they will." Richard stepped closer, drawn by her warm eyes and enticing smile.

She placed her hand on his arm. "Perhaps we should allow things to take their natural path."

Chapter 17

A Terrible Cold

Darcy paced the length of his bedroom. The house was quiet now, the rest of the guests having retired for the night, but sleep was the last thing on his mind. He had not seen Elizabeth since breakfast, and the hours that had passed since then had been filled with an increasing sense of unease. The doctor had been called and returned to the parlor looking grim. "Tis a bad cold. She is robust and will do well, but you must be vigilant with her care. No heavy foods, no open windows, and she must remain abed until the cough subsides." His vibrant, energetic Elizabeth confined to a bed! It was unthinkable.

Earlier that morning, Elizabeth entered the breakfast room looking drawn, her usual brightness dimmed by fatigue. He noticed immediately that something was wrong. She moved slowly and he rushed to pull out her chair. "Miss Gardiner, are you well?"

She attempted to smile but the result was ineffectual. "Only a little tired." It was a lie. He knew it then and was proven correct only a while later, but he did not press her. He had no right... yet.

After helping her into her chair, he signaled the footman to bring coffee. He had noticed her preference for it when she appeared tired. *Had she slept ill?* He pushed the thought away and moved to the sideboard to gather toast and eggs. He sat her plate in front of her and moved back to his own chair. She did not touch her food, choosing, instead, to sip her drink.

Soon, their solitude was broken when Lady Susan, Richard, and the Gardiners stepped in the room. Mr. Gardiner seated his wife next to his daughter. "Toast again, or do you prefer something more substantial?"

Mrs. Gardiner crinkled her nose. "Tea and toast, dear." When Mr. Gardiner left, she turned to her daughter who sat with a hand pressed to her forehead. "Elizabeth, darling, are you well?"

Elizabeth pulled her hand from her head and sat a little straighter. "Only a headache, Mama."

Mrs. Gardiner's expression tightened. "My dear, you appear flushed. Come here." She motioned for Elizabeth to lean closer. Mrs. Gardiner touched her cheek to Elizabeth's. "You are burning up!"

Elizabeth offered a weak smile. "It is nothing. Just a chill from yesterday, I suppose."

But Darcy had seen the worry in Mrs. Gardiner's eyes. "Edward, send my breakfast to Elizabeth's room. She must rest, and I am well aware how little she likes to lie abed."

Mr. Gardiner came to his daughter's side. "My Lizzy, are you ill?" As her mother had done, he pressed his cheek to hers. Feeling the heat on her cheeks he exclaimed, "Oh, my darling. You have not had such a fever since you were a babe."

"I have never seen her such, and I have been her mother since she was six years old." Mrs. Gardiner's face was lined with worry, the same worry that burned in Darcy's stomach. "Off to bed with you."

Elizabeth nodded faintly, too exhausted to argue, and left the room with her mother's support. Darcy watched them go, a sense of helplessness settling over him. He wanted to help, to do something, but boundaries of decorum held him back.

Later that morning, the doctor was called. Nicholas and Lady Susan assured him that Dr. Abel was well-educated and capable of seeing to Elizabeth's needs. Darcy had wished to call for his own man, but it would take days for Dr. Clark to arrive from London.

That afternoon, Lady Susan informed him that Elizabeth was resting, but that her condition had worsened. The doctor had predicted a few very bad days, and it appeared he would be proven correct. Obviously, she had not come down for supper. He had known she would not, yet he missed her anyway.

I need to see her, he thought. Logic told him she suffered only from a cold, but his heart said otherwise. The longer he was removed from her presence, the more restless he became. He knew it was improper to visit her, especially at this hour, but the thought of her lying ill, possibly in pain, was more than he could bear. He had to see her, even if only for a moment.

Making up his mind, Darcy left his room and made his way down the dimly lit corridor toward Elizabeth's chambers. He knew her mother no longer sat with her, for he had heard Mr. Gardiner insist that she sleep in her own bed. Likely a maid had been assigned to watch over. A few well-placed coins would prevent her from saying anything about his midnight visit.

The house was quiet, the only sound his soft footsteps on the carpeted floor. As he approached her door, he hesitated for a moment, unsure if he was making the right decision. But the memory of her frail appearance at breakfast pushed him forward. He knocked softly.

The door opened almost immediately, and Lady Susan appeared, her expression a mixture of surprise and understanding when she saw him.

"Mr. Darcy," she whispered, stepping out into the hallway and closing the door behind her. "You should not be here."

"I know," Darcy replied, keeping his voice low. "But I could not stay away. How is she?"

Her concern was evident by the small lines that formed around her eyes. "She is resting now, but we are worried for her. Her fever is very high."

Darcy's chest tightened. "Please, allow me see her. Just for a moment."

Lady Susan hesitated, studying him for a second before nodding. "Three minutes and no longer."

She opened the door slightly, allowing Darcy to slip inside. The room was dimly lit by the glow of a single candle on the bedside table. Elizabeth lay in the large bed, her face flushed with fever.

He sat on a stool near her bedside and took her hand in his. "Elizabeth," he whispered.

∞∞∞

Elizabeth's eyes fluttered at the sound of his voice. She smiled to herself. *A lovely dream. Speak to me again my love. Come closer so that I can see you.*

"Elizabeth, darling, can you open your eyes for me?" She was tempted to snuggle deeper into her pillow. She would accept a fever if it meant Mr. Darcy would invade her dreams. His thumb rubbed circles on her hand. It felt so real. Too real. With effort she opened her eyes.

"Mr. Darcy," she whispered, her voice was raspy but filled with genuine surprise. "What are you doing here?"

He leaned closer, his eyes never leaving her face. "I could not stay away," he admitted quietly. "I had to check on you."

A warmth bloomed in Elizabeth's chest that had nothing to do with her fever. She had not expected to see him, and certainly not at this hour, but the sight of him sitting by her bedside, his eyes filled with such worry, thrilled her. She looked around the room. It was empty but the door stood open. Suzy must have allowed him in.

"You should not have come," she said, though her heart was far from reproachful. "What if someone catches you here?"

Mr. Darcy gave a small, almost imperceptible smile. "That is a risk I am willing to take."

Elizabeth's heart fluttered at his words, and she found herself unable to look away from him. "Why?" she asked, her voice barely above a whisper. "Why would you risk that?"

He hesitated for a moment, as if gathering his thoughts. When he spoke, his voice was low and earnest. "Because I care for you, Elizabeth. More than I can say. When I heard you were unwell, I could not tolerate the thought of you suffering alone."

"I am not alone. My mother sat with me all day, and Suzy has been here."

He pressed her hand. "Without me, then. I could not tolerate you here.... without me."

Her breath caught in her throat at his confession. "Mr. Darcy..." she began, unsure of how to express the whirlwind of emotions his words had stirred within her.

"Please, call me Fitzwilliam," he interrupted gently, his eyes searching hers. "I need you to know that my feelings for you are real. I have been a fool, Elizabeth."

Elizabeth swallowed, her throat tight. "Your aunt... she wishes for you to be with Suzy. I have seen how she watches you."

Darcy's gaze softened. "My aunt will be pleased for me. She only pressed me toward Lady Susan because she believed that is what I would wish for. My father and grandfather both married daughters of earls, and my great-grandfather married the daughter of a marquess. In the eyes of society they made excellent matches. But..."

"But?" She both longed for and feared his response.

He paused, taking a deep breath as if to steady himself. "But they all also married for love. My parents were deeply in love. My father did not marry her for her position in society. He married her because he loved and adored her, and that is what I truly want for myself. And I have come to realize that I love you, Elizabeth."

Tears threatened in her eyes. "But I am..."

He squeezed her hand once more. "Yes, I know. I thought your father's connections to trade were insurmountable, but that was before."

"Before?"

"Before I contemplated a life without you." He smiled then. "Besides, your father and mother are wonderful people. I would be foolish to reject you because you are the daughter of two such fine individuals."

"Fitzwilliam..." she whispered, the name felt strange yet comforting on her lips. "I... I have grown to care for you deeply as well. But I dared not hope."

Mr. Darcy reached out and placed his hand gently on her cheek. For a moment, the world outside ceased to exist. It was just the two of them.

"Fitzwilliam," she whispered again, her voice trembling slightly.

A sound at the door drew their attention. Suzy stepped into the room. Her eyes widened slightly at the sight of them sitting so close, his hand on Elizabeth's cheek. "Mr. Darcy, it is time for you to say goodbye."

Mr. Darcy nodded, his gaze lingering on Elizabeth's face for a moment longer before he rose to his feet. "Rest well, my love," he said softly, his voice filled with unspoken promises. "We will talk more when you are feeling better."

Elizabeth watched him leave, silently willing herself to quickly overcome her illness. Suzy shut the door behind him. "And you said there was nothing between you two," she snickered.

Elizabeth giggled, then placed her hand against her tender temple. "Do not make me laugh."

Chapter 18

Yuletide Decorations

Darcy could scarcely contain his relief when he saw Elizabeth walk into the breakfast room. It had been a long and worrying week with Elizabeth confined to her bed under the watchful eye of her mother. The entire household had felt her absence, the usual warmth and liveliness of the party replaced by a dullness accompanied by his own palpable tension. But today, that tension broke as Elizabeth entered, her steps still a bit tentative but her smile as bright as ever.

She was immediately enveloped in warm embraces by her father and the Earl of Effington. "I was beginning to believe you would never return to us, my girl."

Elizabeth smiled up at her godfather. "You know me better than that, Uncle Paul."

He chucked her playfully on her chin. "Yes, you are a fighter. Always have been."

Darcy stood a little apart, his heart racing as he took in the sight of her. She was pale, and there was a certain fragility about her that had not been there before, but she was here, and she was smiling.

Their eyes caught as she moved to sit down. For that brief moment, everything else in the room faded away. In the warmth of his gaze, her expression softened into a shy smile that sent a rush of warmth through him. He had not seen her since that night in her room— the night when he confessed his love for her. She had said she cared for him, but was it love? Would it grow to be love? He longed to talk to her again. To ask her what their futures held.

"It is good to have you back," Georgiana said brightly, breaking the spell as she poured Elizabeth a cup of tea. "We have missed you terribly."

"Thank you, Georgiana," Elizabeth replied, her voice still a little weak. "I have missed you all as well. It is good to be up and about again."

Once the meal was finished, Lady Susan clapped her hands together with enthusiasm. "Now that Lizzy is feeling better, I think it is high time we finished decorating the house for Christmas. What do you all say?"

Mrs. Gardiner placed her toast upon her plate. "Elizabeth is not allowed outside to gather greenery," she warned, her tone leaving no room for argument.

Darcy, seeing the faint disappointment on Elizabeth's face, quickly spoke up. "Then we shall gather all the greenery necessary and bring it inside. Miss Gardiner only needs to supervise, if she wishes."

Nicholas and Richard both nodded in agreement. "Indeed," Richard added with a grin. "We can handle the heavy lifting."

"Perhaps we can play a duet while the gentlemen gather the supplies? Then you can supervise, as my brother said, while we decorate."

Elizabeth smiled at Georgiana. "I would be pleased to play with you this morning, but when the men return with the greenery I will assist with the decorating. I have had quite enough of sitting still to last a lifetime. I prefer to be an active participant in the festivities, not just a spectator."

Darcy admired her determination, though he did worry

that she would attempt to overdo things. But he knew better than to argue with Elizabeth. Instead, he would hover near and ensure she did not do too much on her first day away from bed.

The men were gone for no more than three hours. Lady Susan had given them strict instructions to gather as much mistletoe, holly, and other evergreens as they could manage. Several servants accompanied them to pile their cuttings onto a cart. Finally, the party turned back toward the house.

"I am tempted to force you to remain out of doors for a while longer, but even I cannot pretend we have too little greenery. Besides, it would be cruel to keep you from Miss Gardiner's side for so long." Richard clapped Darcy on the shoulder.

"I do not know what you refer to," Darcy evaded.

Richard laughed heartily. "Do you not? I had assumed after a midnight visit to her room, that you two had come to an agreement."

Darcy cursed the heat he felt in his face. "How do you — "

"Lady Susan let it slip one day while we played billiards." There was a story there, but Darcy did not care to probe. He was too excited to return to Elizabeth's side. He hurried toward the house, causing Richard to laugh more.

Lady Susan had hot chocolate and gingerbread waiting for the gentlemen. "At last! I thought you had been swallowed up in a snow drift!"

Lord Effington kissed his daughter's cheek. "Hardly. We simply needed sufficient time to gather the excessive amounts of decoration that you and Elizabeth require."

When hands were sufficiently warmed and bellies sufficiently full, the decorating commenced. The house soon filled with the scent of pine and holly. To no one's surprise, Darcy hovered near Elizabeth, always ready to assist her with any tasks he deemed too strenuous.

"Allow me to do that for you," he suggested.

Elizabeth held a pine garland decorated with bright red ribbons. "Nonsense. I can do this sir. I give you permission to continue your supervision." She stepped up on a small stool and reached high to hang the garland above the mantel.

Darcy hovered near. "Elizabeth," he hissed, "you are not yet recovered enough. Allow me."

She threw him a saucy look and returned to her task. But as she lifted onto her toes to secure the garland to the wall, the stool tipped and she lost her balance.

Darcy moved without thinking, his arms shooting out to catch her before she could fall. He pulled her close, steadying her against his chest, his heart pounding from the sudden rush of adrenaline.

"Elizabeth, are you all right?" he asked, his voice filled with concern as he looked down at her.

She nodded. "I am well. Just… a little unsteady, I suppose."

Their eyes met, and for a moment, neither of them moved. The world narrowed to just the two of them, standing so close that Darcy could feel the warmth of her body against his. Elizabeth's hands rested on his chest.

"Thank you," she whispered.

"You should be more careful," he murmured.

Elizabeth's gaze softened. "I will. I promise."

They lingered there, the proximity making Darcy acutely aware of everything about her—the way her hair brushed against his arm, her floral scent mingling with the fresh greenery around them, her pink lips parted ever so slightly. So inviting. The temptation nearly overwhelming as he dipped his head.

∞∞∞

Mr. Gardiner, standing a few paces away, regarded them with a mixture of concern and amusement. He cleared his throat. "Mr. Darcy," he said, his voice gentle but firm, "I believe Elizabeth can stand on her own."

Darcy blinked, realizing how long he had been holding Elizabeth, their proximity far closer than was proper. He reluctantly stepped back. Elizabeth's cheeks were flushed, though whether from embarrassment or something more, he could not be sure.

Darcy turned to Mr. Gardiner. "Sir, may I have a moment alone with your daughter?"

The room fell silent, all eyes turning to Mr. Gardiner. For a moment, the man regarded Darcy with a thoughtful expression, as if weighing the request. Nearby, Lady Susan and Richard exchanged a quick, excited glance, their expressions betraying their anticipation.

Mr. Gardiner nodded, though his tone remained stern. "You may have five minutes."

"Thank you, sir," Darcy replied with a respectful bow, his heart racing as he turned to Elizabeth.

He offered her his arm, and though she looked slightly disoriented, Elizabeth accepted it without hesitation. He led her out of the room, the eyes of their friends and family following them as they moved into the corridor.

Darcy led her to the library and closed the door behind them. The curtains were drawn, and his eyes took some time to adjust to the darkness of the room. He escorted her to the fire, its light casting a warm glow across her face. She was so beautiful. He took a deep breath and then stepped closer.

"Elizabeth," he began, his gaze locked on hers, "I have thought long and hard about what I am about to say. You must know that from the moment I met you, you have occupied my thoughts in a way that no one else ever has. I have admired your strength, your wit, your kindness, and your beauty. You are, without question, the most remarkable woman I have ever known."

Elizabeth's breath caught as a small smile spread across her face.

"I stand here now, not as a man bound by the expectations of society, but as a man who loves you. I love you with all my heart, and I cannot imagine my life without you."

Kneeling before her, he took her hand in his. "Elizabeth Gardiner, will you do me the great honor of becoming my wife?"

Elizabeth's eyes shimmered with unshed tears. She took a deep breath, as if steadying herself, and then, with a smile that was both radiant and filled with certainty, she nodded.

"Yes, Fitzwilliam," she whispered, her voice trembling with joy. "Yes, my love. I will marry you."

Darcy surged to his feet and pulled her close, pressing a tender kiss to her lips. "You have made me the happiest man in the world."

She smiled up at him, her eyes shining with love. "And you have made me the happiest woman."

He kissed her again, this time, urging her lips apart until she opened for him. "Mmm," she hummed. The soft sound sent a thrilling jolt of desire through him. His hands rubbed circles on the small of her back. He longed for more but was careful to go no further. *Soon,* he told himself.

With great reluctance, he broke the kiss. He pressed his forehead to hers. "I do not wish to wait."

She giggled. "When do you have in mind?"

"Will you marry me on New Year's Eve? Let us begin 1812 together, as husband and wife. I do not want to spend a single day of the year without you by my side."

Elizabeth's smile widened, and she nodded again, her heart full. "Mama will not like it, but I find I agree with you. I am ready to be Mrs. Darcy."

Darcy leaned down, capturing her lips once more. Elizabeth responded with equal fervor, her arms wrapping around his neck as she returned his kiss.

When they finally parted, both were breathless. "I love you, Elizabeth," Darcy whispered, his voice filled with the depth of his feelings.

"And I love you," Elizabeth replied, her voice just as soft, just as certain.

With great reluctance, he stepped away from her. "Our five minutes has long passed. I do not wish to earn your father's wrath, especially when I have something very important to ask him."

To his delight, Elizabeth's smile broadened even more. "I will ask him to join you."

Chapter 19

Christmas

The next day was Christmas, and the inhabitants of Meadow Haven celebrated, but none more so that Elizabeth and Darcy. The day began with a cold trip to the village for church service. Mrs. Gardiner fretted over Elizabeth and wrapped her in so many layers Darcy could hardly see more of her than her eyes. But what fine eyes they were. He sat next to her in church, but dared not touch her, though his fingers itched to take her hand in his own. Her father's watchful eyes prevented him from acting on his desires.

She had been ordered to rest when they arrived home, preventing him from spending the day with her as he wished. But evening was almost upon them, and the various celebrations Lady Susan had planned would allow him the opportunity to be near her.

Lady Susan had invited many neighbors to take part in the evening's meal and festivities but had made plans for a private celebration to begin an hour before the first guests were to arrive.

Darcy walked into the blue salon to find Elizabeth sitting near the fire. She looked radiant. Her eyes lit when she saw him and indicated the space on the settee next to her. Darcy went directly to her side.

Lady Susan clapped her hands to gather everyone's

attention. "It is time for gifts! Elizabeth and I took a trip to the village last week to find something special for each of you. We hope you will like them."

The guests gathered around, curiosity piqued. Georgiana squirmed with excitement. Exchanging gifts was not a tradition in the Darcy household, but perhaps it would become one. Seeing the joy on his sister's face, Darcy promised to always provide gifts going forward, for her and his beautiful wife.

Lady Matlock was the first to receive her present, a beautifully bound journal for the coming year. "I noticed that your current journal is nearly full," Lady Susan said with a smile. "I hope this one will serve you well in 1812."

Lady Matlock's eyes softened as she accepted the gift. "How thoughtful of you, Lady Susan. I do write every day. This will be put to good use. Thank you."

Richard and Lord Matlock each received a box of fine cigars. "Now this is a gift I can appreciate," Richard said with a grin, turning to Elizabeth. "You have outdone yourself, Miss Gardiner. Thank you."

Elizabeth blushed slightly, pleased by his reaction. "I am glad you like it, Colonel. I thought you might enjoy them."

Lord Matlock nodded his approval as well. "A fine choice, indeed. Thank you, Miss Gardiner."

As the gifts were distributed, Darcy's anticipation grew. "Fitzwilliam," she began, her voice soft but steady, "I have something for you as well."

Darcy's heart quickened as he took the gift from her hands, their fingers brushing ever so briefly. He unwrapped it with care, revealing a delicate embroidered handkerchief with her scent upon it and a lock of her hair tied with a ribbon. The intimacy of the gift took his breath away.

"I had cigars for you, but since, well…"

"Elizabeth," he murmured, "This is… this is more precious to me than you can imagine. I shall keep it in my breast pocket, close to my heart, and I will place my hand there whenever I think of you as I travel to London."

"I hope it will bring you comfort while you are away from me," she said quietly.

"It will not be a replacement for you, but it will keep me content. This trip to London is the last time I will be away from your side."

The Earl of Effington, who had been observing the exchange with a pleased smile, cleared his throat. "Mr. Darcy, you mentioned your intention to obtain a special license for the wedding. I will write a letter to help expedite the process."

Darcy turned to the Earl. "Thank you, my lord. That will be most helpful. My uncle also plans to write the archbishop. With two earls on my side, I am sure to be successful."

"Fitzwilliam, must you go to London yourself? Could you not obtain a common license here? I do not like the thought of you being away, especially in this cold."

Darcy took her hand in his. "I must go, my love. Not only to obtain the special license, but also to ensure that the marriage articles are completed to my satisfaction."

Elizabeth sighed softly. "I understand, but I will miss you terribly while you are gone."

"I will be back to you as quickly as I can. The snow has cleared, so there should be no delays. And then we will be man and wife." He leaned close so that no one could overhear. "And then I shall finally have you all to myself. Now that you have promised yourself to me, I find it hard to remain a gentleman."

His words caused her to blush an enchanting shade of pink, but she did not pull away. "I… I do not know what to expect but I find I am looking forward to learning."

"Oh, my dearest, you must not say such things to me. I have too little control where you are concerned."

There was an intriguing gleam in her eye. "Then you must return as quickly as possible, else your control will be tested for longer than either of us likes."

Darcy knew she did not know exactly what her words implied, but he cherished them anyway. Smiling, he brought her hand to his mouth and pressed a kiss to each knuckle. "One kiss for every day we will be parted."

"Miss Gardiner."

With great reluctance, Elizabeth turned her attention to Lady Matlock. "Yes, my lady?"

"You are to be my niece soon, my dear. You must call me Aunt Grace when we are among close friends and relations."

Elizabeth dipped her head. "Thank you, Aunt Grace. Please call me Elizabeth, or Lizzy as Suzy does."

The countess then shooed Darcy away from his bride-to-be as she discussed the twelfth night celebration she wished to host in their honor. "I will send invitations with Darcy to London. It will be a small, private affair. Very elite. Just the thing to make all the ladies of the ton ill with curiosity!"

"But that is so soon. We will barely have time to make it back to London."

Lady Matlock patted Elizabeth's hand. "I know my dear, but it must be done. Your marriage needs to be presented as fait accompli before anyone has a chance to question it. I will ensure the right people are there to witness your success and my nephew's happiness."

∞∞∞

Suzy had invited four families to dine with the Meadow

Haven party for Christmas supper. "Elizabeth, may I have a word, dear." Lady Matlock stood alongside Elizabeth's mother. Elizabeth readily acquiesced, looking from one lady to the other.

"Lady Matlock and I have been talking. There are several well-respected members of the ton here this evening." Elizabeth was aware, having just left a conversation with Baroness Givens and Mrs. Davies. Their invitations were coveted among the highest society in London.

"Although I am thrilled to have you as my new niece and had considered you for a possible daughter, we cannot deny that your father's status as a tradesman will cause some members of the ton to question your suitability as Mrs. Darcy."

Elizabeth felt her anger stir, but before she could allow it to rise, her mother broke in. "And that is why tonight is the perfect time to announce your engagement. Normally your papa would make the announcement, but we have asked your Uncle Paul to do the honors. Having the earl's support will show that you are worthy to be Mr. Darcy's wife."

Lady Matlock nodded. "And my husband will also say a few words. When the party sees that you are welcome by our family and respected by Effington's, the stories told in London will take on a more positive tone."

"But is Papa accepting of this? It is his right to make the announcement."

Mrs. Gardiner placed a loving hand on her daughter's cheek. "He is. He only wants what is best for you, darling. That is all he has ever wished for." The threat of tears clogged Elizabeth's throat, and she had to look away to prevent them from forming in her eyes.

"Here now, none of that." Lady Matlock handed Elizabeth a handkerchief. "Darcy is coming to escort you to the dining room. He will accuse me of saying something terrible. Smile, darling."

She turned to see her handsome suitor walking toward

her party. All worries of the ton's approbation flew away upon seeing his broad smile — a smile that he only ever wore for her.

Soon, the meal began. Elizabeth was situated between Darcy and the Earl of Matlock. The Earl was engrossed in his conversation with Suzy, which allowed Elizabeth ample opportunities to speak with her betrothed. He planned to leave early the next day rendering every moment before his departure charged with urgency.

When the footman took away the remaining dishes from the second course, Lord Effington stood, a glass of wine in hand. Gradually the conversation around the table quieted. "Ladies and gentlemen," he began, "tonight I have the great pleasure of making an announcement that brings me particular joy as it concerns someone who is dear to my heart. My goddaughter, Elizabeth Gardiner." Elizabeth's face heated as the occupants of the table turned to look at her.

"As many of you know, I have had the privilege of watching Elizabeth, grow from a spirited young girl into the remarkable woman she is today. And it is with great happiness that I announce her engagement to Mr. Fitzwilliam Darcy." Mr. Darcy's hand found hers under the table.

"This is all very unusual, sir," the baroness said. "Usually it is the girl's father who makes the announcement."

Effington chuckled. "I know it is traditionally the father's role to make such an announcement, but as her godfather, and since this romance blossomed within the walls of my own home, I demanded the right to do so." The guests laughed lightly.

The earl's face softened. "Seriously, though, I must say that my introduction to Edward Gardiner was one of the most fortuitous meetings of my life. We have been great friends for nearly fifteen years, as have our daughters. When we met, I had just ascended to my position. My father was a good man, but a terrible manager of his funds. Edward allowed me the great privilege of investing in his shipping company. From there our friendship and money grew. At the same time, my daughter finally received a sister of the heart in Lizzy."

Elizabeth's heart warmed as she glanced over at Suzy, who was beaming with pride. Suzy was indeed her sister of the heart, someone who had been with her through the highs and lows, sharing in her joys and comforting her in her sorrows. The bond between them was a true sisterhood.

She felt a pang of sadness as she thought of Jane, her sister by blood. The wound from Jane's betrayal was still tender but not overwhelming. She would always care for Jane, but the trust she had placed in her had been broken. Suzy was the sister she had always wished. She stole a look at Colonel Fitzwilliam who was looking down at Suzy with dreamy eyes. *Perhaps soon we will be more than sisters of the heart. Perhaps we will be cousins, as well.*

When Effington concluded his speech, the Earl of Matlock stood. "My wife and I are very pleased that Miss Gardiner will soon be a member of our family." He raised his glass. "To the future Mrs. Darcy."

"To the future Mrs. Darcy," everyone repeated.

"Congratulations, Miss Gardiner," Baroness Givens said from across the table. Her husband nodded his agreement. "Mr. Darcy, you are a very fortunate man."

Mr. Darcy inclined his head politely, his gaze never straying far from Elizabeth. "Indeed, I am the most fortunate of men."

When supper ended, the gentlemen chose to move to the parlor with the ladies. Elizabeth and Darcy received congratulations from all the guests. They appreciated the good wishes for their future, but with a week apart looming ahead of them, they most wished for a private moment together. It was not to be, however, for soon Colonel Fitzwilliam claimed Elizabeth.

"Darcy, you will have a lifetime with the lady. You must

allow her to play some Christmas carols with Georgiana." Darcy pouted while his cousin escorted Elizabeth toward the pianoforte where a smiling Georgiana waited.

Chapter 20

Separation and Longing

Early the next day, Darcy and Elizabeth met before he departed for London. "You must allow me to remind you that I love you, quite ardently," he whispered.

Her papa had allowed the couple a few minutes alone to say their goodbyes and she took advantage of the opportunity by leaning into her betrothed. "Do not go. We can be married by common license."

He applied a gentle kiss to her forehead. "No, my love. I must have our marriage contract finalized, as well as my will. If something happens to me, I must ensure that you and any children we have together are taken care of."

"Oh, do not say such a thing, I could not —"

He shushed her with a soft kiss on her lips. "Then let us speak of happier things. My valet has instructed me to ask about the color of your wedding dress. He wishes for us to coordinate."

Elizabeth giggled. "The very stern and serious Fitzwilliam Darcy wishes to match his bride?" He attempted a stoic demeanor, but the look was ruined by the upturn of his lips. Seeing that she could not compel him to laugh, Elizabeth answered. "I have not decided. Mama and Suzy wish to visit the modiste today. If you will promise to wear the waist coat with the silver stitching, I promise to purchase a color that compliments it."

The smile that had previously threatened now spread across Mr. Darcy's face. Elizabeth would never tire of seeing the dimple that formed when he grinned at her in that way. "I will spend the long days on the road guessing what color you will choose." In a lower voice, he whispered, "And thinking of these lips." He leaned in for another kiss but was interrupted by the clearing of Mr. Gardiner's throat.

"Elizabeth, allow your young man to leave, else he will not return in time for your wedding."

With great reluctance, the couple stepped apart. "You must hurry back to me, Fitzwilliam, but most importantly, you must be safe." He promised that he would, and with one last squeeze of her hand, he boarded the carriage.

Elizabeth watched until his vehicle was out of sight. Thankfully, the snow that had blanketed the area only a week ago had melted. Elizabeth prayed the warmer weather would continue so that Darcy could return to her on the thirty-first, as planned.

"He will be back, my dear. Not soon enough for you, but all too soon for my tastes."

Elizabeth looked from where Darcy's carriage had last been seen up to her father's face. "You do not wish for Mr. Darcy to return as planned?"

Her papa pulled her into a tight hug. "I like your Mr. Darcy very much, but the day he returns is the day I lose you."

She hugged him back just as fiercely. "Papa, you will never lose me. I will always be your daughter, and I will always love and adore you."

He kissed her cheek. "And I you, my dear. But I will miss having you in the house every day. Breakfast will not be the same for I will have the paper all to myself and will not have to fight you for the best sections."

"Then let us make the most of our time together. First one

to the table gets to read the business page first!" With a giggle she turned and ran up the stairs and into the house. Her father laughed as he followed closely behind.

∞∞∞

After breakfast the ladies of the party called for a carriage. Suzy had a very fine modiste in the nearest town and assured Elizabeth that a suitable dress could be provided in time for her wedding. "I think you should wear blue, Lizzy. You always look so well in it, and it brightens your eyes."

Mrs. Gardiner nodded her head in agreement, but Lady Matlock pursed her lips. "I agree, Elizabeth, you do look well in blue, but I do not believe that should be the color you choose."

"What do you suggest, Aunt Grace?"

The countess pretended to think. "I believe pink would suit you well."

"But what shade of pink should she wear?" Suzy asked.

The countess gave Suzy an incredulous look. "Obviously, the exact shade of her blush."

"But how will we ensure it is correct?"

Lady Matlock laughed. "Simple. We only need ask Elizabeth to remember the most scandalous thing Darcy has said or done."

Immediately, Elizabeth thought of the evening Darcy sneaked into her room to check on her while she was ill. Without intending to, her face heated.

"Aha!" Lady Matlock pointed. "That is the color. Make note, Lady Susan." Together, all the ladies laughed, even Elizabeth's mother.

The modiste's shop was smaller than the ones Elizabeth

favored in London, but it was nonetheless well stocked with excellent sample dresses and the finest materials. It took only a short time to find what Suzy described as "the perfect blush pink" for Elizabeth's dress.

The seamstress fussed over Elizabeth, taking measurements and discussing designs with a speed that belied the urgency of the task. "I realize there is too little time to add embroidery. If possible, I would like it stitched with silver thread so that it will match my betrothed's waist coat." Elizabeth blushed again at the request while Suzy held the material to her skin for another color check.

"Time will be tight, Miss Gardiner," the modiste said with a smile, "but I do love a good challenge. We shall have you ready in time, I promise. And I suspect there will be enough time for us to add a bit of embroidery."

Elizabeth nodded, her thoughts momentarily drifting back to Darcy. She could almost see his face in her mind's eye, his expression as he watched her walk down the aisle in the dress they were now rushing to complete. The thought brought a warm flush to her cheeks, and she silently chided herself for becoming such an easy target for Lady Matlock and Suzy.

"Lizzy, what do you think of this?" Suzy's voice broke through her reverie, drawing her attention back to the present.

Elizabeth turned to see Suzy holding up a length of delicate lace. "I think it will be perfect."

The days wore on and despite the long list of tasks her mother and Suzy had prepared, Elizabeth found herself often thinking of Mr. Darcy rather than attending to her responsibilities. It had been three days since he left. By Elizabeth's calculations, he should be in London by now. *Perhaps, if I am lucky, he will have accomplished his goals and be on the road back to me.*

Elizabeth spent the third morning in the housekeeper's

office with Mrs. Billings planning the meal for the wedding festivities. "Miss Gardiner," Mrs. Billings said, "I was thinking we could serve a roast venison on the wedding day, along with trout from the river. What do you think?"

Elizabeth nodded. Mr. Darcy had shown a preference for venison. "And rum cake for desert? I have noticed my intended has a particular fondness for it."

Mrs. Billings smiled warmly at her. "Do not worry, Miss Gardiner. Everything will be just as you wish it. The staff and I will make sure of it."

On the day before the wedding, Elizabeth and her mother made their way to the Earl's hothouse to select flowers. The warmth was a welcome contrast to the crisp winter air outside. She moved among the rows of blooms, carefully selecting the ones she wanted to use for her bouquet and the decorations.

"These roses are beautiful," Elizabeth remarked, gently touching the soft petals."

Mrs. Gardiner nodded in agreement, her gaze lingering on a cluster of pale pink blooms. "And these lilies would pair perfectly. What do you think?"

Elizabeth had noticed in recent weeks that her mother seemed more tired than usual, and her usual zest for breakfast had been replaced by a desire for dry toast and unsweetened tea. She could no longer keep her worries to herself.

"Mama," Elizabeth began gently, "you have seemed rather unwell lately. Are you certain everything is all right?"

"You need not worry about me. I am just tired, that is all. There is so much to do, and the excitement of your wedding… well, it can be overwhelming."

Elizabeth frowned slightly. "Are you certain that you are not…" She hesitated, unsure of how to finish the sentence.

Mrs. Gardiner's eyes widened slightly before she waved a

hand as if to brush away the suggestion. "If I promise I am well, will you promise to not worry for me? Focus on your wedding and your future with Mr. Darcy. That is what matters now."

Elizabeth wanted to press the issue further, but the look in her mother's eyes stopped her. Her parents were childless after thirteen years of marriage. There had been many pregnancies, but none had lasted more than five months. Perhaps this would be a lucky holiday for both her mother and herself.

Elizabeth snapped the head off a chrysanthemum. Plucking one petal she silently chanted, *A baby.* She plucked another. *No baby.* It was not the flower or the words usually used for this game, but she was very pleased when the last petal remaining was for a baby.

"Elizabeth, what have you done to that poor flower?"

Elizabeth dropped the stem and smiled brightly at her mother. "I believe we have picked the perfect flowers for my bouquet. What else shall you have me do today?"

Her mother smirked. "I suspect Suzy will have plenty for the two of us to do." Together they walked arm in arm out of the hothouse.

∞∞∞

The chill of the London air cut through Darcy's coat as he stepped out of his carriage. The journey from Gloucestershire to London had been made difficult because of short daylight hours. To ensure a timely round-trip Darcy had urged his driver to carry on well into the evening. Despite the challenges, his coachman had brought him safely to town.

"Rest the horses and get as much rest as possible. I am hopeful we can be on our way in a matter of hours. We will not make it far, but every little bit will bring us closer to Meadow Haven." *And to my Elizabeth,* he added silently.

Soon, a stable hand saddled a horse and Darcy made for Doctor's Commons. The Earl of Effington and his own uncle had sent an express ahead of him with a request for the rare permit. Darcy had recently heard the archbishop had suggested that too many people had been requesting special licenses, and he hoped that having two supporters in the peerage would sway the man in Darcy's favor.

He was soon happy to learn that his wish had been granted. The sense of relief that washed over him was profound. This was the key to their future, and now it was safely in his hands. With a broad smile on his face and the special license in hand, Darcy mounted his horse and turned east toward his solicitor's suite of offices. If all went according to plan, he would have everything resolved in a matter of hours and could be back on the road by midafternoon.

Darcy had sent his own express with the details of the settlement and changes to his will. If luck was on his side, his second stop would be as easy as his first. But it was not to be.

"I apologize, Mr. Darcy. We have not yet completed the draft of your document. I treated my workers to a meal at a local tea shop as a belated Christmas gift. Unfortunately, we all became ill afterward. None of us have been capable of work until today."

Though he was disappointed, Darcy could hardly fault the gentleman for delaying the work due to illness. "How long do you anticipate, Mr. Farley?"

"One hour, perhaps two." Darcy nodded. He had not wished for this delay, but it did give him enough time to search for a bride's gift for Elizabeth. She favored blue which matched her vivid eyes. A sapphire necklace and bracelet would be a perfect gift.

"I have another errand to run before I start my trip back to Gloucestershire. Unfortunately, it is nearer to my home than here. When the documents are finalized, will you bring them to

Darcy House? I will review them with you from my office there."

The solicitor readily agreed. "Certainly, sir. I will ensure my team works quickly. I know you are anxious to return to your lady."

Darcy, once again, made his way out into the cold air. He wove his way into traffic and guided his horse toward Hanover Square. The Emanuel Brothers were the most likely to have an appropriate gift in stock.

Though traffic was thick, Darcy managed to weave his way around carriages and delivery carts. He made it to the jeweler's in less than an hour. "Mr. Darcy, how nice to see you, sir. Are you here to look for a gift for your sister or is there a lady who has caught your attention."

Darcy greeted Mr. Emanuel, one of the three brothers who owned the shop. "She has not only caught my attention, but she will also hold it for the remainder of my life."

The shorter man knew that when a gentleman of Darcy's means fell in love, it meant good things for a jeweler's pockets. And this was a customer in love as it was written all over his face. Eager to ensure Emmanual Brothers was the shop that benefited from Darcy's relationship, he escorted his customer to the counter.

"Tell me about your lady, Mr. Darcy. Does she prefer reds or greens?"

Darcy looked at the offerings on display. "Neither actually. She most often wears blue."

The salesman's mouth frowned slightly. "I am afraid, sir, that we do not currently have any blue stones available, but I can certainly put in an order for something if you wish to have an item custom made."

Darcy looked around the shop. "I will do just that, but I also wish to purchase something today, if there is a suitable set." He could not prevent the expression of joy that overcame his face when he thought of Elizabeth. "We are to be married on the thirty-first, and I would like to present her with a gift that no one but she has worn."

The man nodded. "In that case, perhaps something suitable for a blushing bride." He brought several sets of lighter colored jewels to the counter. The third set contained a delicate gold necklace accented with three larger teardrop shaped jewels and several more smaller jewels of the same type between them. It was accompanied by a matching set of earbobs. The cut and design of the set were perfect for Elizabeth, but perhaps most perfect was the color. The pink sapphires were a near perfect match to Elizabeth's lips after she had been thoroughly kissed. He promised to test the closeness of the colors by kissing her often. Darcy purchased the set and placed an order for another set of blue sapphires. Then he rode home, his package tucked safely in his breast pocket. Thankfully, his horse knew the way, as Darcy's mind was too readily occupied by thoughts of Elizabeth's kisses.

When he returned to Darcy House, he found his solicitor waiting with the marriage settlement and Darcy's updated will. He fought the desire to skim them quickly. The documents were too important to Elizabeth's future. Though he wished for nothing more than to board his carriage and head back to her, he gave the review of each document the time it deserved.

When the business was completed, Darcy opened his safe and reviewed the various rings passed down by generations of Darcys. A dainty blue sapphire caught his attention. It was not the grandest jewel in the case, but its delicate band and the small circle of diamonds that surrounded the center stone were perfectly suited to Elizabeth. He placed the ring in a different small bag and stored it alongside the gems he purchased for her.

It was three in the afternoon before Darcy was able to step into his carriage. He calculated the distance in his mind—if they could manage at least 40 miles before stopping for the night, they could reduce their days on the road. After waking early to rush the remaining distance to London, the additional time on the road in the dark would mean a difficult and long day for his coachman. But as the next day was the Sabbath, both men would be afforded a full day's rest. That would ensure they were both refreshed and ready for the remaining day and a half of their journey. If all went well, he would be back at Meadow Haven by the afternoon of the thirty-first, just in time to wed and ring in the new year with Elizabeth.

Chapter 21

Final Preparations

The biting cold of the winter wind cut through Darcy's coat as he rode hard toward Meadow Haven. His decision to forego the carriage on this final stretch of the journey had been impulsive, but he knew it had been the right one. Every muscle in his body ached from the relentless pace he had set, but had he continued his journey in the carriage, he would not have made it in time. A cold rain had delayed them near Burford, leaving the roads deep in mud. It was much easier, though messier, to come on horseback.

He reached the grand entrance of Meadow Haven just two hours before dinner, his horse lathered from the exertion and Darcy's boots and coat splattered in mud. "Cool him down properly and ensure he has a few extra oats for his efforts." Darcy handed the groomsman a coin before bounding up the stairs. The warmth of the interior was a stark contrast to the cold outside, but it was the sight of Elizabeth hurrying toward him that truly warmed him.

"Fitzwilliam!" Elizabeth's voice was filled with relief and joy as she reached him. She stopped just short of throwing herself into his arms, her hands hovering near his chest as she took in the sight of him.

"Elizabeth," Darcy breathed, his voice filled with the emotion he had carried with him throughout the journey. He wanted nothing more than to pull her close, to feel her warmth against him, but he was covered in the grime of the road and her father lingered near. Instead, he reached out and took her hands in his.

"You must be freezing," Elizabeth said, her concern evident as she studied his face.

"It was worth every chill, I assure you," Darcy replied with a small smile. "But I believe you are right—I could use a hot bath."

Elizabeth nodded. "I will have one drawn for you immediately."

"No need, Lizzy. I have already sent a maid." Lady Susan stood near the stairs. Behind her, Richard hovered closer than propriety allowed. Darcy paid them little mind, his attention was too focused on Elizabeth. *His* Elizabeth.

He brought her hand to his lips. "I will not linger, I promise."

Elizabeth's eyes shone with affection. "See that you do not. I have missed you terribly."

"And I you," Darcy replied, his voice softening. He wished to lean closer and kiss her properly, but her father still stood sentinel over their greetings. In two hours he would call her his wife, and never again would he deny himself her kisses.

Stepping away from his soon-to-be bride, he turned to her father. "I realize I am unkempt, but I wish to discuss the marriage articles and Elizabeth's settlement with you immediately. Perhaps you could review them while I refresh myself."

Mr. Gardiner gestured for Darcy to follow him. "Of course, Mr. Darcy. I expected as much. However, I suggest we review together so that you can enjoy your bath."

Darcy followed him to the library. "Here you are, sir." He

handed the marriage articles to the older man. "Everything is in order, as I discussed it with you before I left. Elizabeth will maintain her dowry for her own use, and any daughters we have will have at least thirty thousand settled on them. I have three properties, so at least three sons, should we be so blessed, will have property."

Mr. Gardiner looked over the papers. He was a scrupulous businessman and would approach this contract with the utmost seriousness. Elizabeth was his beloved daughter, and he would not allow so much as an erroneous comma to go unmentioned.

Mr. Gardiner began, "This is exactly as you said it would be. Thank you for your generosity to my Elizabeth. It is not easy to give her up., but I suppose I must. She loves you, and you have proven yourself to be generous."

Darcy inclined his head. "I promise to love her and care for her all my days."

Mr. Gardiner sighed. "There is one matter I wish to discuss further."

"Yes?" Darcy leaned forward.

"There is a possibility," Mr. Gardiner said carefully, "that Elizabeth may end up being my heir. As you may know, my wife and I have been married for many years, but we have not been blessed with any children of our own. However, lately, my wife has shown signs of breeding. While this is welcome news, we have been cautious in our hopes."

Darcy's expression softened as he listened. "Mr. Gardiner, I must make one thing clear: I would take Elizabeth with nothing. I fought the idea for too long, but there is no one else for me. Her dowry, her inheritance—they mean nothing to me in comparison to her."

Mr. Gardiner regarded Darcy with a mixture of respect and gratitude. "She is a treasure, to be certain. I am only glad that someone has seen it beyond myself and her mother. I am pleased to know that she will be well cared for, regardless of what the future holds."

Darcy hesitated for a moment before speaking. "I wish you and Mrs. Gardiner the best of luck in this matter. I have not yet discussed it with Elizabeth, but I know that your happiness is of paramount concern to her. I am certain she will be as thrilled as I am by the prospect of a new addition to your family."

Mr. Gardiner offered a small, nervous smile, his concern for his wife evident. "We have had no luck in the past, and I must admit, I worry for my wife. She is not as young as she once was."

Darcy's voice was filled with understanding. "I may not yet be married, Mr. Gardiner, but I believe I understand the love a man has for his wife. The fear, the hope—it is a heavy burden to bear." Mr. Gardiner nodded.

Darcy rose from his seat, extending his hand. "Let us hope for the best, then, for all our futures."

Mr. Gardiner stood as well, shaking Darcy's hand firmly. "Indeed. And now, I believe there is a bath waiting for you. My daughter is eager to wed so you must not delay."

Darcy smiled at the thought, a warmth spreading through him at the mention of Elizabeth. "Then I shall not keep her waiting a moment longer than required."

He made his way back to his chambers, where the promised hot bath awaited him. The heat of the water worked wonders on his tired muscles, but he did not allow himself the luxury of soaking. Soon, Elizabeth would be his and he would never be parted from her again.

∞∞∞

The parlor at Meadow Haven was quiet. Richard stood near the hearth, his hands clasped behind his back as he watched

Elizabeth's mother whisk her daughter upstairs to prepare for the wedding.

"Suzy, please give us a few minutes before you join us. I would like to some time alone with my daughter."

Lady Susan gave a guileless nod, and Richard had to force back a chuckle. Looking from one maiden's face to the other, it was clear neither understood what conversation Mrs. Gardiner planned to have with her daughter.

Lady Susan, anxious to help her friend prepare for her nuptials, paced to the window and looked out. The house was filled with a sense of anticipation, and yet, in this moment, Richard felt a different kind of hope building within him—one that had little to do with his cousin's impending vows.

When Elizabeth and her mother were out of sight, Lady Susan lingered by the window. The light shining on her face caught Richard's attention, and he found himself watching her, his heart beating a little faster. They had spent so much time together over the past weeks, growing closer with each passing day, but there had always been others around—friends, family, servants. Rarely had they found time alone—except for those cherished moments in the billiards room. Richard knew the time had come to say what had been on his mind for some time.

"Lady Susan," he began, his voice a little more hesitant than he had intended. He cleared his throat and took a step closer to her. "Would you do me the honor of sitting with me for a moment?"

She turned from the window, her expression curious but warm. "Of course, Colonel," she replied, moving to one of the chairs by the fire and settling into it. "Is something on your mind?"

Richard hesitated for a moment, searching for the right words. He had faced battlefields with less trepidation than he felt now. But he could not delay any longer. He took a deep breath and sat opposite her, meeting her gaze directly.

"There is something I have been meaning to say for some time now," Richard began, his voice steadying as he spoke. "Lady Susan... Suzy, you are... you are the most remarkable woman I have ever known. These past weeks, spending time with you, getting to know you better... It has been the greatest joy of my life."

Lady Susan's eyes widened slightly, and she opened her mouth to speak, but Richard held up a hand, gently stopping her. "Please, allow me finish," he said softly, his heart pounding in his chest. "I must tell you how I feel."

He paused, gathering his courage. "I care for you deeply—more than I ever thought possible. I wish, desperately, for you to be my bride." He held his hand up to silence her once again. "Before you say anything, I must be honest with you. I do not have much to offer you in terms of wealth. I have a small estate in Norfolk, enough to live comfortably, but nothing like the life you are accustomed to."

Her expression softened, and she reached out, placing her hand over his. "Richard," she said gently, "do you really think that matters to me?"

Richard looked at her, surprised by the warmth in her voice. "I... I was unsure," he admitted, his voice barely above a whisper. "You deserve so much more than I can give you. I fear that I cannot provide the lifestyle you are used to."

She shook her head, her grip on his hand tightening. "I have never cared about wealth or status. Lizzy and I have always promised each other that we would marry only for love, and I mean to keep that promise. It is your heart, your character, that I value—not your estate."

Richard's eyes searched hers for any sign of deception, but all he saw was sincerity. "Suzy, I... I do not know what to say," he murmured, his voice thick with emotion. "You will marry me?"

She giggled. "I have not yet been asked."

In a trice, he kneeled before her and took her hands in his. "Lady Susan Corwell, I have little to give you but myself. But if you will have me, I will do my best to make you the happiest woman on earth. Will you marry me?"

She leaned forward. "I will." Richard, thrilled beyond words pulled her to him and kissed her sweet lips. The kiss was tender at first, a gentle exploration of the feelings they had both been holding back. But as the seconds passed, it deepened, filled with the passion and love that had been building between them for so long. He knew from her initial reaction that she had never shared this experience with anyone, and he relished the joy of being her first. *Her first and last,* he thought.

With reluctance, the couple broke apart, though their foreheads touched. "Richard, two things I must tell you."

His thumb stroked lazy circles on her temple. "What is it my love."

A playful glint flickered in her eyes. "I told Lizzy that I would marry for love this year. You, sir, are my destiny."

He chuckled. "I am pleased I could help prove you correct. And the second?"

Lady Susan sat back and looked him in the eyes. "Upon my wedding, I will inherit a rather substantial estate in Somerset. Presently, it earns six thousand a year. Together, we will have more than enough to live comfortably."

Richard stared at her, stunned by this revelation. "I… I had no idea."

She smiled softly, her gaze tender. "I know. That is why I am telling you now. I do not want you to fear for our future. We will do very well, I suspect."

The relief and joy that washed over Richard were overwhelming, and before he knew it, he once again closed the distance between them. Suzy's eyes fluttered closed as he cupped her face in his hands. "I love you," he whispered before joining their lips.

When they finally broke apart, they were both breathless. They sat there for a moment longer, simply holding each other. Finally, she pulled back slightly, a thoughtful look crossing her face. "Richard, there is one more thing."

"What is it?" he asked.

She hesitated for a moment, then smiled. "I think we should wait until after Lizzy and Mr. Darcy's wedding to make our engagement official. I want them to have their day, without any distractions."

Richard nodded, understanding her reasoning. "That is a wise idea. We will give them their day, and then… tomorrow we will begin our life together."

"I suspect it will be a while before our life will begin, in truth. Your mother will, no doubt, wish for a society wedding." Richard groaned.

Chapter 22

The Wedding

Elizabeth's heart fluttered with a mixture of nerves and excitement as she finished dressing for the ceremony. The light pink dress she wore fit perfectly, its delicate silver embroidery catching the light as she moved. It would be the perfect complement to the waist coat Darcy had promised to wear.

As she adjusted the folds of her dress, there was a soft knock at the door. Suzy hurried over to answer it. When she returned, she held a small velvet bag in her hands, her eyes wide with excitement.

"Mr. Darcy's valet delivered this for you." Suzy's voice was filled with curiosity.

Elizabeth's heart skipped a beat as she untied the delicate ribbon. Inside, nestled against the dark velvet, was the most exquisite set of pink sapphires she had ever seen, all perfectly matching the shade of her gown.

"Oh my," she whispered.

Her mother stepped closer, a knowing smile on her lips. "It seems Mr. Darcy has an excellent eye for such things," she said gently. "And perhaps he was also inspired by the color of your blushes." She touched her finger to Elizabeth's pink cheek. Elizabeth felt her face warm even further at the suggestion.

With her mother's help, Elizabeth put on the jewelry. She took one last look in the mirror to admire the effect the jewels had on her appearance.

"Lizzy, are you ready?" Suzy stood by the door, holding Elizabeth's bouquet.

Elizabeth smiled, smoothing down the front of her dress. "To be Mrs. Darcy? Yes, I am quite ready for that."

Suzy kissed her friend's cheek before she handed her the bouquet. "You look absolutely stunning, Lizzy. Mr. Darcy will be speechless."

Elizabeth blushed slightly at the thought. "I just hope I do not trip on the way down the stairs."

Suzy laughed and took her hand. "You will be perfect, as always. Come, everyone is waiting."

Mrs. Gardiner and Suzy made their way to the top of the staircase, followed soon after by Elizabeth. When Elizabeth looked down, her breath caught in her throat. The party had gathered below, but at the bottom of the stairs, standing tall and handsome in his finely tailored jacket, was Mr. Darcy.

Elizabeth's eyes locked onto his, and in that moment, the world fell away. Mr. Darcy's gaze was so intense it set her heart aflutter. His eyes never left hers as she descended the stairs. The warmth that spread through her at his unwavering attention made her forget the others. It was just the two of them.

As she reached the last step, he stepped forward, his hand outstretched to help her down the final distance. "Elizabeth," he murmured, his voice filled with emotion as he opened his hand to reveal a dainty blue sapphire ring, its design intricate and feminine. "This belonged to my great-grandmother. Of everything in the Darcy jewelry safe, I thought this one would best suit you. The color reminds me of your eyes."

Elizabeth's breath caught as she looked at the ring, the sapphire glinting in the light. "I…" Words caught in her throat.

Suddenly nervous, he said, "If you prefer something different for your betrothal ring, we can choose another one when we return to London."

"It is beautiful, Fitzwilliam," she whispered, her voice trembling slightly.

Relieved, Mr. Darcy took her hand and gently slid the ring onto her finger. He looked up at her, his eyes shining with love. "You are beautiful," he said softly.

She leaned in, momentarily forgetting their audience. When she pulled back, Georgiana darted forward. "Oh, Elizabeth, you look so beautiful!" she exclaimed, wrapping her arms around Elizabeth in a tight hug.

The suddenness of Georgiana's embrace took Elizabeth by surprise, and she laughed softly as she returned the hug. "Thank you, Georgiana. You look lovely as well."

Georgiana's joy was contagious, and soon everyone around them was laughing, including Mr. Darcy, though his laugh was tinged with the slightest bit of frustration. He had clearly been about to embrace her himself, but his younger sister had beaten him to it. "Georgiana, must you always be so eager?" he teased.

Georgiana stepped back, grinning unabashedly. "I could not help myself, brother. You will just have to wait your turn."

He took Elizabeth's hand once more, his thumb brushing gently over her knuckles. "I suppose I will," he said, his voice deepening with a hint of anticipation that sent a shiver down Elizabeth's spine.

"Shall we proceed?" Mr. Gardiner offered his arm to Elizabeth.

The guests moved toward the drawing room, which had been transformed to resemble a small chapel for the occasion. While everyone found their place, Mr. Gardiner stood with Elizabeth in the entryway. He cupped her beloved face in his hands. "You have been my greatest joy, Elizabeth. The day I took you home with me was the day I learned to live." He kissed her cheek. "I will miss you, my girl."

Elizabeth wiped at a threatening tear. "Papa, I cannot know what my life would have been had my parents lived, but I could not have loved my birth father any more than I have loved you."

"Your father would have adored the woman you have grown up to be. I think I did his honor credible justice in the raising of you." Mr. Gardiner dabbed his own eyes which were suspiciously wet. "Shall we?"

Though their sentimental conversation had brought tears to her eyes, Elizabeth's face glowed with joy as her father escorted her down the aisle. The room was filled with the scent of flowers from the earl's hothouse, but Elizabeth could hardly focus on anything but the man standing before her. His smile broadened as she walked toward him, revealing a deep dimple. *That is my dimple,* she thought. *He only shows it for me.*

Soon, her father placed her hand in Mr. Darcy's. The minister spoke about love and a couple's duty to grow their family, but Elizabeth heard none of it. She was far too focused on the man beside her. Suzy quietly prompted her to repeat her vows, earning a chuckle from the assembled group. She offered an apologetic smile to the parson, before repeating the words. When it was Mr. Darcy's turn, he spoke in a voice laced with reverence, sending Elizabeth's heart racing.

Finally, the parson pronounced them husband and wife, and Mr. Darcy wasted no time in pulling Elizabeth into his arms. "You are mine now, Elizabeth," his voice a low murmur that only she could hear. "And I am yours. Forever." Elizabeth's heart skipped a beat at his words.

She took her husband's arm and allowed him to escort her out. Colonel Fitzwilliam and Suzy followed. The trailing pair exchanged a look so full of understanding that everyone in the assembled group immediately understood its meaning. A slow, knowing smile spread across Lady Matlock's face. "Perhaps there will be another wedding soon," she whispered to her husband.

"I believe they think it is a secret." The two tittered quietly at the folly of their youngest son and his soon-to-be bride.

∞∞∞

Darcy led Elizabeth into the library for a moment of privacy before the wedding supper. He gently closed the door behind him. "Alone at last, Mrs. Darcy." The soft glow of the firelight danced across Elizabeth's features, highlighting the delicate pink of her lips—a color that had only deepened since their last kiss. Darcy could not resist pulling her into his arms once more, his lips finding hers.

She responded eagerly, her arms encircling his neck and her fingers curling into his hair as their kiss deepened. When they finally broke apart, both were breathless, their hearts pounding in unison. Elizabeth's mouth was swollen from the intensity of their kisses, and Darcy could not help but smile at the sight.

"I regret that we must join the others for supper," he murmured, his voice husky with desire. "But I cannot help but admire the color of your lips, my love. It was that very shade that inspired the jewels I bought for you." He fingered the necklace at the base of her neck.

Elizabeth giggled softly, her eyes sparkling with affection. "And it was the color of my blushes—those that you inspire—that led me to choose this fabric."

Darcy's eyes darkened with a mixture of curiosity and teasing intent. "I have often wondered about those blushes, Elizabeth," he said, his voice dropping to a low, intimate murmur. "Do they extend below your neckline?" Instantly he regretted his comment. She was a maiden and, as such, was far too innocent for his innuendo.

Elizabeth's cheeks flushed a deeper pink at his bold question, her innocence battling with the newfound thrill of their intimacy. "Fitzwilliam," she whispered. A sudden boldness prompted her to add, "You shall have to wait and see."

Darcy's heartbeat quickened at her response. "Then I look forward to that discovery, my love." He leaned in to brush a tender kiss against her forehead.

They shared another kiss before reluctantly parting. "I suppose we should join everyone for supper." He pouted, which made Elizabeth laugh.

He offered his arm, and together they made their way to the dining room. When they entered, a rousing round of applause greeted them.

"To Mr. and Mrs. Darcy," Richard called, raising his glass.

"To Mr. and Mrs. Darcy!"

Darcy could not prevent the smile the spread across his face, or the feeling of pride he felt when he seated himself beside her at the table. He moved his chair closer than was strictly appropriate, causing his uncle and cousin to snicker. Darcy did not mind. The arrangement allowed him to continue his private connection with his bride, even in the midst of gathered company.

Ever the gentleman, Darcy served Elizabeth first, his hand brushing hers as he did so. Under the table, his hand found its way to her thigh, resting there with a casual possessiveness that sent a fresh wave of blushes to her cheeks.

Darcy's eyes gleamed with satisfaction. In a voice barely above a whisper he teased. "There is that lovely blush again." His thumb rubbed gentle circles on her leg.

Elizabeth bit her lip, her pulse quickening at his touch.

"Fitzwilliam, you must stop. My father is looking at us." That had a sobering effect, and Darcy immediately removed his hand from her knee. He looked down the table toward Mr. Gardiner who sat in happy conversation with his uncle. Elizabeth giggled.

"Sprite," he laughed before tapping her on the nose. "You will pay for that… later." Elizabeth swallowed, and Darcy felt pride in knowing that he had disconcerted her, confident that her passion for him mirrored his own.

The food was delicious but neither of them paid much attention to the fare. Their minds were occupied with thoughts of one another, their hands occasionally brushed under the table, sending little shocks of pleasure through them both. Elizabeth's blushes, which Darcy had so admired, seemed to be a constant companion throughout the meal, much to his delight.

"I do believe I am becoming addicted to your blushes, my dear. They are the most exquisite shade of pink, and I find myself wanting to see them again and again."

He was thrilled when his bold wife replied. "And I find that I am becoming rather fond of the way you make me blush."

Chapter 23

Celebrations

Noticing Darcy's reluctance to be away from his wife, Effington suggested the men forego their cigars and join the ladies in the parlor. Darcy was quick to offer his arm to Elizabeth. "Shall we, my love?"

After a few moments of conversation, Georgiana suggested a few songs. "Does anyone have a recommendation?"

"Play something for dancing, Georgiana. It is a celebration, after all." Georgiana hid a smile at her cousin's obvious ploy to dance with his lady.

Darcy squeezed Elizabeth's hand, his eyes glinting with a playful energy that she once would not have believed possible. "What do you say, Mrs. Darcy? Shall we take to the floor and show them how it is done?"

Elizabeth's heart fluttered at the way he said her new name. "If you think you can keep up with me, Mr. Darcy, I suppose I am willing."

As the couples began to pair off, the room filled with the rustle of skirts and the sounds of furniture being pushed aside. Richard took Suzy's hand, his eyes warm with affection as he led her to the center of the room. Mr. and Mrs. Gardiner joined them.

With a shy smile, Georgiana took her place at the piano. The first notes of a lively tune filled the room, and the couples began to dance. Elizabeth found herself laughing as Darcy twirled her around the room, his steps confident and sure.

"You are quite good at this, Mr. Darcy," Elizabeth teased as they moved together.

"Only because I have the best partner," Darcy replied, his voice warm with affection.

As the dance came to an end, they all found themselves breathless and smiling, the joy of the moment shared among them. Georgiana's fingers stilled on the piano keys, and for a moment, the room was filled with the comfortable silence of companionship.

It was Richard who broke the quiet, his eyes twinkling with mischief. "You know, all this talk of music reminds me of something. Darcy told me about a song he once heard. An ode to the new Mrs. Darcy. I wonder if my cousin here might give us a performance?"

Darcy raised an eyebrow, immediately understanding Richard's intention. "Ah, yes. I believe I know exactly the song you are thinking of, Richard." He turned to Elizabeth, a mischievous grin on his lips. "Shall I serenade you, my love?"

Elizabeth's eyes widened, already guessing what he was about to do. "Oh no, Fitzwilliam, please do not—"

But it was too late. With exaggerated solemnity, Darcy began to sing in a deep, dramatic voice, doing his best to imitate Mr. Collins' infamous ode to Elizabeth.

Elizabeth, my wife so dear,

You walk the fields to exercise.

"Enough, enough. We have not yet been married a day and already you treat me so."

The room erupted in laughter, and Elizabeth could not help but join in. "I do commend you for choosing all the correct words, however."

"Ah yes, perhaps I should have said 'you walk the fields to alchemize'. I think that would have been a more authentic choice."

Elizabeth and Darcy shared another laugh, as Richard joined in. "Oh, that horrid, imbecilic man!" Lady Susan harrumphed from beside Richard. "Lizzy told me all about his little songs. How dreadful! Though I did enjoy it when she included Collinsisms in her letters to me. I believe he once referred to your aunt as 'The Venereal Lady Catherine de Bourgh."

This caught the Earl of Matlock's attention. He laughed heartily. "I shall never think of her differently now!"

Elizabeth, still laughing, shook her head. "Mr. Collins' grasp of the English language was tenuous at best. And his little songs were truly abysmal, but," she added with a soft smile, "they offered me a chance to first form a connection with my dear husband."

Darcy cocked his head. "How so, my love."

She placed her hand on his. "You offered me comfort and distraction during the worst of it. I was pleased by your gentlemanly manners. It is what first caused me to hope."

Darcy, clearly pleased with her response, raised an eyebrow. "Then I have outdone you, my dear. My interest was piqued during our first dance, but my feelings have been engaged since I encountered you on Oakham Mount."

Elizabeth looked up at him, her laughter fading into a soft smile. "So soon?"

Darcy's eyes softened, and he nodded. "Yes, so soon. You captivated me from the very beginning." Elizabeth wanted nothing more than to kiss him. Here, in front of everyone. But good manners prevailed.

∞∞∞

When the maid brought in the tea tray, Elizabeth found herself being gently pulled aside by her mother, who had a tender look in her eyes. "Lizzy, my dear," Mrs. Gardiner began, her voice filled with emotion, "from the look in your husband's eyes, I suspect you will not join us for much longer. Before you go, I must tell you how much I will miss having you so near."

Elizabeth's heart tightened with emotion, and she took her mother's hands. "But perhaps you will soon have another son or daughter to occupy your attention?"

Mrs. Gardiner's eyes softened with tears, and she smiled faintly. "I fear to wish for it, Elizabeth, but oh, how I hope."

Elizabeth hugged her mother close. "It has been a privilege to be your daughter, Mama. You have taught me everything I need to know about love and family."

Mrs. Gardiner pulled back slightly, a mixture of pride and love shining in her eyes for her daughter. She then moved her gaze to Mr. Darcy who was standing nearby. "And as I predicted, your husband is eager to steal you away," she whispered. "Trust him, Lizzy. He will not hurt you. He loves you dearly."

With her mother's blessing, Elizabeth allowed herself to be secreted away by Mr. Darcy, their hands intertwined as they quietly left the room. The two said nothing as they walked up the stairs and down the hall to Elizabeth's new suite. Suzy had arranged for the new Mrs. Darcy to have the room next door to her husband. Mr. Darcy turned to her, his eyes filled with longing. "How much time do you need, my love?"

Elizabeth swallowed, feeling a rush of warmth spread through her. "Half an hour. Possibly less," she replied, her voice barely above a whisper.

He nodded, his gaze never leaving hers. "Take your time, my darling. And leave the necklace on." He brought her hand to his mouth and kissed it, allowing his lips to linger. Elizabeth's toes curled in anticipation.

Inside the room, Milly had laid out a new silk nightgown and wrapper, and a set of soft white slippers, trimmed in rabbit fur. "Mrs. Darcy," she said in reverent tone as she offered a proper curtsy.

Elizabeth eyes danced. "I am the same as I have always been, Milly, though I do love hearing my new title. I shall never tire of it."

Milly gave a wry laugh. "That is good, ma'am, as you are now stuck with it."

Milly's deft hands soon had Elizabeth out of her dress and into her nightgown. "This red looks mighty pretty on you. Mr. Darcy will be beside himself." Elizabeth looked into the mirror as her maid brushed her hair.

"He asked me to wear the necklace, but it does not match."

Milly smoothed Elizabeth's hair into soft waves before putting the brush upon the table. "I doubt Mr. Darcy will care one jot for that. He will simply wish to see you wearing the jewels he bought for you. Men are like that."

Elizabeth's response was stalled by a light knock upon the door. Milly gave Elizabeth's shoulder a reassuring pat before opening the door. "Good evening, sir." She bobbed a curtsy before leaving.

Elizabeth's pulse quickened at the sight of her husband standing in the door frame. His shoulders were so wide, she could hardly see around him. She had wondered about those shoulders many, many times. Elizabeth had run her hands over them during kisses, so she knew he did not pad his coat as so many gentlemen did. *Perhaps he is built as the Greek statues are in the museums I have visited.* A thrill of hope ran through her.

"Are you cold, Mrs. Darcy?" he asked softly, his voice sending another bout of shivers down her spine.

Elizabeth shook her head, her voice failing her as she stepped to him. He crossed the room in a few quick strides and gently cupped her face in his hands.

"My beautiful wife," he murmured. "I will warm you."

He leaned down, capturing her lips in a tender kiss. As the kiss deepened, Darcy pulled back slightly, his voice husky with desire.

"Let us get you to bed, Mrs. Darcy," he said, his eyes darkening with a mixture of love and longing. Slowly, he walked her backwards until her legs hit the mattress. "So beautiful." Darcy's hands moved from her face to her shoulders, sliding over the silk of her nightgown and down her body with deliberate tenderness. The warmth of his touch caused goosebumps to rise on her flesh and made her heart race even faster.

"I have waited so long for this moment," he whispered, his voice thick with emotion. "To finally call you my wife, to touch you like this, to know that you are mine, now and forever."

Elizabeth's breath caught in her throat. "I am yours, Fitzwilliam. And you are mine."

Darcy smiled, the dimple in his cheek deepening as he gazed at her with an affection that left her feeling cherished. He leaned down, pressing soft kisses along her jawline, trailing them down her neck, each touch sending a shiver of anticipation through her.

Elizabeth felt her hands move of their own accord, slipping beneath the fabric of his dressing gown to feel the solid warmth of his back. She reveled in the sensation of his muscles tensing beneath her fingers, the reality of him, so close, so strong, so undeniably hers.

He moved them toward the bed, his hands never leaving her, his kisses growing more insistent. When they reached the edge, he paused, lifting her slightly to remove the fur-trimmed slippers from her feet. His gaze flicked to her necklace, and he smiled. "Your lips grow brighter after kissing, my love. I must purchase another set of jewels to match this exact shade." He ran his thumb along her swollen mouth. "The color will be beautiful against your skin, but not as lovely as my Elizabeth."

In a breathy voice, she responded. "You flatter me, Fitzwilliam."

"I speak only the truth," he replied in low voice.

∞∞∞

Darcy lowered her onto the bed, careful to keep his body from fully touching hers. His intrepid Elizabeth did not appear fearful, but he wished to go slow for her sake. And, if he was truthful with himself, for his own. He wished to savor every second. Elizabeth's hands moved to his lapels, pushing his robe open to expose his chest. Darcy assisted her, untying the sash and allowing the garment to fall carelessly to the floor.

Her eyes were hooded as she brought her hands to his shoulders. Her touch sent thrills through his body, and he reminded himself to be gentle. She was a treasure, and she was all his. "Elizabeth," he whispered, his voice nearly breaking, "I will spend every day of my life making you happy."

Tears welled in her eyes. "And I will spend every day loving you, Fitzwilliam."

Darcy lowered himself to her, his lips capturing hers in a kiss that conveyed all the love and desire he held for her. The kiss deepened, and soon they were lost in each other, their hands exploring, their breaths mingling, until there was nothing left between them but the sheer intensity of their need for one another.

∞ ∞ ∞

Darcy pressed a tender kiss to Elizabeth's forehead. Her hair was a riot of curls spread across the pillow, her skin glowing with the aftereffects of their joining. "I want you to always wear your hair down for me when we are in our chambers."

She lifted her hand to her hair and attempted to smooth it. "It will become a tangled mess. Jane always chided my unruly locks."

He stilled her hand with his own. "Your sister was wrong. Your hair has long captivated me. I have wished to run my fingers through it for months."

She giggled. "For months? That would certainly have thwarted Jane's plans."

He leaned down and kissed her plump lips. "I believe we gave your sister exactly what she wished for."

Elizabeth looked perplexed. "How so?"

"She wished you to marry a gentleman, did she not?"

He thought back to the months that had led them to this moment, the twists and turns of fate that had brought them together. He silently thanked his Aunt Matlock for her interference in his love life, for inviting him and Georgiana to that fateful tea where he had first seen Elizabeth again. Even if his aunt had intended to match him with Lady Susan, it had all worked out exactly as it should have. He now had his lovely Elizabeth by his side, until the end of their days.

Elizabeth stirred in his arms, and Darcy tightened his hold on her, feeling a swell of protectiveness. This was where she belonged, where she would always belong—in his arms. In his bed. In his life.

"Are you happy, Mrs. Darcy?" he whispered, his voice filled

with tenderness.

Elizabeth looked up at him, her eyes shining with love. "Happier than I ever imagined, Mr. Darcy."

Darcy smiled, the dimple in his cheek appearing once more as he pressed a lingering kiss to her lips. "As am I, my love. As am I."

Somewhere in the house the distant tones of a grandfather clock struck twelve. Elizabeth lifted her head to listen. "Uncle Paul should just now be opening the front door to usher in the new year."

"Are you sorry I forced you to leave the celebration early?" He ran his thumb across her cheek, stopping at her plump bottom lip.

She kissed the digit. "I believe this is exactly how we should usher in the new year, my love."

He kissed her then before settling himself above her. "Happy New Year, Mrs. Darcy."

Chapter 24

London

The next day the couple rose earlier than desired and joined the rest of the household for breakfast. Meadow Haven bustled with activity as the servants rushed to and fro to prepare the residents for travel. Despite the late breakfast and lingering celebrations of the previous evening, the time had come for everyone to make their way to London. Lady Matlock's Twelfth Night celebration awaited them.

Darcy brought his wife's hand to his lips. "I am sorry to rush you from our bed and into our carriage, my love, but it seems Aunt Grace has dictated we attend her dinner."

Elizabeth smiled. "It is in our honor, darling." He acknowledged the truth of her statement before tucking a blanket around her legs.

Elizabeth sat back against the plush cushions of the carriage, her gloved hands resting on her lap. The warmth of Darcy's hand next to hers provided a steady comfort, though the reality of their new life together filled her with a sense of nervous anticipation. The gentle clatter of the horses' hooves and the rhythmic motion of the carriage should have soothed her, but she could not stop the butterflies in her stomach.

"Is something the matter?"

Elizabeth gave him a shy smile. "It is odd being here... alone I mean. I suppose the idea of being Mrs. Darcy has not quite settled yet. It's as though I am living in a dream."

Darcy smiled, his expression one of quiet contentment. "I do hope it is a pleasant dream, my love. For I fear you will never awaken from it. You are mine now, Elizabeth, and I am yours."

Elizabeth's heart fluttered at his words, though she quickly masked her emotions with a teasing smile. "Do not think that simply because I have taken your name, you will have your way in all things, Fitzwilliam."

"Ah," Darcy replied, his voice filled with mock seriousness, "I had hoped that as my wife, you would at least allow me some small victories."

"Perhaps," Elizabeth mused playfully, "though I do not believe it will be so easy for you."

Darcy's gaze lingered on her, his smile softening. "You blush still, Mrs. Darcy."

Elizabeth turned to him, her cheeks indeed warm, though she raised an eyebrow in mock indignation. "You know why I blush, Fitzwilliam."

Darcy chuckled, leaning a little closer to her. "Is that so? I do not recall doing anything that would merit such a reaction."

Elizabeth gave him a knowing look. "Your memory must be short, then. Or perhaps you simply choose to forget."

"I will never forget, my darling," Darcy replied, his voice dropping to a low murmur. He touched her cheek. "It has yet to fade, my love."

Elizabeth raised an eyebrow, her lips curving into a playful smirk. "It is hardly a fair game when you insist on staring at me with such intensity. You know very well what effect that has."

Darcy leaned closer, his voice dropping to a low murmur. "I do know, my love, and I confess I am rather addicted to that particular shade of pink."

Elizabeth's heart skipped, but she would not give in so

easily. "You should be careful. I may grow immune to your charms if you keep at this pace."

Darcy chuckled, his breath warm against her skin. "I would wager you are far too fond of me for that to happen."

Elizabeth leaned back into the soft cushions, her hand still resting in Darcy's. "It feels strange, does it not?" she mused. "To think that only yesterday, I was Elizabeth Gardiner. Now I am Mrs. Darcy, and my entire world has shifted."

Darcy turned to her, his expression softening. "You were always meant to be Mrs. Darcy," he said quietly. "It was simply a matter of time."

Elizabeth smiled at his words. "I do not know if I will ever tire of hearing you say that."

"Good," Darcy replied, his eyes twinkling with amusement. "Because I plan to remind you of it often."

After many hours of travel, Darcy called for his coachman to find an appropriate inn. He had no intention of subjecting Elizabeth to an uncomfortable journey. Soon after, the couple pulled into the receiving yard of the Black Goose, an establishment Darcy had frequented in the past. The innkeeper was beside himself at the number of richly appointed carriages that arrived after the Darcy's. Lord and Lady Matlock ascended first, followed soon after by Lord Effington's and the Gardiner's carriages

For the three days it took to travel from Meadow Haven to London, Darcy and Elizabeth rarely saw their family, though they made all the same stops along the way. It was, perhaps, an unconventional honeymoon, but the couple was desirous of time alone, as so many newlyweds often are. Each night at the inns, Darcy arranged for the lushest and more private accommodations. Though he was a private man, he did not blush when his cousin and uncle teased him for rushing Elizabeth up to their quarters. Elizabeth insisted on taking supper each night with their family and friends, but Darcy had his way each morning by treating his wife to breakfast in bed.

On the second night, as they settled into their room at an inn tucked away on a quiet road, Elizabeth found herself smiling as she watched Darcy stoke the fire.

"Fitzwilliam," she said softly, drawing his attention away from the fire.

He turned, his eyes filled with warmth. "Yes, my love?"

Elizabeth hesitated for a moment, unsure of how to put her feelings into words. "It has been... rather easy, has it not? These last few days. I thought marriage would feel more... I do not know. Different. Not difficult, but... But this... this feels so natural."

Darcy crossed the room, sitting beside her on the edge of the bed. He reached for her hand, his fingers lacing through hers. "That is because it is right," he said quietly. "I was always meant for you. And you, my love," he stopped to kiss her lips, "were always meant for me."

By the time they reached the outskirts of London on the third day, Elizabeth found herself almost wishing the journey would not end. There was a quiet magic to these early days of marriage, and she was in no hurry to leave it behind.

∞∞∞

The carriage pulled to a stop in front of Darcy House. Elizabeth had paid little attention to the stately home until a few weeks ago. After he brought her back from Hertfordshire, she had found ample reasons to ask her coachman to drive her the long way home in hopes of catching a glimpse of Mr. Darcy. Her heart fluttered in her chest. *Now it is my home,* she thought. And more importantly added, *Now he is my husband!*

Fitzwilliam, for that is how she now thought of him, placed his hand gently over hers. "We are home," he said softly. "Our home."

A faint smile played about her lips. "Yes, our home."

When the carriage door opened, Mr. Darcy stepped out first before offering his hand to his wife. As they ascended the steps the door swung open, and they were greeted by their butler. His face showed great relief upon seeing his master.

"What is it Bates?" Before the man had a chance to respond, a shrill voice pierced the air.

"Fitzwilliam!"

Elizabeth froze, her eyes widening as a wiry lady in her middle years swept into view. The woman's face contorted with fury. Mr. Darcy's grip on Elizabeth's hand tightened. From somewhere behind them, the door shut and Elizabeth could just see Bates's form slink off in her peripheral vision.

"Lady Catherine," Mr. Darcy greeted her with a stiff nod. "I had not expected you to be here."

"Obviously," Lady Catherine snapped, her eyes blazing with indignation. "And yet, here I am, just in time to stop this utter travesty of a union!"

Mr. Darcy's expression darkened in a way Elizabeth had only seen once before — the night of the Netherfield ball. "Which union do you mean? Surely you do not disparage my relationship with Elizabeth, for that is no travesty at all. It is my great joy to call her my wife."

Lady Catherine's eyes flicked toward Elizabeth, her mouth curling into a sneer. "Wife! So you have done it already, then. You have married this... this woman. I could not believe it when I saw the engagement announcement. I thought you had lost all sense!"

Mr. Darcy's eyes flashed with anger. Elizabeth gently

squeezed his hand, a silent reminder for him to keep his temper in check. But before he could say anything, Lady Catherine pressed on.

"I am ashamed of you, Fitzwilliam. You have brought disgrace upon our family! This—this daughter of a tradesman will never be accepted into proper society. You have tarnished your name, and the name of your father, by tying yourself to such a low connection!"

Elizabeth's heart raced, but she remained silent at her husband's side, her eyes fixed on Lady Catherine as the tirade continued. "And what of my brother, the Earl of Matlock?" Lady Catherine spat. "He will never sanction such a marriage! The entire family is humiliated by your poor judgment. It is not too late, Fitzwilliam. You must end this farce at once!"

Mr. Darcy's voice was low and dangerous. "My marriage is not a farce. Even if it were, I assure you it is far too late to do anything about it."

Lady Catherine gasped. "You crude boy! Your mother would be ashamed of you."

Mr. Darcy pulled himself to his full height. "You are wrong. My mother would be ashamed of *you*. In Elizabeth she would find the greatest joy. She is my wife and you will show her the respect she deserves."

It was not the proper time, but Elizabeth could not help but remember all the things her brother-in-law had said about Lady Catherine. *It seems in this Mr. Collins was correct,* she thought. *She is Mr. Greene's exhausting patroness. I certainly find her so.* Elizabeth lips twitched.

"Respect?" Lady Catherine laughed bitterly, her gaze shifting to Elizabeth with disdain. "I will not show respect to a woman who has clawed her way into a position far above her station. Even now she stands with a stupid smirk on her face! She is an upstart, plain and simple, and no matter how much you try to polish her she will never be fit to stand as Mrs. Darcy!"

At that, Elizabeth could remain silent no longer. With a steady voice, she addressed the lady. "Lady Catherine, you may call me an upstart if you wish, but I must tell you that my birth father was a gentleman."

Elizabeth felt her husband's hand tighten on hers, but she ignored it. "My uncle, indeed, is a tradesman. But my father was a gentleman. Until his death, he ran Longbourn in Hertfordshire, just as six generations of Bennets did before him. Given that my husband's own deceased father was also landed but without title, then I must point out that my husband and I are, in this respect, equals."

Mr. Darcy's eyes shone with pride as he looked at Elizabeth. Lady Catherine, however, flushed with indignation.

Elizabeth pressed on, her gaze unwavering. "As for your brother, both he and Lady Matlock attended our wedding. They are quite pleased with the connection. In fact, they will be hosting a dinner on Twelfth Night in honor of our nuptials."

"You... you are lying! My brother would never—"

"I assure you," Mr. Darcy interrupted, his voice cold and authoritative, "my uncle and aunt are fully supportive of our marriage. And until you can also find it in your heart to support us, you will be removed from our lives."

Lady Catherine sputtered, her fury bubbling over. "You will regret this, Fitzwilliam. You will regret this marriage, mark my words! This woman—this *upstart*—will never be accepted by proper society. She will bring nothing but disgrace to your name!"

Mr. Darcy stepped forward, his voice as sharp as a blade. "Enough. I will not tolerate any more of your insults. You have overstayed your welcome. It is time for you to leave."

Lady Catherine looked as though she might explode, but something in her nephew's hard gaze silenced her. Without another word, she turned on her heel and swept toward the door.

Darcy followed her to the entrance, his expression hard. "Goodbye, Aunt."

Lady Catherine turned once more, her eyes narrowing as she gave one final, scathing glance at Elizabeth, but to the couple's surprise, she said nothing further.

"Do you believe we have heard the last of her?"

Mr. Darcy grimaced. "I will, undoubtedly, receive a copious number of letters on the topic, but that is easily dealt with. I will simply consign each missive to the fire."

Elizabeth stood in the middle of the foyer, willing her heartbeat to slow. "I am sorry that your aunt is displeased, though not so sorry that I would give you up."

He moved toward her, taking her hands in his. "I would not allow you to give me up. You are mine and I am yours." He kissed her forehead, allowing his lips to linger. "But why did you never mention your father's status as a gentleman?"

She pulled back, her eyes locking with his. "Did it matter?"

A smile tugged at his lips. "At one time, I foolishly thought it did. But now I see that it was never important."

Chapter 25

Twelfth Night

The glow of candles filled the grand salon of Matlock House as Elizabeth entered with Mr. Darcy by her side, her arm resting lightly on his. The buzz of conversation, laughter, and the clinking of glasses filled the air. Elizabeth's heart raced, not out of fear but excitement. It was her first formal event as Mrs. Darcy, and though she had attended many such events in her lifetime, this one felt different. Before she was the goddaughter of an earl and the best friend of his daughter. Tonight she was Mrs. Darcy, causing the eyes of the ton to settle upon her in a different way.

Her husband leaned toward her as they entered. "You look radiant tonight, my love." She wore a red gown that highlighted the creaminess of her skin and the subtle sheen of red in her hair.

Elizabeth smiled, glancing at him from the corner of her eye. "And you look the part of a very proud husband, Mr. Darcy. Is it such a surprise that I can manage to dress myself properly?"

Darcy's lips quirked into a half-smile. "It is a surprise that I allowed you enough time alone in order to dress." Elizabeth blushed slightly but kept her composure.

They moved through the room, receiving nods and greetings from various guests. Familiar faces dotted the space, including Mr. Bingley, who offered them a broad, friendly smile.

"Congratulations, Darcy!" he exclaimed. "I must say I was not as surprised by your wedding as I was by its haste. I knew you preferred Mrs. Darcy as early as the party at Lucas Lodge, but I thought it might take you longer to act upon it."

Mr. Darcy pulled Elizabeth closer to his side. "If you ask me, I waited too long as it is. Once I secured Elizabeth's acceptance, I could wait no longer before I made her my wife."

Bingley laughed heartily, so pleased was he by his friend's felicity. To his left, Caroline Bingley stood, her expression carefully composed as she watched Mr. Darcy with thinly veiled desire. Her sharp gaze flicked to Elizabeth, and her smile tightened.

Elizabeth lifted her chin, meeting Caroline's gaze head-on. Tonight, she was not just the daughter of a tradesman. She was Mrs. Darcy, goddaughter to an earl and niece to another. She would not let Caroline's disdain rattle her.

"Mrs. Darcy!" a familiar voice called out.

Elizabeth turned to see Lady Matlock gliding toward them with an elegant grace that befitted her station. Her warm smile was genuine as she embraced Elizabeth. "Come. There are some people I am most eager for you to meet."

Elizabeth allowed herself to be drawn deeper into the room, leaving Mr. Darcy standing with the Bingleys. As they approached, Lady Matlock introduced Elizabeth to several distinguished guests, including Lady Jersey. She was a striking woman, with sharp eyes that seemed to assess everything around her, and yet there was a warmth in her gaze as she extended her hand to Elizabeth.

"Mrs. Darcy," Lady Jersey said, "it is a pleasure to finally meet you. Lady Matlock has spoken highly of you."

Elizabeth curtsied. "The pleasure is mine, Lady Jersey."

Lady Jersey's brow lifted slightly, a hint of amusement in her eyes. "My friend has spoken to me of your charm and natural grace. I suppose that is how you captured your husband. He has been notoriously difficult to secure. The young ladies of the ton will not be pleased to learn of your marriage, my dear."

Elizabeth chuckled softly. "I am sorry for their loss, but I cannot repine my own gain."

"I daresay you cannot," Lady Jersey said, her gaze sweeping over the room before returning to Elizabeth.

"My husband is currently speaking to your father. It seems Earl Jersey has a keen interest in your father's investments."

Elizabeth's eyes widened slightly, surprised by the connection. "Indeed? I was not aware." Lady Jersey gave a slight nod.

Elizabeth's smile was genuine, though she felt the heat of another's gaze upon her. She glanced around the room and found Caroline Bingley lingering nearby, her expression cold and calculating. Elizabeth turned away, choosing to engage more deeply in conversation with Lady Matlock, Lady Jersey, and Suzy who had just entered their circle of conversation.

Yet, Miss Bingley's presence loomed closer. When the conversation lulled, she took her opportunity. She stepped into the circle with a delicate laugh, her eyes sharp and glittering with malice.

"Lady Matlock, thank you for inviting me to your party."

Lady Matlock stopped her conversation with Suzy to look at the woman. "Miss Bingley, you should thank your brother for bringing you. It was his name addressed on the invitation since he is my nephew's dear friend."

Miss Bingley's cheeks pinked, but that did not prevent her from continuing. "My lady, were you as surprised by Mr. Darcy's marriage as I was?" When Lady Matlock did not reply, she persisted. "It is rather curious, is it not? Mr. Darcy could have anyone, and he chose Eliza Gardiner." She looked to Lady Jersey as if they were the best of friends. "I have heard that Mrs.

Darcy was given up by her aunt as an infant for being... what was the word? Ah yes, so ugly." She smiled, as if sharing a piece of harmless gossip. "How fortunate for her that her tradesman uncle took pity on her."

Elizabeth's spine stiffened, but she kept her expression neutral. Before she could respond, Miss Bingley continued, her voice turning sweeter. "Her own sister, I understand, was so concerned for Mrs. Darcy's future that she attempted to have her compromised, lest she never marry. A tragic story, is it not?"

Lady Susan's eyes flashed with anger. "Tragic? Not at all, Miss Bingley. I would say it is a story with a most delightful ending. Lizzy did marry, after all. And quite well, I should say."

Miss Bingley's smile faltered, but Suzy pressed on, her tone sharper than before. "Perhaps it is time you examined the difference between outward appearances and true character, Miss Bingley. You see, Lizzy's beauty—both in appearance and spirit—is obvious to those who truly matter."

Lady Matlock, who had been watching the exchange with raised eyebrows, joined in. "Indeed. One should never judge a person by their family, Miss Bingley. If we did that, I daresay your brother might never receive another invitation."

Miss Bingley's face flushed with embarrassment, but before she could respond, Lady Jersey, who had been listening quietly, turned her head with the elegance of a queen. "Quite so. But it seems the conversation has turned tiresome. Perhaps we should find something more pleasant to discuss, Lady Matlock?"

With that subtle dismissal, Lady Jersey effectively excluded Miss Bingley from the conversation, leaving her flustered and humiliated.

"Thank you," Elizabeth whispered under her breath as Miss Bingley retreated.

Suzy gave a soft laugh. "It was my pleasure. I would not allow anyone to speak so of my dearest friend."

Soon the party was informed that it was time for supper. Though Mr. Darcy did not like it, he relented when his uncle asked to escort Elizabeth into the dining room. The earl was not so cruel as to prevent his nephew from sitting with his bride, however. "Darcy, sit here next to Elizabeth, else you will pout the entire evening." Everyone laughed at the earl's jest, including Mr. Darcy, who was happy to laugh at anything as long as he could be near his wife.

When the first course was served and the room had quieted, Lord Matlock stood. "I would like to propose a toast. To Elizabeth and Darcy. I have never seen my nephew so happy, and for that I heartily thank Mrs. Darcy. When Darcy found her, he found a partner, someone he can rely on through good times and bad. And he continues the Darcy tradition of marrying for nothing less than the greatest of love. May all our children, nephews and nieces be as lucky and happy as they are."

"Here, here!" Lord Effington echoed. And soon the entire room was repeating the same sentiments.

Lord Matlock remained standing. When the room quieted once more, he spoke. "And at the risk of sharing too much joy in one evening, I wish to inform you that my own son has found his great love. Later this spring, Lady Susan Corwell will become Lady Susan Fitzwilliam. Richard, Lady Susan," the earl tipped his head in the couple's direction, "I wish you great happiness and a lifetime of love."

Suzy beamed while Richard smiled down at her with love in his eyes. Darcy whispered in his wife's ear. "You do not seem surprised by this, my dear."

Elizabeth chuckled. "We are as good as sisters. She told me the day Richard proposed."

"But that was on our wedding day!"

They both chuckled this time. "Never let either know that the other shared the secret before they agreed. Suzy said she and Richard promised to wait until after our ceremony to tell anyone."

Darcy grinned. "Richard told me the same thing on the same day. In his defense, I know how happy an engagement makes a man. I wanted to shout ours to the world."

∞∞∞

When the gentlemen joined the ladies after supper, Lady Matlock rang for tea. Darcy leaned toward Elizabeth, his breath warm against her ear. "Shall we slip away, my love?"

Elizabeth blinked, surprised. "Slip away? Fitzwilliam, we must say our goodbyes. It would be most improper to leave without doing so."

Darcy chuckled, the sound low and warm. "I am quite certain everyone will understand. We are newlyweds, after all, and I believe they will forgive us for seeking a moment of privacy."

Elizabeth opened her mouth to protest, but Darcy put his finger to his lips, entreating her to be quiet. He held his hand out to her. She hesitated for only a moment before taking it.

"Very well," she said with a soft laugh, "but I do hope your aunt does not take offense."

"She will not," Darcy assured her, leading her quietly through the grand house and out toward the waiting carriages. "She is too wrapped up in Lady Susan and Richard to worry with us."

The cold night air greeted them as they stepped outside, the stars twinkling above in the clear winter sky. Their carriage awaited them, and he helped Elizabeth inside before climbing in beside her.

Elizabeth leaned her head against Darcy's shoulder. "You

are quite the rogue, Fitzwilliam," she murmured, her eyes closing as she relaxed into him. "I should have known you would find a way to steal me away."

Darcy smiled, his hand gently stroking her arm. "I could not help myself. You looked so beautiful tonight, and I found it impossible to share you with everyone for so long."

Elizabeth's lips quirked into a smile. "And what, pray tell, was different about me tonight?"

Darcy chuckled, his voice deep and affectionate. "My love, I always find you irresistible, however, that red gown… it suits you perfectly."

Elizabeth lifted her head slightly, glancing down at the rich fabric of her dress. "Do you think so? I was not sure if the color was too bold."

Darcy shook his head, his eyes darkening with appreciation. "It is perfect. I believe I shall need to take a trip to the jeweler tomorrow."

"The jeweler?" Elizabeth asked, raising an eyebrow. "Fitzwilliam, you have already given me so many jewels. Surely, I do not need more."

"Ah," Darcy replied with a playful smile, "but you do not have rubies to match that gown. And I will not rest until I see you adorned in them."

Elizabeth laughed softly, her fingers tracing a pattern along the sleeve of his coat. "You will spoil me if you continue in this manner. If you buy me so many gems, there will be no funds left for our children."

Darcy's eyes softened, his gaze full of love and amusement. "I promise you, Elizabeth, there will be plenty left for our children. I will spoil them as well. But I shall never stop spoiling you."

Elizabeth smiled, her heart swelling with affection. "You

are impossible, Fitzwilliam."

Darcy lifted his hand to brush a stray curl from her face, "You are mine to spoil." He paused for a moment, his eyes searching hers, before he spoke again. "I cannot believe you are mine," he whispered.

Elizabeth's breath caught in her throat at the depth of his words. She felt her fingers intertwine with his. "Forever and always, Fitzwilliam."

Darcy leaned down, pressing a tender kiss to her lips.

They rode on, wrapped in each other's arms. Darcy swore to end every day with her in his arms.

Forever.

Epilogue

In July of 1812, when the sweltering heat of summer typically sent society fleeing from town, Darcy made a rare exception. Instead of retreating to Pemberley or some other cool country estate, they remained in London. Elizabeth had been adamant—her mother was expecting her first child, and Elizabeth would not miss the occasion for anything. Darcy, who had become deeply fond of Mrs. Gardiner and respected the bond Elizabeth shared with her, did not hesitate to agree. He was content to linger in the city, though it was against his usual habits.

On the third of August, Mrs. Gardiner gave birth to a healthy baby boy, christened Thomas Edward Gardiner. Elizabeth had been utterly enamored with the child, though it was not lost on Darcy that part of her joy stemmed from the knowledge of her own condition. Her pregnancy had only just begun to show, and Darcy delighted in the way Elizabeth unconsciously touched her belly whenever she held little Thomas.

"This baby brother of mine," Elizabeth had said with a smile as she gazed down at the infant, "has completely stolen my heart."

"You say that now," Darcy replied with a teasing smile, "but I suspect our own child may compete for that affection soon enough."

Elizabeth's eyes twinkled as she glanced at him. "Our

children shall never lack for love, Fitzwilliam. Of that, I am certain."

In those early days of their marriage, nothing seemed to dampen the light in Elizabeth's eyes. But some shadows, however faint, did linger from the past. Mr. and Mrs. Collins had sent multiple letters since the wedding, filled with words of remorse. Mrs. Collins, in particular, had expressed deep regret over her role in the failed attempt to compromise Elizabeth's reputation. Elizabeth, always willing to forgive, had allowed the correspondence to continue, though she confided in Darcy that their relationship would never be what she once hoped.

"I will write to her, of course," Elizabeth said one evening as they sat by the fire. "But it will not be the same as it is with Suzy or even with Georgiana. There is something missing between Jane and me—something I fear cannot be restored."

For Darcy's part, it was more difficult to forgive his wife's sister. When he thought about what might have been had their plan succeeded, he grew angry, but he tried to hide his feelings from Elizabeth. He knew she loved her sister, despite Jane's selfish ways. "You owe her nothing more than your peace of mind, my love. You have built your own family here, with me. You have the love you deserve."

Not all relationships in Meryton were strained, however. Though she never again spoke to her aunt, and only kept up with Jane through correspondence, Elizabeth's friendships with Miss Lucas, Miss Goulding, and Miss King grew. All three ladies visited her in London when Sir William Lucas attended business meetings with Mr. Gardiner. They became regular correspondents and saw each other at least once annually, when the Darcys were in London.

Georgiana had flourished under Mrs. Annesley's influence. That lady became the girl's companion when Elizabeth married Mr. Darcy. Georgiana had always been shy, but Mrs. Annesley's quiet guidance combined with Elizabeth's outgoing nature, ensured that Georgiana grew in confidence, eager for the next chapter of her life.

Georgiana adored her new sister and took great pleasure in the prospect of soon becoming an aunt. More than that, she was thrilled to have Elizabeth by her side as she prepared for her own *come out* the following year.

Meanwhile, in April of 1812, another joyous event took place: Suzy and Colonel Richard Fitzwilliam were married at Meadow Haven. It had been a glorious affair, though not without its challenges. Richard had wished for an engagement as short as Darcy's, but Lady Matlock had firmly opposed the idea, insisting on a proper engagement. In the end, they had compromised with a four-month engagement. After their wedding, the couple escaped town and settled happily on their estate in Somerset.

Suzy and Richard's marriage had been as lively as everyone expected. They welcomed five children into their lives, starting with their son, Paul Richard Fitzwilliam, and followed by four daughters: Elizabeth Mae, Lillian Grace, Eloisa Rose, and the youngest, Cassandra Jeannine. Little Cassandra, from the moment she could toddle, showed a fiery spirit not unlike her mother's. She was saucy, quick-witted, and surprisingly good at billiards—a talent Richard proudly boasted about at every opportunity.

Though Richard adored all his children, it was Cassandra who claimed a special place in his heart. Father and daughter were often inseparable, and Richard took great joy in teaching her everything from riding to strategy, both on and off the billiards table.

Darcy and Elizabeth, too, were blessed with children — four in total. First came Edward Fitzwilliam, who looked remarkably like his father but possessed his mother's lively spirit. Then Alexander James, the second son, who was a mirror image of Darcy in both looks and temperament. Gregory

Thomas followed, a spirited mix of both his parents, full of laughter and mischief. Finally, their only daughter, Anne Susan, arrived. At the age of six, Anne bore such a striking resemblance to Elizabeth that Darcy often found himself recalling the first time he had seen Elizabeth so many years ago, dusty from playing and missing her two front teeth.

Though their marriage had been filled with love and joy, there were occasional times when Darcy and Elizabeth had to endure days apart. These moments were brief, often due to Elizabeth being with child and unable to travel with Darcy for business. But no matter the distance, Darcy always rushed back to her side, never allowing their separation to last long.

"You spoil me, Fitzwilliam," Elizabeth said with a soft smile one afternoon, as Darcy returned home after a short trip. "I think you might miss me too much."

Darcy gathered her in his arms, pressing a kiss to her temple. "Not possible, Mrs. Darcy. My greatest joy when traveling alone is when I return to you."

As their family grew, so did their love. The grand halls of Pemberley echoed with the laughter of children, and the warmth of their home reflected the bond they had built—strong, unbreakable, and full of the quiet contentment that comes from knowing you have found your other half.

Darcy and Elizabeth were bound, not by duty or circumstance, but by a love that would endure forever.

And that was all that mattered.

Afterword

When I first started thinking about "Christmas with Elizabeth", the idea that really intrigued me was the separation of Elizabeth and Jane as children, and their eventual reunion. I wanted to explore what would happen if their lives took drastically different paths. At first, I planned for Jane to remain the sweet, kind character we know from "Pride and Prejudice". But as I thought more about it, I realized that growing up as the only child in Mrs. Phillips' household would change her drastically from the Jane we're used to. In canon, Jane is not only naturally sweet, but she also takes on the role of caretaker as the eldest daughter, watching over Elizabeth and the younger Bennet sisters. In this version, Jane is the only child and without that responsibility or her Aunt Gardiner's influence, she becomes a bit more spoiled. In some ways, she's more like Lydia than the kind and compassionate Jane we know (though I admit, I do enjoy a good "bad Jane" story!).

I had a lot of fun writing the other characters, too. Miss Goulding was especially enjoyable to create. I wanted her to be a bit like Lydia but with none of the malice or self-centeredness. She's a little loud, a little prone to saying the wrong thing, and definitely skirts the edges of propriety, but in a way that's lovable. For instance, she immediately starts calling Elizabeth by her first name without asking permission, which could have been a major faux pas, but she does it with such charm that it's easily forgiven. She's a character I might want to explore more in the future, maybe even give her a sidekick role.

And of course, we have to talk about Mr. Collins. His songs and his misuse of words were a delight to write. I took a lot of inspiration for his character from Mrs. Malaprop, the famous character in Sheridan's "The Rivals". That play was written in 1775, so it would have been familiar enough to the characters in this story. But fun fact: the word "malaprop" wasn't actually coined until 1814 by Lord Byron, so it's unlikely that any of my characters would have used it. Instead, Suzy calls his little verbal stumbles "Collinsisms," which I thought was a fun way to acknowledge his blunders without being historically inaccurate.

As for Mr. Collins' songs... well, I must thank my husband for that one. We were at our favorite Mexican restaurant, and I was telling him about a scene I had planned where Mr. Collins would make some sort of embarrassing mistake (as he usually does). My husband, who has zero clue who the character is, suggested that he should sing. The idea stuck with me, but I wanted it to be more ridiculous. Mr. Collins is so pompous that just singing wouldn't be enough—he would need to go further. That's when the idea of having him write his own songs came to mind. I chose "Greensleeves" as the tune because it's something most readers would recognize, and hopefully, when you got to those parts, you couldn't help but hum the lyrics to yourself!

Finally, let's talk about the wedding night. I've steered away from those scenes in my previous two books. It didn't fit at all in "Georgiana Darcy's Magical Meddling", and I was unsure about it in my first book "Trust & Honesty". To be truthful, I notice a recent leaning toward sweet, clean romances in this genre, but I cannot deny that I like a little spice. None of my books have been marketed as clean reading, but I suspect many readers expect that after publishing two books without any hint of bedroom affairs. I hope I didn't cause anyone to reach for their smelling salts. That said, I'm not sorry for putting it in. Darcy and

Elizabeth's attraction started right from their first meeting, and I wanted to know where it would go on the wedding night.

I admit, I first wrote a very open door, explicit scene, but I decided that was for my consumption only. It didn't quite fit with the rest of the book, so I rewrote it to a more sedate level of steam. Once I finalize everything with this book, I plan to start a series of paranormal witch romances set in my home state of Kentucky. There will be lots of steam in those, so keep an eye out in case you read multiple genres like I do.

About The Author

Leah Page

Leah Page loves books, hiking, and the Bengals (Who Dey!). She has a passion for travel, is doing her best to learn Spanish, and has plans to live "a little bit of everywhere" when her husband retires. For now, you can find her sitting at her writing desk in Kentucky while her sidekick pup sleeps in her lap.

Find Leah online at www.leahpageauthor.com.

Praise For Author

Praise for Georgiana Darcy's Magical Meddling.

This was a delightful, adorable little story. While I usually do not enjoy first person pov, in this case, it was wonderfully done.

Georgiana is a sweet menace, bright with personality and good intentions. The author really did an excellent job with characterizations. This is an author to watch.

- LT

Praise for Trust & Honesty.

This story reaches down and plucks out characters we've come to love so we can have a closer look at certain situations and how these characters move to find their own happiness amidst the struggles and situations they face. It gives us an up close and personal look at how our ODC dealt with the good, bad and the ugly as their relationship grew into a beautiful love story. Very well written and a joy to read.

- ARKANSASAUSTENFAN

Books By This Author

Trust And Honesty

COMING TO AUDIBLE DECEMBER 2024!

Where trust is woven in words and proven in actions, there lies the path to true love.
Inspired by his friend's unconventional romance, Darcy is determined to win back the only woman who's ever captured his heart. Yet, finding the right words proves challenging for him. Will he manage to push past his reticence and prove that he is her perfect match?

In an act of courage that defies the strictures of decorum, Elizabeth Bennet pens a letter to Mr. Darcy, hoping to heal the wounds of a proposal gone awry and her own hasty rejection. But will her nerve falter in the face of her family's disgrace?
"Trust and Honesty" weaves a captivating retelling of the timeless romance between Elizabeth Bennet and Mr. Darcy, proving that sometimes, love's truest expression is found in the words we dare to share. This novella-length book spans 54,000 words, delivering a heartfelt journey of love and redemption.

Georgiana Darcy's Magical Meddling

Sixteen-year-old Georgiana Darcy harbors a secret—she's recently discovered she is a witch! Under the tutelage of a wise and witchy companion, she spends her days casting spells and plotting the occasional hex against the irksome Miss Bingley.

When the tea leaves reveal that her brother, Mr. Fitzwilliam Darcy, is destined to meet his one true love at a local assembly, Georgiana cannot resist using her newfound powers to eavesdrop. Unfortunately, the encounter is far from magical. Fitzwilliam's clumsy attempts at affection are doomed without her intervention. Armed with her trusty diary and a knack for magical mischief, Georgiana vows to document—and secretly improve—each of her brother's courtship efforts, ensuring he never strays from his path to true love. But when Lady Catherine de Bourgh senses a budding romance, the stakes rise.

Will the fledgling witch secure her brother's happiness and manage the magical realm's unpredictable twists? Or will her enchanted endeavors fizzle just when she needs them the most?

Humorous, heartfelt, and utterly enchanting, Georgiana Darcy's Magical Meddling invites you to experience Darcy and Elizabeth's romance through the eyes of a clever, charming, and slightly meddlesome young witch. Her diary isn't just a record of magical mayhem—it's a confirmation of the love, laughter, and lunacy that make up her witchy life.

Follow Me

Facebook

Instagram

Thank you for reading!

It's tough trying to carve out a space for myself in the world if Indie publishing. Thank you for supporting a self-published author. Readers like you make me happy, and happy is a great thing to be.

Printed in Great Britain
by Amazon